WHY THEY CALL IT FALLING

CHRISTINA SINISI

Christina Sinisi

Anaiah
Press
Books that Inspire

WHY THEY CALL IT FALLING by CHRISTINA SINISI

ANAIAH FROM THE HEART
An imprint of ANAIAH PRESS, LLC
7780 49th St. N #129
Pinellas Park, Florida 33781

Edited by Kara Leigh Miller
Cover art by Laura Heritage
Book design by Anaiah Press, LLC

To Carol — Sisters are a blessing from God, and you are one!

"God...is able to do far more than we would ever dare to ask or even dream of..." Ephesians 3:20 TLB

PROLOGUE

"It's better to seek forgiveness than ask permission," Emma whispered near Justin's ear.

"What?" He leaned back, his blond bangs falling across his palmetto-green eyes.

His eyes were half-closed, the result of her kissing. She'd been kissed before, but this was their first kiss and she would remember. She'd wanted to date him since he'd asked her to marry him in kindergarten, but her parents only let their daughters start dating at age sixteen. She wouldn't hit that milestone for months.

"We may be out past my curfew," Emma said.

Justin jerked away from her and scrambled for the car door handle. "Why didn't you say something? I don't want to get you in trouble on our first date."

Emma twirled a curl around her finger. "Um, I might not be allowed out on a school night, either."

The boy looked like he might have a heart attack at sixteen. He was almost a full year older than she was, but the timing of their birthdays put them in the same year in school.

"So, we're in trouble no matter what?" He groaned, and then winked at her. "But it was worth it, right?"

He did have her heart stuttering and butterflies doing forward rolls in her belly, but he didn't need to know that. He was already a star tight end playing varsity even though they were only sophomores; there was no need to make his head any bigger.

"Maybe." She did a little dance with her shoulders.

The front porch light flickered on and off, rapid, like machine-gunfire. Emma ducked her head and reached for the door. "Busted. I got to go."

"Wait," he yelled. "I have to get the door for you. My mama would kill me if I didn't."

Emma leaned back against the head rest and laughed, thrilling in the power of being young and treasured. "We wouldn't want that now, would we? By the way, one final thing."

He jogged around the front of the car, his body highlighted by that infernal porch light. He jerked the door open. "One more thing? What else, Emma?"

She slid one long leg out of the car and framed the pose. He gulped. She grinned, the devil rising up in her. "I'm not supposed to date at all yet. Not until I'm sixteen."

His eyes shot to the sky. "What in the world? Emma, you'll be grounded for months. What were you thinking? What will your parents think of me?"

She shrugged. "I'm the bad sister. I'll take the blame, and they won't know it was you because you won't come in. I wanted to go to the movie with everybody else. It was my decision."

Justin shoved his hands into his pockets and rocked back in his boat shoes. He held out a hand. "Naw, that's not how I roll. I should have asked when your curfew was. Real men don't run from their mistakes. I'll face the music with you."

Emma took his hand, her thoughts jumping over each other like wild rabbits.

The porch light went into apoplexy and then stopped flashing altogether when they started walking up the sidewalk. She'd given her parents a heart attack, according to the flickering light.

Her father met her at the door. "Emma." His gaze raked over Justin. "Justin Lee. I thought better of you, son."

Justin tightened his grip on her hand. "Yes, sir. No excuses, sir."

"Okay, then, I'll let your parents deal with you. Drive safe."

"Yes, sir." Justin took his life in his hands and kissed her on the cheek. "Good night, baby girl. Call me." He jogged back toward his car. "Good night, Mr. and Mrs. Marano."

"Emma, get your hind end in the house," her mother said from a few feet inside a living room lit by one solitary lamp. "Your daddy is about to leave for his shift at work. He don't need to be distracted by wondering where you are and what you're doing. He needs to have his mind on his work, and you're driving us both out of our gourds."

She started to defend herself, but her father in his security guard uniform stopped that long black train on its tracks. He moved past her toward the kitchen, checking his belt for the taser he wore since he wasn't a real cop.

"I'm sorry, Daddy."

"Are you?" He rested his thumbs in his belt loops. "Are you really, Emma? Seems to me that you enjoy putting yourself in this bad daughter role. I'm wondering if that young man even knew you aren't allowed to date yet. Did it matter to you that you got him in trouble as well? Or do you just care about ruining your own reputation?"

Emma almost snorted. "Dad, we just went to the movies with a group of kids. Everybody else I know is already dating. If you weren't so—"

He held up one finger. "Stop right there. Not only are you grounded for a month, but I'm going to watch you talk to that boy on the phone tomorrow. You are going to explain our rules to him, and he can protect himself if he decides to pursue a relationship with you in the future. He might decide you're not worth it, pumpkin. You need to think about the consequences of your actions."

Tears came down her cheeks from nowhere. Emma didn't cry. Tiffany was the weak one. "I'm going to bed."

"Not before you kiss your old man good night." Her daddy tilted his head toward her. "We all mess up, Emma. It's what you do with your mistakes that matter."

Emma shook her head. "You can't do that. You can't ground me for a month and then act all nice." She pushed past him and stormed toward her room.

"Good night, pumpkin." Her father sounded worn out, not a good thing for a man working night shift.

Emma kept walking. Her father and his ridiculous rules. None of her friends had so many rules.

"That girl's going to give us the gray hair everybody talks about, hon." Her father spoke to her mother, behind Emma's back. "Well, I best be off."

The smack of a full-blown kiss between her parents made Emma cringe.

"You be careful, Clinton. Don't let worrying about our girls distract you."

"I won't, honey. See you in the morning."

The back door opened and closed with a soft tick. Emma sank against the hall wall. When her mother had warned her father about worrying about the girls, she'd lied. Tiffany and Shelby didn't cause their parents a moment's worth of worry. She was the one to blame.

She was the problem child.

∾

The high nasal sound of their broken doorbell jarred Emma from a deep sleep. Sunshine poured through her bedroom window, the blinding light infiltrating no matter how hard she squeezed her eyes shut. Emma stretched her arms out and pushed at the sheets with her toes. She'd been dreaming of Justin.

Sunlight? Horror had her tossing back the blankets and falling out of bed. "No, no, no." Nine o'clock. They'd missed the bus. "Tiffany! Shelby! We're late. So very flipping late. I have a test."

Hopping around her room, one arm in her robe and one out, she stopped talking. Missing a test could be a good thing. She hadn't studied the night before because, well, Justin.

Tiffany stumbled into her room, sock feet skidding on the floor and sending her crashing into the dresser. "Emma. We missed the bus."

Emma grinned. "Yeah. Maybe it's a holiday, and we didn't know it."

Tiffany rubbed her ribs. The girl was a walking bruise. "No, I'd know it. Something must be wrong. Dad was supposed to wake us up. Come on, maybe he's sick or something."

"Maybe he's tied up at work, or maybe he forgot to set his alarm." Emma bit her lip. "Hey, we haven't missed a day all year. No big deal."

Shelby appeared in the hallway, corkscrew curls sticking out like the hands of the clock that hadn't worked this morning. "Where's Daddy? What's for breakfast?"

A horrible sound pierced Emma's eardrums before drifting down to a guttural moan.

The three of them froze in place, pillars of salt from Sunday school stories.

"No, no, no." Their mother moaned.

Shelby started crying. She was little. She didn't need to know why.

Emma wanted to know, but then again, she didn't.

"Emma?" Tiffany's voice was small.

"Come on." Emma grabbed Tiffany by the upper arm and tugged her down the hallway. "Let's go find out what's wrong with Mama this time."

Some part of her insides clenched at the disrespect in her tone, but then again, her mother had dropped to a chair and bawled when her cake flopped into a goo last week before church. They crept down the hall, the old brick ranch had just a few steps between their bedrooms and living room. The front door stood half open, broad daylight pouring in and a police cruiser parked at the curb.

"Why is there a police car outside?" Shelby peered around her two older sisters.

"Girls. My girls." Their mother sat on the couch, still in her robe, with a police officer sitting across from her on the recliner. "Your daddy's dead."

Emma couldn't breathe. "No. You're lying."

Her mother's mouth fell open, and the police officer jerked to a stand, as if he'd stop the words spewing from her mouth.

"I'm not. I'm not." Her mother wailed. "I'm so used to him waking you girls up. I slept late and didn't even know he didn't come home. I can't live without him. I can't."

Tiffany glared at Emma and then walked across the room as if there were broken seashells on the oak planks. "Mama, we love you. What happened?"

"You have to be lying." Emma stood in front of the policeman, time coming in and out. "Daddy's not a real policeman. Why would he be dead? What happened?"

The police officer sank back down, his elbows on his knees, his fingers interlaced together. "I'm sorry, miss. Your father interrupted a robbery on campus early this morning, and he was shot. He wore a name badge, and co-workers identified the body."

"My father is not a body." She backed away. If she just rewound, she'd wake up to her daddy's off-key singing of the good morning song, and they'd make the bus. She'd fail the test.

The last sight she saw before she disappeared into her room was her mother burying her face in Tiffany's hair, Shelby burrowed into her side.

No one followed her because she had done this.

Her daddy was dead because of her.

CHAPTER 1

Ten Years Later…

"Haley," Emma griped. "If you don't put your little patootie in gear, we're going to get there too late, and the place will be closed."

"I'm coming!" Haley shouted. "I just need a hat so I won't get sunburned."

Her daughter raced into the living room with a ski hat in the shape of a bunny rabbit, complete with floppy ears and cotton yarn tail in the back. The thing didn't offer protection from the sun and would have sweat dripping down her little face before they even got out of the car.

"Um." Emma had to laugh. "Darling, that's a winter hat. We don't even need those in Charleston at all. No way are you wearing that to pick strawberries."

Haley crossed her arms over her chest and stuck out her bottom lip. "Yes, I am, and you can't stop me."

Red spots swam in front of Emma's eyes for a few seconds; her daughter got on her nerves that bad. She'd given birth to herself in miniature and that might be fair, but raising herself wasn't fun. "You know what, go ahead and wear it. When it gets too hot, you'll need to carry it around with you, and maybe you won't be able to pick strawberries because your basket will be full of hat." She grabbed her purse and started for the door. "Up to you."

Haley huffed. "Meanie."

When Emma turned to hold the door open, Haley was hatless. She'd take the motherhood "win" for the day. "I have a sun hat for you in the bag. You know the one we got at Simply Southern?"

Haley recovered her bounce. "Yay! I love that hat. I just want to kiss the frogs on there. They're so cute."

Emma grinned. "I just want to kiss you all over your smoochy face."

Haley jumped into her car seat as soon as the back door opened. Emma leaned over and planted a raspberry on her daughter's cheek, loud and prolonged.

Haley squealed and squirmed. "Yuck, Mama. Stop."

Emma laughed and pulled back. "Now, that's some kissing."

Haley rubbed her cheek. "You're a silly mommy."

"Yep, and don't you forget it." Emma clicked her daughter's buckle and closed the door. She swung her tote bag into the back of the SUV before sliding into the driver's seat. She stared at the rearview mirror, drinking in her daughter's toothy smile. She'd done that, all by herself.

Yeah, Justin had been there at the making of their daughter, but he hadn't been around long after and didn't even know she existed. That was on her, too, but she was good with that.

"Are we ever going to move?" Haley grumped. "I thought we were going to miss it if I didn't get a move on."

"Yes, ma'am," Emma said. "You're right, you're right. I just couldn't stop staring at this beautiful little girl in the rearview."

Haley twisted in her car seat and looked behind her. "Who? Where?"

Emma smiled and put the car in reverse. "You, silly. You're my beautiful little girl."

Haley plopped her bottom back down. "Humph. You say

that now, but what if you have another baby? My friend Ashley at Christ's Kids said she's going to be a big sister, and she's going to have to share her toys. I said that doesn't sound like a good time to me."

Emma laughed so hard she snorted. Thank the Lord another car didn't come from the other direction. The mile before Dorchester Road passed before she could gather her wits.

Haley wasn't fazed. She kept up a steady chatter all the way down Dorchester and when they merged with I26. Emma tried to pay attention, knowing from her own strained relationship with her mother that if she didn't listen when they were young, they'd return the favor when they got older.

The exit to Mt. Pleasant loomed, and she made the right and then the left on Long Point Road. The road fascinated her, the shoulder inches away from the marsh. Oak trees the size of guardians loomed over the road. Then, they reached the plantation. The historic grounds spread a vivid green in front of her. Giant branches dripped with swamp moss, but there was also Pick Your Own strawberries in the summer and a pumpkin patch in the fall. Both were highlights of her year now that she had Haley to share them with.

"I want to make myself sick with so many strawberries." Haley stretched her arms as wide as her double straps would let her go. "How many are you going to eat, Mama?"

"None." Emma wasn't critiquing; she was excited. "I want to take some home and make strawberry shortcake. That stuff is what dreams are made of."

"Oh, you're right." Haley jumped out of the car seat when released and almost tumbled to the ground, catching herself with her hands. "Phew. That was close."

"Yes, it was." Emma adopted her serious Mom voice. "Stand still, sweetheart. I'm going to get the sunscreen out of my bag and our hats. We have to lather up and lady up before we go out in the sun."

"Yes, ma'am!"

Emma looked around the parking lot. Two rows of vehicles lined up with no moving traffic. Still, that signaled a lot of people up and down the rows. She hated arriving so late in the day, but she'd had the day shift at Jasmine's, the Italian restaurant where she waited tables on the weekends. Hurrying, she grabbed the bag.

She slathered lotion on her dancing monkey and then tried to get the back of her own neck without much hope. Haley tried, but her flirting from foot to foot didn't inspire much confidence. So, Emma did her own little dance and tried to reach all the difficult places and said a little prayer for the pale skin that hadn't seen the sun all year.

"Where are we going to eat dinner?" Haley gave every evidence of going through a growth spurt, and two months of summer remained. "I want chicken nuggets."

Haley would eat God's chicken every day of the year, but Emma might be growing tired of it. "We'll see." Emma checked her purse for her keys before she locked up. "I'm in the mood for Mexican."

"Anything but Italian!" They both raised their voices, in a chant. Not because they had anything against Italian food, but they'd had enough leftovers from Jasmine's for a lifetime.

They bumped elbows and walked down the path. Emma paid for two buckets, and they headed out to the field, the air still muggy in the late afternoon sun. The Lowcountry of South Carolina, being so close to the beach, meant living with humidity thick as she-crab soup.

"Okay, this row looks good." Emma scanned the area for an unoccupied stretch of green leafy plants with their ruby jewels. "You get on the other side and stay close by me."

"Yes, ma'am."

"Good answer." Emma squatted and flipped over a leaf. "Look, that's a fat, juicy one."

They picked berries in a happy partnership, commenting the whole time on the quality of this specimen or how plump that one was. Haley hummed to herself, off-key and sometimes loudly, so at first, Emma didn't hear him.

"Do you think we have enough?" The male voice came from two rows behind her.

Emma fell backward, bottom smacking the dirt. She jumped up, scrambling after the berries she'd spilled from her half-filled basket. She felt close to fainting, and her face flushed… had to be the summer heat. He couldn't be here.

"I don't know. What are we going to do with them when we get back?" The female voice held no accent, so she was definitely not from around here.

Emma snuck a sideways look. Her worst nightmare came to life. She locked eyes with the man she'd tried to forget but failed.

"Mama? Are you okay?"

Haley. He couldn't see Haley. Emma scrambled to hide her child in the middle of an open field.

"Emma? Is that you?"

"Yes. No," she answered one after the other. Haley was her spitting image. He could never guess.

"Emma." Justin Lee, blond hair glinting and tanned face red in the sun, stepped over two rows of strawberries to stand an arm's length away. "That is you. How are you?"

"Mama." Haley jumped between them. "Who is he?"

Haley had her hands on her scrawny hips and her chin jutting out. Emma was wrong. Her daughter had his chin.

"I'm Justin Lee, an old friend of your mama's. Who are you?"

Haley squinted so hard she was close to being warned about her face freezing that way. "I'm Haley Grace, her young daughter."

Justin laughed and reached out to touch her hair. Haley evaded his reach, but he managed to mess up her bangs before she got away.

"Emma, you have a daughter?" Unbelievable hurt and disbelief battled in eyes that, up to this point, had been warm and happy to see her. "You never told me you had a child. How old is she?"

"She's almost five," Emma's answer came out in a scratchy whisper.

Emma watched the knowledge seep in, the touch, the realization, the bleaching of all color from the man's face. He looked up at Emma, down at Haley, up, down.

"We were together then. Did you... was there someone else?" He pitched his voice low, as if Haley, who stood right there, wouldn't hear.

"No. I never."

"If you didn't. Then?" He glanced back and forth between the mother and daughter. "Emma?"

Emma bit her lip, tasted sweat and blood. She could lie.

"Emma? Please answer me. Is she...?" He stood there, hands clenching and unclenching, gaze boring into her like he'd find the answer behind her eyes, and she couldn't form a word.

"Hey, Justin, babe, do you want to introduce me?" The muscular woman swung her overflowing basket of strawberries and came to stand behind Justin, given there was so little space between the plants.

"Sure." Bitterness cracked his voice. "Kristi, this is my old girlfriend, Emma, and if I'm not mistaken, this is Haley, my daughter." He closed the gap between them to inches. "Am I right, Emma? Am I right?"

CHAPTER 2

*J*ustin swayed where he stood, couldn't stand up straight. He sank down to his knees in front of the little girl. "Emma? Am I right?"

The answer came in a barely-there breath. "Yes."

He shoved a hand in his hair, stared at Emma. "She doesn't know?"

"No," Emma said in a barely audible voice. "I never told her."

"And why is that?" he asked. "I never did anything to you that would deserve this."

"You left."

Kristi grabbed his upper arm, trying to tug him to a stand. "Justin, stand up. We need to leave before they call the cops or something."

He blinked at Kristi, having forgotten she was there at all. "What are you talking about? Why would someone call the police? I just found out I have a daughter I knew nothing about. I'm not going anywhere until I get this straightened out." He lifted his hand, and Haley scowled at him. A hug was out of the question, clearly too soon, so he extended his hand to shake, like he would to an adult. "My name's Justin Grady Lee. It's very nice to meet you."

He gave her a lopsided grin, trying to appear less large. Haley hesitated for a few seconds, gnawing on her lower lip, and then she placed her hand in his. Her hand was warm and small, and he did his best not to bawl.

"Nice to meet you, too." Haley glanced up at Emma. "Is he my daddy?"

"What? How?" Emma stuttered. "What makes you think that?"

"Because he told the other lady that I'm his daughter."

Pride puffed up Justin's chest. His daughter was a cracker jack. He'd tried to talk around the truth, to protect the child, but at some point, he must have slipped.

"Yes, yes, he is." Emma was crying, and all he could do was stare.

He wanted to break down. He wanted to scream at the woman who had robbed him of years of his child's life. He wanted a time machine, for God's sake.

"Daddy? Why are you making that face?"

"Because my knees are starting to hurt," he lied. He let go of her hand and pushed to a stand. "Emma, can I have your phone number?"

"Justin." Kristi spoke from somewhere behind him. He probably shouldn't ask for one woman's number while on a date with another. He didn't care.

"What?"

"There's a park ranger coming over here. Are you sure you want to get involved?"

"I don't care," he yelled, knew he was out of line, but couldn't take his voice down a notch. "I need to have a relationship with my daughter. Can't you understand that?"

The park ranger drew even with them across a row of strawberries. "Is everything all right here?"

Kristi pressed her lips together in a tight, thin line, and her exhale sounded like steam coming out of her ears.

Emma wiped tears from her face and nodded.

"I just met my new daddy. I didn't know I had a daddy. I never met him before," Haley answered for everyone.

The poor ranger's shocked eyes stretched his tanned skin thin. "Okay. All righty, then. Just let me know if there's anything I can do." The man tripped over the strawberry plants between him and escape.

Haley had escaped back to her mother, and Emma rested a protective hand on the child's shoulder.

He sucked in a breath. He had not done anything to make her feel she needed protection from him, ever. "Your phone number?" His voice was gruff, but he managed an indoor voice at least and that made him proud. "Please."

Emma placed her basket on the ground. A bell rang off to the side of the field. Her head jerked in direction of the sound. "They're closing."

"Oh, no," Haley groaned. "We didn't finish."

"Here, you can have mine." He'd dropped his basket two rows over and went to retrieve it. "Don't go anywhere," he tossed the words behind him, like a grenade, but at this point, he trusted Emma less than he could throw her.

"I'm not moving," Emma said.

He'd spilled several plump berries in his earlier surprise, and he clawed them out of the dirt. Five seconds and he was back. He dumped his strawberries into Haley's mostly empty basket. "Phone number?"

"You can put your number in my contacts. I'll text you when I get home."

He literally saw spots. On deployment, he'd joked around and made the men in his squad laugh until they spit beer on each other. Now, he went from zero to sixty in seconds. "It's not going to work that way. I'll put my number in your phone, but

17

then you're going to stand there and call me so I have your number. I'm sure you can understand why I don't want to trust that you'll get in touch with me when you didn't bother five years ago."

Emma stiffened. "You weren't around. Besides, I don't think you have much choice. Legally, Haley is my daughter, not yours."

He forced himself to take a breath; counting to ten was beyond him. Instead of answering when he might regret whatever spewed out of his mouth, he grabbed her phone and typed his number. Then, he hit send. The park ranger was heading their way, ready to shoo them off the property, so he motioned toward the parking lot.

"Let's walk and talk." His brain worked overtime with possibilities. She could always refuse his calls. "Where do you work now, Emma? Where do you live?"

As a group, they paid before making their way to the one remaining car that wasn't his truck. Tight-lipped, Emma stowed the berry baskets in the back of her SUV. Kristi said nothing and walked on to his truck.

"I don't think it's any of your business where I live or where I work." Emma gifted him with a glare as she walked to the rear passenger door. "Haley, get in, please."

The little girl had been quiet for some time. "Can Daddy come to dinner with us, Mommy?" Now, she scrunched her nose in his direction. "We're going to Mexican."

"I don't think that's a good idea," Emma said before he could put two neurons together to form a response.

"Why not?" he blurted.

"Your lady friend, for one." Emma twisted her lips to one side. "Shouldn't you be thinking of her?"

"Right now, all I can think of is Haley. I have a lot of lost time to make up for." He started to reach for her, dropped his hands. "I asked where you lived and where you work because I need a backup plan in case you don't answer when I call, Emma."

She shrank away from him, and he was baffled. He'd been the one to break up with her, and up to that point, she'd been all over him. "I don't blame you."

"Don't make me call your mother." The threat had been an inside joke, and the words just slipped out.

She winced. "Please don't. She doesn't know."

"She doesn't know about Haley?" He couldn't process all of this at one time.

Emma reached for the driver's door handle. "Of course she knows about Haley. She doesn't know that I didn't tell you."

Acid bubbled in his gut. "She thinks I just abandoned the two of you? That I couldn't even be bothered to take care of my own child?" Shock waves went through him as other possibilities occurred to his overloaded brain. "What about Tiffany and Shelby? Do they think I'm a deadbeat dad, too?"

He could read the answer on her face. Exhaustion rode through him, and he ran his fingers through his hair. Glancing back at Haley, he spoke in a quiet voice. "Haley, I think your mom is right, and it's not a good idea for us to have dinner together tonight. Us grownups need some time to figure things out, okay?"

He could almost see the wheels turn. His girl was a smart.

"Yes, sir. You're going to come see me, though, right? We have some things to talk about."

"Yes, ma'am." He smiled for the first time since this whole epiphany started. "Yes, we do."

Emma took advantage of his distraction and swung open her door. She slid behind the steering wheel and gave him a blank look. "I have two jobs—waitressing at Jasmine's on the weekends and office manager at Oxmoor Insurance. My address is 108 Brickyard Way, Apartment A, Summer Creek like always."

"You never left."

She'd wanted to live in New York and Hawaii and anywhere but Summer Creek. His anger dissipated a bit in the face of what had to have been her disappointment.

"108 Brickyard Way. Got it."

Emma moved to shut the door. "You'll need a lawyer, Justin."

His throat convulsed. "To see my daughter? What happened, Emma? How did we get here?"

"You left, Justin. You left."

CHAPTER 3

*J*ustin walked to his truck and tripped over gravel. He was in the best shape of his life, but he had the terrible urge for a nap. His legs felt heavy, and a weight sat on his shoulders like a gunny sack.

Normally, he'd act the gentleman and go around to open Kristi's door. She'd protest because she was a soldier, same rank as him, and didn't need a man to hold a door for her. He'd have done so anyway. Right now, he clicked the button on the fob and slid behind the steering wheel. Kristi stared at him through the passenger window for a minute, slack jawed. So much for not needing a man.

A few seconds later, she jerked open the back door and stowed her basket on the back floorboard. Without speaking, she slammed the door and climbed into the passenger seat.

Justin started the engine, backing out of the now empty parking lot. He knew he should ask what she wanted to eat or maybe even if she just wanted to go back to the house. He didn't because he sort of liked the silent treatment. It was a welcome break.

"I can't believe how you acted back there. I mean, I understand it had to be a shock to find out you were a father, but it was like you forgot I existed." Kristi would come up for air at some point, and then he'd have to form a coherent response. "I can't tell you how embarrassed I was, and I want you to know I won't tolerate being treated like that. I mean, you acted like I didn't even exist."

He opened his mouth only to shut it when she started in again.

"I bet you still have feelings for her, even though she treated you like this. I mean, what kind of woman doesn't tell the father of her child that he's a father? I bet you knew she was going to be there, and that's why we ended up doing something I never even wanted to do."

"What?" he sputtered. "How did you even get there? And I thought you wanted to go strawberry picking. It was something cool to do on a date weekend."

"Some date weekend this turned out to be." Kristi sat back, arms crossed, barriers up. "Well, we're stuck with each other for the next day and a half. So, where are we going for dinner? I'm in the mood for Japanese. How about you?"

"Japanese is fine." Justin could have patted himself on the back for answering in a tone that at least resembled cool and collected. He really wanted to say some things his mother wouldn't approve of, but she would find out. Kristi had friended his mother on social media.

"Okay, I'll plug it into my phone." Kristi sounded chipper, as if every mile put between them and his newly-discovered daughter would make the whole ugly scene go away. "Ooh, this place has five stars. Have you heard of the Ming Sun Café?"

Justin didn't even try to rake his memory. "No. I haven't lived here for a long time."

"Turn right on Coleman Boulevard. Then, you'll want to get in the left lane. The turn is in a mile and a half." She turned her body to face him. "I'm sorry if I wasn't very patient back there. I was obviously as shocked as you were. I mean, I didn't plan on becoming a stepmother."

He concentrated on searching for an opening in traffic. The blind spot on this truck was the size of a house so he looked multiple times before merging into the left lane. He drove in silence for a few minutes, knowing she wanted a reaction.

"I'm sorry." Her voice dripped with self-pity. "I guess I jumped the gun. I know we haven't talked about the future, but that's where we're headed, right? I'm down here to meet your family. You came to the lake house and met my mother last month. I'm not out of line here, Sergeant Lee."

She was, in so many ways. "What street am I looking for, Kristi?" Out of the corner of his eye, he saw her studying the phone.

"Boone Avenue."

"At the light?"

"The next one."

These pockets of normalcy were surreal, sandwiched between her bizarre reaction to the upheaval in his life. "Thank you."

"It's not that I don't like kids." She must have misinterpreted something. "I love kids. It's just that parenthood was something way off in the future. I mean, you have OCS in just a few months. How will that work?"

"If I get in." He sucked in a long inhale of oxygen and waited for the light to change.

Kristi's voice might irritate like fingernails on a chalkboard right now, but she wasn't wrong. His whole life plan was all Army, all the time.

"You'll get in." Kristi pointed. "The restaurant's down that frontage road. By the way, I'm paying tonight, Lee. Don't even think about tricking the server." Kristi grabbed her purse from under the seat where she'd stashed it earlier. The bag resembled a rucksack, typical of a woman who could out-press half the unit. "We make the same salary, don't forget."

"Yes, ma'am. I won't forget."

How could he? She pointed that out every time they turned

around. He exhaled. He wasn't being fair to her, even if most of the nastiness had stayed in his head.

"Ma'am?" Kristi laughed. "I thought I'd browbeat that out of you. I'm not your mama."

"No, you're not." He exited the truck and waited for her to catch up. He recovered enough to hold the restaurant door for her.

They didn't wait long, which didn't bode well for Mt. Pleasant on a Saturday night. He kept his mouth shut and followed the hostess to their seats. Kristi sat herself.

Justin shook his head and told himself to do better.

"I am so hungry." Kristi's voice sounded brittle now. She had to know he wasn't happy with her, and the forced cheerfulness would come to a screeching halt. "I think I want sushi. How about you?"

"Steak. Hibachi steak is good." Justin didn't bother with the menu. "I'm not a fan of sushi."

"Hmm." Her finger was tracing the menu. "I forgot."

Her bangs fell across her small face, and he couldn't help comparing her short-cropped, no-nonsense style with Emma's almost waist-long blonde hair. Her hair hadn't been that long in high school. Her features had become more defined, her body a little curvier.

"Hello? Earth to Justin?" Kristi waved a hand in front of his face. "I was asking if you'd like to share an appetizer."

"What?" He searched the menu for something that didn't involve seafood. "Sorry. How about some egg rolls?"

"Boring." Kristi rolled her eyes. He tried not to be insulted. "How about some wasabi snow peas?"

Justin could do spicy, just not slimy. "Sure. That sounds good."

The server came by and took their orders. She left, and they were left with nothing to talk about. Justin felt no pull of attraction to the woman across from him and wondered if he ever had.

The server came back with her beer and his diet soda. Kristi gave him a sideways glare. He couldn't explain his compulsion, but he felt like if he was a father, he wasn't going to be drinking all the time anymore. *If* he was a father. He'd been a father for years and hadn't known.

"Thank you," he said and smiled at the waitress.

"Wow." Kristi almost growled at him. "I can't believe you just did that."

Justin had no idea. "Did what?"

"You totally flirted with that waitress. I'm sitting right here, and you flirted with her." Kristi sloshed her beer on the way to her mouth. "First, you go crazy over your ex and now this. Why am I even here?"

Justin's brain was so blank that he had nothing to say in reply.

Kristi was on a roll, though. "And what's the deal with ordering a soda? You always get the most interesting beer on tap. Who even are you?"

He almost shushed her, which probably would have lit a match to an incendiary device.

She stood. "I'm going to the restroom. I hope you'll be the Justin I know and love when I get back."

His pulse drummed to the beat of a heavy metal song in the back of his mind. They hadn't been seeing each other for more than a few months, and most of that had been as buddies. Love wasn't even on his GPS, not with her.

He took a healthy dose of soda and almost choked. Kristi was right. He hadn't bypassed a beer in a long time. The stuff tasted foul. At the same time, she was very wrong. He wasn't going back. He couldn't. He was a totally different person than he'd been a few hours ago.

The second sip went down a little easier. He couldn't fathom what being a father meant for his immediate future. All he knew was that he wanted to spend time with Haley, as much time as possible. His knuckles whitened around the clear glass. He hadn't been there to help choose a name. He hadn't been there when she was born. He had missed her first ever-loving steps.

"Whoa. You look like you just saw the enemy in your crosshairs." Kristi was back.

Justin closed his eyes. *Dear Lord, I need help. I'm going to need to find a way to deal with all this anger. Thanks in advance. Amen.*

"Are you okay?" Kristi slid into her spot across from him. "Can I get you something?"

Justin took a breath. "I'm getting there. Listen, I didn't flirt with the waitress. I was trying to be kind. I didn't go crazy over Emma. I went *crazy*," he emphasized her poor choice of wording, "over Haley. I'm having a very hard time adjusting to finding out I'm a father a few years late."

Kristi reached across the table and rested her hand on his, the one still getting too close to shattering a glass in the middle of a restaurant. He tried not to flinch at her touch.

"I can only imagine. I'm sorry I wasn't more supportive." She squeezed his fingers and then sat back.

The server placed their appetizer in front of them, asked if they needed anything else, and hurried away.

Kristi dropped her hands in her lap. "Do you want to say grace?"

He released the glass and gave her a good look. She wasn't a believer and was undoubtedly trying to placate him. At the same time, right now, he needed all the prayer coming his way.

"Yes, thanks." He bowed his head. "Dear Lord, thank You for this food and this day. Thank You for my being a father. Please guide us and keep us. Amen." Their eyes met. "Thank you," he said.

"You're welcome."

He dove into the wasabi without really thinking, took a bite, and tried to come up for air. "Hot, hot."

Kristi grinned. The rest of the meal went by in neutral, friendly conversation. They pretended Haley still didn't exist, and nothing had changed. They drove in complete silence, interrupted only by the country music on his playlist.

When he parked the truck at his mom's house where they were staying, he sat frozen in his seat. At first, Kristi was so busy unloading her carton of leftovers that she didn't notice his lack of progress.

"Hey." She stuck her head back inside. "Aren't you coming in?"

"No, Kristi, I don't think I am." He stared straight ahead. His subconscious must have been working on its own. "I'm going to Emma's. I have so many questions, and I need answers."

"Wow." Her face closed off. "Way to make me feel special. I'll see you in the morning."

"Yeah." He shifted to reverse and then paused. "Hey, Kristi. Don't say anything to my folks, okay? I can't imagine how they're going to take this."

"Oh." She glanced at the house. "I didn't even think of that."

He didn't blame her. There were so many implications of this afternoon's revelation. "It's a lot to take in. I'm sorry. Good night."

"Good night."

He made sure she was out of the way before backing out, but he didn't look back.

CHAPTER 4

*E*mma tucked a very excited Haley into bed and tried to leave the room for the third time. Her head pounded, and her neck was so stiff she leaned to one side. Ibuprofen beckoned in the bathroom medicine cabinet, if she could just make her way down the hall.

"And do you think he will take me to the water park? Meggy says her daddy takes her fishing and swimming. He also sneaks her cookies when her mama isn't looking."

Emma lifted two fingers to her right eyebrow and massaged. "Haley, I know it's a big deal, finally getting to know your father. I know you're excited, but it's time to go to sleep now."

"Wait. You didn't read me a story."

The pain intensified, if that was possible. "Honey, I can't read you a story tonight. My head hurts too much. Go to sleep, and I'll read you two stories tomorrow. Deal?"

"Do I have a choice?" Haley crossed her arms over her chest, outside the blanket.

Emma had no idea how she'd raised such a smart aleck child. She did know there would be no going to sleep with her arms outside the covers. Somehow, the child had inherited her superstitions. She might as well have her hand hanging off the edge of the bed for the monsters to nibble on her fingers in the middle of the night.

Sighing, Emma retraced her steps. "Haley. I love you, and you love me, right?"

Haley pressed her lips together and had the good grace to look ashamed. "Yes, Mama. I love you to the moon and back."

"So, what should you do when I tell you I have a headache?"

"I should care."

"And maybe understand when I can't read you a story?"

"Yes, ma'am." Haley lifted her arms toward the ceiling, and Emma picked up the pink lace comforter. Haley scooted her hands underneath, tucked and rolled beneath the blankets, and folded her hands under her cheek.

"Good night, sweetheart." Emma leaned over and kissed her. She tiptoed to the door and turned out the light, pulling the door almost closed, careful to leave enough of a gap so the hall light shone through the crack.

"Good night, Mama."

Emma stumbled to the bathroom and flinched when she turned on the bright florescent light. The pain killer was up front, maybe because she got these headaches often. The stress of having two jobs showed up behind her forehead and at the back of her neck. Still, life had been good. Her sister, Tiffany, volunteered to babysit and gave her a weekend every other week so she had time to herself sometimes.

So what if she had no time for friends and hadn't been on a date since right after Justin had left? Her life was full. All she needed in her life was Haley and her family.

Only a little after eight, two hours until she could sleep. Part of her wanted to lie down in bed and curl into a ball, but that was the path of her demons. She knew those demons well.

Instead, she forced herself to wander around the apartment, picking up toys, putting away dirty socks. Her conscious goal was to stay awake and keep moving. Her ulterior motive was to avoid the phone charging in her bedroom, pretend this afternoon hadn't happened, and avoid any texts.

The phone rang.

"Who actually calls anymore?" she groused, then realized the noise from the phone might wake Haley. Emma took off at a run, quiet in her sock feet as possible.

She slammed to a halt next to her bed and jerked the phone off the charger. One swipe of the thumb and she was whisper-yelling, "What are thinking, calling at this hour? Don't you know it took me forever to get Haley to sleep?"

"Whoa, sis," Tiffany answered in a joking voice. "Put the brakes on. As far as I knew, this was a perfectly acceptable time to call since your phone is usually glued to your fingertips, and Haley would normally have been in bed for a good half hour. What's up?"

Emma sucked in air. "Oh, Tiffany, I'm so sorry. It's just been a day."

As soon as the vague words left her mouth, a hard knot formed in her stomach. She couldn't tell her sister. If she told Tiffany that Justin was back, she'd have to explain why she'd lied all those years ago.

"I'm sorry. What happened?"

Emma's brain scrambled for a feasible explanation. Shame filled her that this was part of her background, but she'd learned the best option was to stick as close to the truth as possible. She needed to keep her lies straight. "I took Haley to the strawberry patch after work. She got all wound up, and it was hard for her to settle down. I just took my frustration out on you. I apologize."

"I forgive you. But that was a lot of angst for a Haley bedtime. I haven't heard you that angry since I don't know when." Tiffany paused, and Emma waited.

She didn't want to go into any more detail because that's what got her in trouble.

Tiffany filled the silence. "Okay, so you're not going to tell me anymore."

"Tiffany." Emma put in enough force to make her wishes known. "There had to be a reason you called."

"Fine." Tiffany's sigh sounded more like a huff. "So, I called to see if you wanted to go with me to the church picnic next Saturday. It's going to be at Lake Moultrie at one of the pavilions. It's going to be beautiful weather. I'll do all the cooking."

The woman knew how to bribe. "That's super sweet of you, Tiffany, but..."

"Don't say no, Emma. It's been forever since we've done something together."

"Haley can go," Emma answered but couldn't see keeping this large of a secret from her sister and actually spending bonding time with her. "She loves when you take her to church events. There's this little girl she talks about, Sandy... what's her name?"

"Sandy Diamond. Yes, they love playing together, but that's not you and me, Emma. We're sisters, and you wouldn't know it by how little time we spend together. I don't even know what's going on in your life lately."

"Not much." Emma tried a distraction. "Maybe we can have dinner together next week. I'm not working at night during the week."

"That's not church." Tiffany was like a dog with a bone. She asked the same thing, in different guises, every few weeks. Emma didn't seem to have the option of a permanent "no."

"Really?" Emma needed sleep and patience, probably not in that order. "I honestly think I should turn the question around. How can you go to church? After what happened to Dad? What kind of God would let something like that happen?"

"Ah, Emma." Tiff's voice dropped in pitch. "What kind of God would let us choose whether to love Him or not? It's the same thing. Either we have freedom, or we don't."

Emma's mouth dropped open and stayed that way. Her big

sister had come back at her. She understood God gave them free will but also didn't feel comforted. She just wanted her Daddy back.

The silence dragged on too long. "I'm sorry, Emma. I miss him, too." Tiffany's voice was laced with concern.

Emma lowered herself to her mattress and leaned against the upholstered headboard. "Anyway, Tiffany. I'm not ready to go back to church."

"Okay, I'll come get Haley." Tiffany started talking about pickup times and what Haley would need to bring.

Emma pretty much ignored her since they'd have this conversation again, closer to the date, knowing her super-organized sister. "Thank you," Emma said when Tiffany paused. "She'll love it. Listen, Tiff, I need to get to bed. I have a raging headache."

"I'm still picking Haley up in the morning, though, right?"

Emma had forgotten the next day was Sunday. Her phone buzzed in her hand. Justin. She let his call go to voicemail. She couldn't very well hang up on her sister.

"Right." Her hesitation probably made Tiffany think she was reconsidering their weekly routine. "Thanks for everything, Tiff. I don't know what I'd do without you."

"I'm glad to do it." Her sister's smile shone through the cell phone. "You know I love that girl as if she was my own."

"I know." Emma closed her eyes, already regretting the sharp words of just a few minutes earlier. "I'll have her ready at nine. Sweet dreams, big sis."

"You, too, little sis." Tiffany ended the call.

Jimbo barked at her feet. He was too small to jump up on the bed, but that didn't mean the Yorkshire terrier pup was happy with being consigned to the floor or his crate.

"Come on, you." Emma scooped up his little warm body and cradled him on her lap. Justin had called three times—once while Haley had been in the tub and twice during her conversation with Tiffany. He had to think she was avoiding him.

A gentle knock echoed through the still apartment. Jimbo set off in a barking frenzy and rushed toward the door. Emma ran after him. Without checking to make sure who stood outside, she ripped open the door. "What do you think you're doing?"

Justin stood on the other side of the door, as expected, but his appearance took the wind out of her sails. He wore his uniform and had his cap in his hand. "I have to be back on base by morning. I just got called back." He tipped his chin up an inch. "You didn't answer your phone."

Emma realized he still stood outside in the concrete hallway. "Um, why don't you come in?"

"Thank you." He seemed humbled, the anger from earlier nowhere to be seen.

He moved to enter, but she was so out of her normal that she forgot to retreat. They ended up a few inches away from each other, and a woodsy scent assaulted her senses.

"Emma?"

"I'm so sorry." She shook her head as if clearing cobwebs rather than shaking off an attraction that should have been destroyed when he broke off their relationship. She gestured to the couch and shut the door. "Have a seat. Can I get you something to drink—coffee, a beer?"

He gave her a strange look, which she fully deserved. "No thanks. I just need to talk about Haley, about us coming to some sort of arrangement for visitation."

Emma waited until he took a seat before coming to a perch on the edge of the loveseat on the other side of the coffee table. "What do you mean?"

A spark of irritation lit his eyes. "Emma, you know what I mean. For the life of me, knowing how I was raised, I can't understand why you didn't tell me about Haley. The last thing I would want is to be a deadbeat dad."

"I know." She tucked her feet beneath her.

"You know?" He raised his voice a notch before dropping the volume and staring down the hall. "You know? That's all I get?

The least you could do is explain. I can't promise to understand, but I deserve an explanation."

"You left me." Emma stood. "You broke up with me, right when all my friends started disappearing. I had no one."

Justin's nostrils flared. "I broke up with you, not a child I didn't know existed. Big difference. It's perfectly okay to decide you don't want to be with someone when you're not married."

She said nothing because, while society might have approved, the general masses didn't know how much she'd depended on him. He had known.

Justin faced her. "Why didn't you tell me? If not for my sake, then Haley's. She has a whole other family who would love nothing more than to love her."

The black air pockets threatened the side of her vision. She fought to keep control. "You left. When you left, I couldn't." How did she explain without telling him what she told no one? He might have deserved to know about her deepest darkness at one point, but not now. "I had a hard time. I didn't even acknowledge I was pregnant for a few months." She didn't leave the house for weeks when she did. "By the time I went to the doctor and knew for sure, you'd finished basic training and had been deployed."

Justin's fingers worked at his cap, folding and unfolding. "You had my phone number. My mother loved you. How do you think she's going to react when I tell her she's been a grandmother for years and didn't know?"

The shame she'd felt, the distance between the person she'd expected to be and the scared teenager she'd become, created too many barriers to overcome.

"Help me, Emma."

"I couldn't." Emma knew tears ran down her cheeks like rain in a ditch. "I felt so stupid, Justin. With my mom offering to get me birth control since we started dating, and me insisting we could wait, how could I have been so dumb?"

Justin lifted his hand to wipe off the tears, but his hand froze midair. "If you were dumb, I was right there with you."

"I couldn't face you. I didn't want you to only come back because of Haley. It'd be like I forced you." She hiccupped. "I couldn't face reality for so long."

"But you had to face it eventually. What then, Emma?"

She couldn't make eye contact. "By then, I had a baby to raise."

He lifted her chin so she couldn't avoid his gaze. "That would mean you lived in denial for months. Did you get prenatal care? Were you okay?"

Emma flinched away from his touch. "Yes, I'm fine, and Haley is fine. I've been fine, ever since she was born. She's my anchor."

He looked skeptical.

"I did get prenatal care, maybe not as early as I should have, but Haley was born right on time and healthy. She's in the 50th percentile in height and weight and off the charts in sass. She's already reading some words. You'll have to be careful, or she'll find every bit of junk food you've hidden in the house."

She took a breath, and Justin held up a hand. "Whoa, Emma. You don't need to convince me. I saw with my own eyes. She's a beautiful, smart child. I want to know everything about her. When?"

"When what?" Emma rested a hand on her stomach. She'd always hidden a part of why she hadn't worked too hard to find Justin, even from herself. Haley belonged to her.

Justin held up his phone. "I can ask for family leave. I can be back here in two weeks. I will take as much time as you can give me. How do we arrange this?"

Emma's headache raged. "Whoa. I didn't say."

"You didn't say?" His lip curled in a sneer. "Didn't say what? I don't want to get a lawyer, and I don't want to take you to court, but I will if I have to. Don't make this ugly, Emma. Give me dates that work for you."

She pressed her fingertips to her forehead. "I didn't say you could take Haley away." Emma knew she wasn't making sense. He just wanted to spend time with Haley, not kidnap her.

"I'm not taking her away, Emma." Justin ran his hand through his hair, again, causing it to stand at attention. "I wouldn't do that. She needs both parents, and I want to get to know her. Don't you think that's reasonable given how much time I've lost?"

Emma's throat constricted. She'd done this. She'd deprived Haley of a father because of her inability to function half the time. "Yes, it's reasonable, but I don't want you to take her by yourself. I need to be there."

Justin's whole body tensed. "You think I need supervision? Are you saying you don't trust me? Yeah, I was a bit wild and crazy as a teenager, but I'm a grown man now. The Army straightened me out where I needed it. I'm not going to steal her, for God's sake."

She didn't know what she was implying, only that she was terrified.

Justin's shoulders slumped, and he pushed past her to the door. "I'll call tomorrow, give you more time to adjust to the idea. Then, I'll plan on being here the Friday after next, unless Haley has big plans."

Emma watched his every move. "Haley doesn't know you. She needs time."

"Does she?" The intensity of his glare had her reeling away. "Or do you? I'll do whatever's best for her, but at some point, I want full visitation. Whether we have to go to court over this is entirely up to you."

"You're not going to want to push this," Emma heard herself saying, but the cold voice belonged to someone else. "You've not been around. You have no rights."

Justin's jaw worked, and she was glad for the short distance between them. "Whoa. The only reason I haven't been around is you didn't bother to tell me I was a father. You know full well that I would be there if I knew I had a daughter. Am I even on the birth certificate?"

They were standing in the open apartment doorway. Emma looked from one end of the deserted concrete walkway to the other before whispering her answer back in anger. "Of course not. I've never." She didn't want him to know more than necessary. "No, you're not on the birth certificate. I didn't want you to be notified."

He closed his eyes for a few seconds and then opened them with a world of hurt behind those green eyes that had mesmerized her as a teenager. "I'm going to leave now. Before I say something I'll regret. I'll call tomorrow night. Please be ready to set up some dates." He crossed the threshold but looked back. "She has my dimples. She's mine."

The door shut. Emma reached for the back of the couch for support. Of course, Haley was his daughter. He was the only man she'd been with, the only man she'd ever loved.

So, why was she making this so hard on all of them?

"Is Daddy coming back?"

Of course, Haley had overheard. Emma bent down and held out her arms. Haley ran into them and buried her face in her mother's neck.

A few seconds later, much too quick for Emma's wishes, Haley pulled back. Her little girl scrunched up her nose and put her hands on her hips. "Why did you make Daddy leave? I didn't even get to show him my room."

Emma truly had no idea.

CHAPTER 5

*E*mma wiped crumbs off a table into the bin and headed for the kitchen. Jasmine's had been super busy this morning, just what she'd needed to take her mind off the day before. Tiffany had taken Haley to church and would have her all day.

Emma was working brunch. Mimosas and peach Bellinis were the order of the day, and the special was a collard green and roasted sweet potato salad complete with plump blackberries and local goat cheese. Southern cooking had come a long way since Granny Linda's kitchen where Sunday breakfast had been biscuits and sausage gravy before everyone rushed out the door to church.

"Miss?" Customers hovered near the hostess' desk, dressed in their Sunday best. "We've been here awhile, and no one's come to seat us."

Emma scanned the area and located the owner/manager standing with some regulars by the bar. He tended to get involved in conversation and forget everything else. Emma picked up the pace. "Three? Do you prefer a booth or a table?"

"Booth, please."

Emma checked the seating chart and grinned when her own name came up. "This way, if you'll follow me."

The woman followed right behind her, her husband trailing with a toddler in his arms. "Excuse me, but don't I know you?"

"I don't think so," Emma started and then tripped over a non-existent wrinkle in the carpet. "Sandra?"

"Emma."

Just as she stopped to let them slide into their booth, Emma found herself enveloped in a long-lost friend hug. She patted the other woman's back with one hand and held out the menus with the other. Her mind tried to reconcile the warm greeting with the years of being ignored.

Sandra gave her a quick squeeze and then scooted into place opposite her husband. "Girl, how long has it been? At least since high school."

"Yes, at least. Five years?" Graduation happened and her so-called friends had disappeared to larger universities while she'd dropped out of community college.

"Yes." Sandra smiled, dark brown hair framing a pretty face. "Summer Creek High graduation. Somehow, it's so hard to keep in touch, everybody going off to different schools."

"Yes, it's hard." Emma set a menu in front of each of them. "If you look at the paper insert, our specials of the day include our never-ending mimosas and a summer salad. Our fish of the day is red snapper caught off Folly Beach. The owners are friends with a ship captain who brings his catch by early in the morning."

"Oh, I'll have the summer salad, and Lauren here will have the kid's mac and cheese," Sandra said. She patted a flat abdomen that could not have given birth. "What about you, Scott?"

Emma blinked. She'd been so focused on the female in the equation that her exhausted brain hadn't computed the identity of the man. Scott Sample had been Justin's best friend in high school. "Scott. Believe it or not, I didn't see you there."

He gave her a plastic smile that didn't reach his eyes. "Hey, Emma. I can't complain about being overlooked when my lovely wife is present."

Cheesy, but sweet. Emma cleared her throat. "I didn't mean it that way. Um, have you heard from Justin lately?"

The heavy stare coming her way did not bode good things. Scott tapped his menu a couple of times and then closed it. "I'll have the snapper. What sides come with that?"

"Yes." Emma scrambled to remember what they were. His lack of an answer said so much, including a more general knowledge of what she'd done. "The snapper comes with corn aioli, pickled onions, and roasted parmesan asparagus."

"Sounds good." Scott combined his wife's menu with his and held them out to her. "Oh, and I'd like sweet tea with that. Sandra prefers half and half."

Emma blinked. She was off her game. Drink orders should have come first. "I can't believe I forgot to ask. I'll get those orders in as soon as possible."

Scott took an audible breath. "Actually, Emma, it would be real good if someone else could wait on us. Justin called me last night. I know what you did."

Sandra had been in the process of buckling her child into the booster seat hurriedly brought over by another server. Now, she froze in mid-air and stared at Emma. "I didn't know. This one has me in bed early every night. What?"

Emma couldn't control her face, but her words came out low and professional. "I'll be sure to get Donna over here. I'll put your order in and let her know your drink requests. I hope you enjoy your meal."

Walking away, she couldn't help but overhear Sandra repeat the question. "Scott, what did she do? It's not like you to be rude, and I wanted to catch up, find out what she's been doing."

"Trust me, honey. You don't want to renew your friendship." Scott sounded angry, as if he could complain to her boss.

Emma moved out of hearing distance and grabbed her coworker just as she and Donna almost collided. "Hey, Donna. I need your help. I just seated this couple in my section, but the gentleman holds a grudge against me from high school. Can you take them?"

Not exactly the truth, but close enough.

Donna couldn't help but sneak a peek behind them. "Really? From high school?"

"Yeah, and he wants someone else to serve them. Can you do it? I'll take your next table."

"Uh." Donna checked the order. "Sure. I'm sorry to hear someone would do that to you, after all this time. Well, I'm off to pour some tea."

"Thank you." Emma rushed to the kitchen and grabbed another table's appetizer. Out of the corner of her eye, she watched as Donna delivered Scott and Sandra's drinks. Even though she had no business taking a break during the mid-morning rush, she headed for the bathroom. Small miracle, no one else in there, and she stumbled into a stall.

Emma let herself cry for a few minutes, her shoulders shaking. She rolled out toilet paper to wipe her eyes, trying not to make a sound. This shouldn't hurt so much. She hadn't seen either of those people for years.

"Emma?"

Emma sniffled, blowing her cover. "Yes?"

"Emma. I'm sorry for what Scott did." Sandra was standing on the other side of the stall door, which Emma hadn't even bothered to deadbolt before having a meltdown. "I mean, I can't understand why you would do that to Justin, but you had your reasons. Right?"

Did the woman expect her to confide her deep, dark secrets to a virtual stranger? "Watch out, Sandra. I'm coming out."

"Okay. Sure." Sandra backed up, her pink toes in her gold flip flops scrambling.

Emma took the few steps needed to stare at herself in the mirror. "Wow. I really did a number on my makeup."

"Here." Sandra held up a shiny designer purse. "What do you need? I keep everything in here, powder, blush, mascara, you name it. I have samples if you're worried about germs."

Emma widened black-streaked eyes. "You have all that in there? How?"

"Don't you remember?" Sandra giggled. "I can pack a purse like nobody's business."

Emma felt teary-eyed again, for a totally different reason. "I remember. I do remember. That one time, at the away game, you had five shades of lipstick, for every girl there."

A makeup wipe came at her. "Here. And I planned it that way. I wanted to be helpful."

"Thank you." Emma started to clean up. "I've missed all of you."

"All of us?" Sandra held up eyeliner. "This one would work with your lighter coloring. Anyway, Scott doesn't know I followed you in here to talk. So, we don't have a lot of time."

Emma outlined her eyes. "I appreciate the gesture, but I don't know that I want to talk about it. I'm not going to pretend that what I did was right. I think I went a little crazy when I found out I was pregnant, and then it was easier to just stay the path. Plus, Justin had broken up with me. I didn't want to go begging."

Sandra held up a hand in the classic stop signal. "Hey, you don't have to justify yourself to me. I just know that Scott shouldn't have taken out his anger on you in your workplace."

Emma couldn't form a response because Scott could be viewed as a loyal friend, or human.

"Hey." Sandra rested a hand on her arm. "I'd like to reconnect, to get together some time. I miss seeing you."

Emma contemplated both of them in the mirror—both young mothers who probably had a lot in common. "Um, sure. That sounds nice."

"Here." Sandra pulled out her phone. "Give me your number, and I'll text you. We can set up a lunch or tea or something. Lauren goes to preschool three days a week. What's your daughter's name?"

"Haley Grace." Emma patted her apron, came up empty. "I forgot, which shows how close I am to losing my mind, again. We lock our phones in the back when we're working. But I can give you my number."

Which put any future interaction totally in the other woman's power. The echo of what Justin had said the day before haunted her. She didn't want to sympathize with the man who was flipping her world off its axis.

Sandra tilted her head to the side—cute, like a little bird. "Shoot."

Emma gave her the number. "I'll look forward to hearing from you."

"I'm so excited to catch up." Sandra's smile held so much sincerity Emma found herself feeling better.

A third woman entered the restroom, unknowingly signaling the end of their conversation.

"Okay," Emma said, reaching over to turn on the faucet. "I better get back to work. Thank you, Sandra, for reaching out."

Sandra touched her shoulder and stuffed her phone in the bottomless purse. "I'll text as soon as we get home. Have a good rest of your day." She gave a little wave and left.

"Bye." Emma tore off a paper towel and dried her hands. Other than some red tinge to the white of her eyes, no one would be able to tell she'd been crying. She hoped.

The rest of the afternoon passed in a blur. When she walked into her apartment, knowing she had maybe an hour before Tiffany brought Haley home, she curled up on the couch. At some point, Justin would call, and she needed to have some dates ready. She had so little time with Haley, but she didn't want to cling to her daughter like a burr in the field.

Without knowing her own intentions, she closed her eyes. "Lord, help me."

As soon as the plea escaped her lips, her eyes flew open.

Praying was Tiffany's thing, not hers. Jumping to her feet, she raced to her room and changed out of her uniform. She sorted laundry and emptied the dishwasher. She often got more chores done in this one hour gap than she did the whole rest of the weekend with Haley underfoot.

Five minutes before it was time to leave, she recalled their regular routine. Tiffany would want to hang out. She might lie over the phone, not so much straight to her sister's face.

The doorbell rang. Tiffany ushered Haley inside and then gave Emma a side hug. Her other arm was weighed down with Haley's overnight bag. "This thing gets heavier every time."

Emma snorted. "What did you buy her this time, Aunt Spoiler?"

Tiffany splayed her slender fingers across her chest. "Me? What makes you think I bought her anything?"

"She got me church coloring books!" Haley danced from foot to foot. "And some coloring pencils. She says I'm getting too good for old baby crayons."

Emma felt a pang of misplaced jealousy. She hadn't even touched her own art supplies. Time was in short supply, and what was the point?

Haley started tossing things out of the bag, including her discarded church dress. "Oh, this dress is too small. And I need new shoes."

The growth spurt had come to fruition. Emma groaned. She already worked two jobs and could barely keep her daughter clothed. The costs of preschool alone ate up all the tips and the pitiful check from Jasmine's.

"I put a skirt of mine in there." Tiffany caught one of the flying missiles Haley launched. "It's too big for me so I hope you can get some use out of it."

Her sister had the bad habit of sneaking charity presents and disguising them as favors to her. Often the tags were still on the items, and the size matched Emma's figure, not Tiffany's.

Emma wasn't stupid, but neither was she going to let

misplaced pride get in the way of accepting help. "Thank you, sissy."

"You're welcome." Tiffany ducked her head, always uncomfortable with extra attention. "Hey, I'd hate for it to go to waste."

Emma grinned. "Yeah, right. Do you want to stay for dinner?"

This was another game they played. She'd ask, and Tiffany never stayed. Not that they didn't love each other. They were both so infernally busy.

"Yes, but I can't." Tiffany pressed her lips together. "You'd think, since it was summer, that I'd have all the time in the world, but I have a dozen orders for monograms. I'm swamped." She was a first grade teacher but had a second job in the summer. The hours were flexible but still took time.

Emma gave her a hug. "I understand. I have to prep meals for the week, finish the laundry."

Tiffany squeezed her back and then stepped away. "Love you, Emma. Next Sunday, what about I get here early and bring breakfast?"

Emma blinked. That was new. "That would be great. Just let me know what time. Haley, do you have something to say to your aunt?"

Haley ran over and clutched Tiffany around the waist. "Thank you, thank you, thank you," she sang.

"Love you, love you, love you," Tiffany sang back. "See you next weekend, Haley boo."

"See you then, Aunt Tiffy." Haley ran back toward her pile of loot.

Emma held the door for her sister. "Really, thank you, Tiffany. I don't know what I'd do without you."

Tiffany bowed her head and hurried away.

Emma watched the retreating back for a minute. That hadn't been so hard. Justin had been out of their lives for so long that there was no reason Tiffany would have asked about him. Emma relaxed shoulders that had been drawn up and tight.

A half an hour went by, past dinner and during bath time as she dumped in her bucket of rubber duckies, for Haley to ask the question. "Did Daddy call yet?"

Emma picked up the wide-toothed comb stored next to the tub. She started to run the comb through Haley's wet hair, only advanced maybe an inch before snagging a tangle. Sighing, she flipped open the lid of the tangle-free conditioner and squeezed a blob on the tines of the comb. "No, he hasn't called yet. Do you want him to?"

"Well, duh. Of course I want him to call. He's my daddy." Haley squeezed the mother duck until she squeaked. No symbolism there. "I've never had a daddy before. All the other girls have known their daddies their whole lives. Why didn't I know him before?"

Emma concentrated on the massive spider web of hair, teasing it apart with her fingers. "You've always had a daddy. You have to have both a mommy and a daddy for a baby to be born." She almost choked. In order to avoid one difficult question, she'd opened a can of worms the size of a milk jug.

"Why?" Haley was drowning the mother duck, whether purposefully or not. "Oh, I know. Mommies and Daddies have to kiss in order to make a baby. Ashley's mama and daddy kiss a lot. She's going to have a baby sister."

"I remember. You already told me that having to share toys didn't sound like a good idea to you." Emma could have pumped her fist. One hard conversation postponed.

"Well, I don't know about that." Haley grinned. Now, Mommy duck carried five babies on her back, all at once. "I think it would be worth sharing your toys to have a baby sister. Not a baby brother. Boys are gross."

Emma dropped her head in defeat. Once Haley wanted something, she usually got it. This might just be the first time the spoiled little girl didn't get her wish. "Honey, your daddy and I don't really like each other anymore so we won't be kissing any time soon. No baby sisters."

The ducks went flying, and Haley almost got scalped when she leaned forward to retrieve the toys. "Ouch. Well, maybe you can get a different boyfriend and kiss him. I'd really like a sister."

Emma had maybe half the kid's head tangle-free. There was no escaping the train of thought. "Honey, I don't need a boyfriend. We're happy together, just the two of us."

Haley turned a scant few inches and rolled her eyes. "Mommm. You couldn't kill the spider in my room the other day. We don't know where that thing went. We need a man."

Emma surrendered, rested her head on her arm, and started laughing. Her shoulders shook, and she snorted, twice. "Oh, honey. Oh, Haley."

"What?" Haley grinned and put soap bubbles on her cheeks. She pursed her lips like a fish. "Am I funny, Mama?"

"Girl, you are hilarious." Emma caught her breath after a few minutes. She'd untangled Haley's hair three quarters around the child's head. Good enough. "So, Haley, do you want to go places with your daddy? Spend time with him? Because you don't have to if you don't want to."

She tugged at her daughter's elbows, a signal for her to pack up the ducks and get ready to rinse. Silent signals had turned out to be a way to lessen the nagging and threatening. The hint worked, and Haley scooped up ducks, dumping them on the side of the tub.

"I think I have to." Haley perched on her knees, ready to get splashed with clear water. "My Sunday school teacher says God commands us to honor our father and our mother. A father is a daddy, right?"

Emma switched from side-splitting laughter to tears burning at the back of her throat. Her child was so precious. "Yes, a father is the same thing as a daddy."

Haley stood up in the tub. She put her little hands on her skinny naked hips. "Then, I need to spend time with him if I'm going to honor him. Don't I?"

"Yes, yes, you do." Emma dropped the comb in the water and lowered the drain. She grabbed the towel with the bunny head on top and wrapped Haley in the soft, fluffy goodness. "He might want to see you next weekend. Would you be sad if you couldn't go stay with Aunt Tiffany?"

She didn't think she was trying to undermine Justin. She just wanted to do the right thing and warn her daughter of the possible repercussions of bringing her daddy into her life, their lives. Because like it or not, if Justin was going to be in Haley's life, he'd be in Emma's, too. There would be the pick-ups and the drop offs and the coordination of both.

If part of her was excited by the possibility of seeing him again, another part told the first part to shut up. Justin had dumped her. Period. End of story.

"Mommy, you're suffocating me." Haley's voice was muffled by the towel covering her face.

"Dear Lord, so I am." Emma was horrified. Thinking about Justin made her lose track of what she was doing. "I'm sorry, sweetie. I just have a lot on my mind."

"It's okay." Haley patted her face. "I have a lot on my mind, too. I mean, what shall I wear when Daddy comes to get me?"

The towel was now properly wrapped around the child's body but with her arms inside. She veered around the room like a zombie mummy. A few minutes in, the covering lost the knot, and she streaked to her room.

Emma wiped down the tub and stashed toys away before following. "So, what story do you want tonight?"

Haley was wearing a short baby shark nightgown. "I want a princess one. And the real kind, not one where the girl saves herself. What good is that? If it's a story, I want a prince."

Emma cackled. "Did Aunt Tiffany read you a strong woman story last night?"

Haley made a googly face. "Yeah. And I told her that saving yourself sounded like work. I don't want to work in my stories. I want to have fun."

Emma picked up her copy of the Hidden Princess from when she was a little girl. "What did your aunt say when you told her that?"

Haley scooted under the covers. "She said that it was too fun buying your own stuff. I don't believe it. That's real life where women aren't princesses, and you have to work all the time. Give me fun."

Emma was torn between being proud and crying. "You have a point, baby girl. Every grownup you know is a woman taking care of herself."

Herself, Tiffany, even their mother, Haley's grandma, who had remarried, worked outside the home. She didn't spend much time with Haley because Emma had been such a disappointment, and Haley really didn't know her grandfather at all.

"Mama?" Haley squeezed her face. "Read the story."

Emma startled, embarrassed. "I'm so sorry. I really am. Now, where did we leave off?"

Haley settled in against her pink ribbon pillows. "The girl just met the cutest boy."

They might need a man in their lives eventually, if only to beat off the boys who would come chasing after this little firecracker.

Maybe ten minutes in, Haley was fast asleep. Emma kept reading until the bottom of the page, just to be sure. Sometimes, her daughter fooled her, and her eyes would pop open, asking why she'd stopped reading. A few minutes more and she drank in her little girl's beauty. Tomorrow, they'd be apart for most of the day with only dinner and this evening ritual to glue them together. If she gave Justin some of her time with Haley, there would be so little left.

On the other hand, she might be angry with God, but she knew the Ten Commandments. The one about honoring your mother and father was the only commandment with a promise attached. If Haley's days were going to be long, she needed time with her father.

Her phone rang in the other room.

She sighed and inserted the book back into its spot on the shelf. Her decisions weren't based on faith, since hers was rocky. She made her decision based on the right thing to do, finally.

And the fact that she couldn't have time with her own daddy, even if she wanted to.

CHAPTER 6

*J*ustin stood outside Emma's apartment door. The bureaucracy had taken two weeks to get the paperwork pushed through for him to take some time off. When he'd told his NCO why he needed more time, the man's eyes had almost jumped out of his bald head.

"Father?" *Sgt. Sanderson had yelled loud enough to wake every man in the motor pool.* "What have you done, Lee?"

The man had been a second father to him for the last few years, and his guidance had been needed since Justin's own father had been angry that Justin had enlisted rather than attending his alma mater. The shame of being a deadbeat dad surged from his stripes to his shiny black combat boots.

"Sir." *Justin looked down, realizing he was folding and unfolding his head cover like a napkin.*

"Sit down, Justin." *Sgt. Sanderson rubbed his face a couple of times.* "We've been to hell and back together. I thought I knew everything there was to know about you. Do you want the door shut?"

"No, sir." *He knew he shouldn't be calling a sergeant sir.* "Everybody will know soon enough. I just found out that my high school girlfriend and I have a daughter she never told me about. Haley's four, almost five. I don't even know her birthday."

Sanderson rocked back in his wooden chair. "Wow, that's rough. That's real rough. I can't believe."

Justin was still reeling himself. He'd had days to adjust and try to understand Emma's point of view, but he couldn't.

His mother had told him that no matter what, he needed to get along with Emma. He hated what she'd done, not so sure how he felt about her, but he had to play nice.

She held all the cards.

He held daisies for Emma and a backpack full of stuff for Haley. He juggled to press the doorbell.

Emma opened the door so fast she must have been standing on the other side, just waiting for him to arrive. There were circles under her eyes, but she still radiated beauty. That was another thing that mystified him. After what she'd done, why was he noticing her looks?

"Hi." Emma motioned for him to enter.

"Hi." He shoved the flowers in her direction. "These are for you. I appreciate you making time for me to see Haley."

She took them. "I'll get a vase. I think Haley's changing her clothes again." Emma smiled, maybe for the first time since they'd met again, at least in his direction. "It's like she's going on her first date. Ever since she found out you were coming to take her to the park, she's been trying on outfits."

Justin tightened his grip on the pink sunburst backpack. "I get it. I kept going to the store, trying to figure out what to bring her. It took me hours."

Emma narrowed those summer sky blue eyes. "Tell me you just brought her a backpack."

He smirked, revenge being sweet and all. "Uh-uh. No way. I've got missed birthdays and Christmases to make up for. You are going to have to live with one spoiled little girl, at least for a while."

Emma dropped the flowers on the counter and whirled on him, anger flying. "Don't you dare come in here throwing presents at her, trying to buy her love. I can't afford a lot of extras because I'm the one paying the bills. So, don't you dare."

Justin crossed the gap in two easy steps. "Don't you tell me not to dare. You stole her from me. Years I can never get back. I cannot fathom–no, I can't excuse how you did this to me."

Emma backed up. "I didn't."

"Yes, you did." Justin loomed over her, and when had this happened? He didn't want to threaten her. He turned around, took in his surroundings.

The apartment was neat and clean, black and white. There weren't any candles, any extras, but there were plenty of pictures of Haley. He went to the end table next to the couch and picked up a baby picture. He'd been shot at in Afghanistan. He would not cry.

"As far as expenses, I talked to military legal and tried to find out what my rights are. Regardless, I'll pay child support. I want to be declared her father."

"I didn't mean to hurt you, Justin. I thought you wouldn't care."

If Haley hadn't bounced in the room at that exact moment, he couldn't have accounted for what terrible words would have erupted from his mouth.

"Hi, Daddy." Haley stopped a few feet into the room and posed. She stuck out her front leg and pointed her toe, propped her hands on her hips, and batted her pale eyelashes at him.

"Hi, Haley." Whatever he and Emma had been talking about flew out of his brain to be replaced by mush. She was the most beautiful thing he'd ever seen. Her blonde hair gleamed in the morning sun, and she lit up the room. "How are you?"

"I'm fine. How are you?" She switched front legs and hand on her hip.

"I'm fine. You look pretty in that dress."

Haley dropped the pose and fingered the ruffle on the sunflower sundress. "Thank you. My Aunt Tiffy gave it to me for my birthday. So, you like it?"

"Yeah, I do." Justin held out the backpack like a peace offering. His hands shook. "I'm sorry I missed your birthday, but I'd like to give you something anyway. A late birthday present."

He didn't have to tell her twice. Haley grabbed the gift and ran. He followed her to the couch like a puppy. His hands were sweating, and he would have laughed at himself if it had been the two of them, but Emma hovered only a few feet away.

Her disapproval hung over their heads like the dark cloud in the comics.

Haley patted the backpack. "I love it, Daddy. It's a beautiful color, and I need one for school."

She sounded like such a small grownup that he finally let go and laughed. "I'm glad you like it." He reached out and touched her dimple. He'd give anything to pull her into a bear hug, but he needed to take things slow. "Do you want to open it?"

"What? There's more?"

"Yeah, sweetheart, there's more."

Emma shuffled in place behind them. The woman needed to calm down. She was lucky he hadn't stashed a pony in the back of his truck.

Haley unzipped the main compartment and squealed. She pulled out a doll, a pack of colored pencils, crayons, tiny erasers, a coloring book, a sketch pad, and a huge pack of sugar-free gum. Every item, she shrieked. "Look, Mama."

Haley scrunched her nose at him. "How did you know I like drawing and coloring? Did Mama tell you?"

Justin froze. He'd just assumed. "I guess in a way she did. Your mama loved art when we were kids so I guessed you might, too."

"That makes sense." Haley's face cleared. She seemed to really have a need to understand. Guess she got that from him.

Haley stood, as if some signal had been given that it was time to go to the park.

"Wait." Justin held up his index finger. "Two things. One, you're not done. There are small compartments in the front."

Haley's eyes about bugged out of her head.

He held up a second finger. "Two, you're going to have to change. As pretty as that dress is, I bet your mama wants you to keep it pretty for church or something. You should wear shorts or something to go to the park. Am I right?" He glanced at Emma. Instead of the anger from earlier, her face looked haggard and hurt. "Emma?"

"Yes, you're right. First, Haley, find out what else is in there." She faked excitement for her daughter's sake, and he gave her props.

Whatever was going on behind that beautiful face—and he'd never been able to figure that out—she was doing right by Haley. "And then go back to your room and change into the blue shorts you had on earlier."

"Yes, ma'am." Haley was eager to unzip the smallest compartment first. There was a pair of earrings in the front pocket, even though he hadn't remembered if she'd had her ears pierced yet. She hadn't.

"You can put those away for when you're older," he said, holding his hand out for safe keeping. "I just thought of your eyes when I saw them."

Haley dropped them in his palm and moved to the next, larger zipper. When she pulled out a long, thin jewelry box, Emma gasped. "Justin, what did you do?"

He never stopped looking at his daughter, *his* daughter. Her eyes lit up, and she stared at the box. "How do I open it?"

He took the box, showed her where the edge of the top ended and lifted it off to show an engraved bracelet. "Hold out your arm, please." The small clasp almost did him in, but he persisted, and it clicked.

Haley held out her arm, admiring the bracelet. "What's it say?"

"It says, 'Daddy's girl.'"

Emma flinched.

He ignored her. "Haley, I know you don't know me much,

not yet. But I wanted you to have that so you will always remember that you have a daddy who loves you very much. And I'll always be here for you."

"As much as you can," Emma blurted the words, and then covered her mouth with her hand.

Justin could either argue with her, and taint his first real memory with his daughter, or let it go. "As much as I can." He nodded. "I am in the Army, Haley. Sometimes, I have to go train or fight the bad guys and you won't see me for a while. But I will always be back. Okay?"

"Okay." Haley threw her arms around his neck. "Thank you, Daddy. I'm going to go change. I can't wait to get to the park."

Emma gave him a brittle smile. "I'll go with her and supervise. Otherwise, we may never make it to the park, and that would be a shame."

After she left the room, Justin snorted. He just bet she would cry in her sleep if Haley spent all her time in her room and wiped out his plans. Him not getting to spend time with their daughter would be such a shame.

He gathered Haley's gifts and placed them in a neat pile on the coffee table, tucked the backpack off to the side. Hearing no signs that they'd be joining him soon, he stood and wandered around the living room. He went from framed photo to framed photo, piecing together his daughter's baby and toddler years. If he asked, would Emma give him copies?

"Here we are." Haley came back in, sporting blue shorts and a flowery T-shirt, and posed anyway. "Are you ready? I bet I can swing higher."

"That's not how physics work," he joked. That one sailed right over the girl's head. So, he needed practice. "I bet you can," he tried again.

She grinned and ran for the door.

Emma motioned to a tote bag the size of a carry-on suitcase by the door. "If you'll carry that, I'll grab my purse."

Justin eyed her askance. "Are we really going to do this? You know you can trust me to bring her back."

Emma rolled her eyes. His pulse picked up, and he opened his mouth to let off some steam, but she cut him off.

"It's not that, Justin." She pointed to the bag. "You're new to this parenting thing. Sunscreen. Hat, if she'll keep it on. Sunglasses, ditto. A change of clothes for when her ice cream melts all over or when she falls in the dirt. Bandages, same reason."

He blinked, then held up his hands in surrender. "Okay, okay. I get it."

"Good. Now, we'll be taking my car." Emma swung the shoulder strap of her purse across her body. "Haley still needs to be in a booster seat. Did you get one?"

Justin wanted to pull out his phone and take notes, but he also didn't want to look like an idiot. "No, I didn't get one." He motioned for them both to precede him through the door. "Ladies first."

Haley giggled. "I'm not a lady. I'm just a girl."

"You're a lady in training." He pulled the door almost closed. "Does it automatically lock?"

"I've got it." Emma reached for the doorknob, and their fingers grazed.

Her touch brought on sparks, followed by the urge to curse. The woman had done him wrong six ways to Sunday, and he was not going to revisit an old attraction.

"So, which park did you want to go to?" Emma seemed unaffected and that was definitely a good thing. If she had no feelings for him, no scraps from the past, then that would be the end of it.

"Which park?" Justin followed in her wake. He needed to buy a car seat before they did this again. Sitting in the passenger seat while she had the wheel was not his idea of fun. "Is there more than one?"

Emma twisted her lips as she backed her SUV out of the

parking space. "There are three water parks in the Charleston area, and more playgrounds than you could shake a stick at. How about the one at Gahagan?"

His mother had always been busy with committee meetings and charities when he was a kid, so if an activity hadn't involved a sport, he didn't know his way around town. "Sure, whatever you say." A scary thought had his stomach seizing. "Um, Emma. A booster seat is safe in a truck, right?"

The woman looked angelic and evil in one grin. "What? Oh, no, you'll have to get a minivan."

They were sitting in a jeep. He settled down. "Yeah, right. You almost had me there."

Emma gunned the engine and roared into traffic.

"Whoa. What's the hurry?" He'd heard stories about soldiers getting back from deployment only to be killed in random car accidents.

Haley giggled in the back seat. "She always drives fast. Aunt Tiffy says Mama is a speed demon."

Justin clutched the safety strap hanging above his head, exaggerating a little, but not by much. "Woman. You do realize you're not driving the safest vehicle in the world, right?"

Emma slowed down and flipped on the radio. Justin's phone buzzed in his pocket, and he ignored it. There was no one he wanted to talk to right now that wasn't in this car. The country radio host broke into a commercial segment. He recognized the voice as the same man who'd read his name over the air waves when he'd won those tickets for a concert under the Cooper River Bridge.

He glanced at Emma to see if she remembered, but her eyes were on the road. Of course, she'd never left the area. She'd been listening to TJ, and this wasn't a trip down memory lane for her. He'd been the one who had left. He'd been the one who'd spent months on another continent, a world away, and years bouncing all around this one.

Gahagan Park was to the side of some Little League baseball

fields. He knew them well, even if he'd never played on the playground. Baseball had been his passion up until middle school when he'd switched to football. Every memory, he glanced at Emma and wondered if she remembered, too. He didn't ask, though, since they were co-existing in peaceful silence, and he wasn't going to be the man breaking the accord.

"Daddy, we're going to have so much fun!" Haley chattered. "There are swings and a slide, but best of all, there are drawbridges. I'll be the princess, and you rescue me."

"Got it." He could follow orders with the best of them. He flexed his arm and showed off a bicep built the old-fashioned way. "I'll fight your dragons."

Emma switched off the ignition. "She can fight her own battles. She doesn't need a man."

Justin almost groaned. The Emma he remembered had been more fun, when she hadn't been crying at the drop of a hat.

"Mama." Haley unbuckled herself and placed a hand on both adults' shoulders. "I told you last night. It's more fun to be rescued."

He laughed and gave Emma a "so there" look. "All righty then. Let's go fight some dragons."

"Tote bag, sunscreen."

As if he'd forget. Okay, he'd forgotten.

They exited the vehicle. Emma popped the hatch and ruffled through the bag. She held out the bottle of sunscreen, and Haley held out her arms like she was about to be handcuffed.

Justin took the bottle and found himself choked up at the thought of rubbing lotion on this small person that somehow belonged to him. With both him and Emma fair skinned, Haley was blonde and blue-eyed and prone to burn crispy-fried.

Justin slathered lotion on his own arms and neck after he'd finished with Haley. He'd actually formed the habit in the Middle East. He'd worn his BDU jacket a lot, covered his arms, but any skin showing was in the danger zone from that blistering heat.

Haley grabbed his hand and dragged him forward. Someday, this would be commonplace, but right now, every touch of her small hand sent dueling thrills of love and regret racing through him.

The playground walls rose up two stories with rope bridges and plank walkways and small forts. Emma had picked one of the coolest playgrounds he'd ever seen. There were poles to slide down and the typical swings, but the hiding places and portholes were anything but boring.

"Where to first, Haley girl?" He'd worn gym shorts, a T-shirt, and his athletic shoes with the idea of keeping up with her as best he could.

"This is the way in." She was all seriousness that there was a right way and a wrong way to do things.

"I'll just be over here on this bench," Emma said, the tote bag in one hand and a book in the other.

"What?" The one word blurted out before he could rethink the implied judgment. "I mean, don't you want to play? If it's because I'm here..."

She shook her head in denial. "No, it's not that. I just don't have the energy. You'll see."

Justin contemplated the woman he knew for a fact was in her early twenties and should have all the energy in the world and the child hopping from one foot to another in anticipation. "Well, I guess I'll have to learn my lesson the hard way."

He ducked his head and followed Haley up the curving staircase where strange children pretended to shoot arrows in their direction.

The next hour was one of the best times in his life. Haley led, he followed. They ran along the bridges, galloping, pretending to vanquish dragons and mermaids, even though he didn't know what the pretty ladies with fish tails had done to deserve their fate.

He drew the line at swinging himself, if only because he didn't fit. He pushed Haley. He noticed Emma looking at him funny. He lifted his chin in silent acknowledgement. He wouldn't push their girl too high, no matter how vociferously she pleaded.

And bribed. "Daddy, if you push me higher, I'll kiss you on both cheeks."

"Nope, this is far enough."

She drove a hard bargain, though. "I'll clean my room."

He caught her, held her up high so they faced each other, and pretended to consider her offer. "Naw, that would work with your mom but not with me. I've never even seen your room. Is it messy?"

"The messiest," she said, but her eyes sparkled. He let her go.

The release had her shrieking in glee. On the backswing, she started singing nonsense songs, and he laughed like he hadn't in years.

The sun gleamed at its peak when Emma called out to them from a few feet away. "I think we should head out and have lunch now. Are y'all hungry?"

"I am positively famished!" Haley yelled and giggled.

"Famished?" Justin glanced at Emma. "Who says famished anymore?"

"Tiffany." Emma led the way back to the parking lot. "She has her most weekends while I'm working."

Justin held the door for both of them in turn and then made his way to his seat. When he finally leaned against his own seat, the air conditioning made him realize just how hot he'd gotten.

"Where to?" Emma sounded resigned.

He'd have thought she would welcome someone else paying for lunch for a change. "Ye Castle Confections. Do you remember that superhero ice cream?" He was asking Emma, but she seemed determined to say as little as possible to him all day.

Haley jumped back into the middle, even from the back seat. "Yeah, their ice cream is the best. They have a cotton candy and a princess unicorn flavor. I want two scoops."

"Only after you eat some real food," Emma said to the

rearview mirror, her tone dry. "Wait. When have you ever been to the Castle?"

"With my class at school. We went there after we went to the water park."

"Oh." Emma bit her lip and started driving.

Justin couldn't take his eyes off her. She barely knew her own daughter. "Where did you say you work, Emma?"

He worked to keep his tone gentle, but her answer still came through clenched teeth. "I work at an insurance company nine to five Monday through Friday, then Jasmine's on most weekends. I take one weekend a month to myself."

This weekend. "Is it the money? Will child support help?" His intelligence quotient dropped a standard deviation as soon as the words left his mouth.

"Of course, it's the money, and of course it would help." Emma stopped at an intersection. "But..."

Haley listened and absorbed every word. Haley butted in. "I go to Aunt Tiffy's after school on Fridays."

"But what?" Justin didn't let himself get distracted.

"But when will this get old? When will you leave again?" A curl fell into Emma's line of vision, and she blew it out of the way.

If the Army had taught him one thing, it had been to pick his battles. Sometimes, he had to hurry up and wait. The only way to prove his staying power to her was to stick around. Why she felt like he was going to walk away, that was something to discuss when Haley didn't sit in the back seat.

"Never." He turned toward his daughter. "What do you like for lunch, before the ice cream?"

"Chicken nuggets and macaroni and cheese." Hayley gave a typical kid answer from what he'd seen with his buddies' kids, and he nodded. "And fried okra."

Justin grinned as big as he could go. "Yeah, now, that's my girl."

"You hate fried okra," Emma argued, then pressed her lips together as if shutting herself up.

"I changed."

The rest of the afternoon passed in a junk food induced blur, and then they pulled into the apartment complex parking lot. Justin and Haley kept up a running conversation.

"Do you like hamburgers?"

"How about hot dogs?"

"French fries?"

"Salad?"

Turned out his girl liked pretty much everything, except mustard. Since he thought the stuff was a gift from the gods, they didn't have everything in common. But they had a lot and any differences wouldn't have mattered anyway; his newfound love deepened every minute.

When the car came to a complete stop, Emma stared straight ahead and spoke to the windshield. "I've got it from here. She's going to need a nap, so I guess we'll see you tomorrow."

"She's already out like a light." Justin was halfway out of the car. "Just let me carry her inside."

If Emma protested, he didn't stick around to hear it. The woman had been giving him the cold shoulder most of the day. She'd also seemed withdrawn from her own daughter, but Haley didn't act like her mother's attitude was anything unusual.

When he pulled a drowsy Haley out of her car seat, small arms went around his neck. He took a deep pull of oxygen, just wanted to breathe in this moment and hold it.

"Thank you, Daddy."

"Any time, sweetheart." If his voice cracked, so be it.

"I'll just get the bag," Emma said, sarcasm soaking her tone. "And the leftovers."

Since the leftovers were hers, he didn't know what her problem was.

"You smell good," Haley whispered against his neck, and her breath tickled.

"I don't know how," he joked. "You gave me a good workout, and I stink."

They had reached the door, and he had to wait a few seconds for Emma to catch up. She dropped the tote bag on the concrete landing with a huff, and he got the message. He probably should have let her carry Haley and offered to get the bag. Should have, would have, could have. He wanted to hold his daughter every chance he could get.

"Her room is the second door on the left down the hall." Emma moved toward the kitchen. "I'll put everything away and let you tuck her in. You can show yourself out."

"Out?" Haley lifted her head off his shoulder, eyes half closed. "Where's he going?"

"He's going home, Haley." Emma sounded tired.

"But daddies and mommies live together. Isn't he going to stay for a sleepover?"

Justin met Emma's shocked gaze with what had to be complete disbelief on his face. "I didn't say anything that made her think..."

"Neither did I." Emma came closer, reaching out a hand to touch Haley's cheek. "Baby, mommies and daddies live together when they're married. Your daddy and I are not married. He's going to go back to his own house."

Haley gripped his neck tighter, but he kept his inability to breathe to himself. "I want him to stay. You said you'll always be with me."

Justin's chest hurt. "Honey, I will always love you, and I'll be with you when I can. But this is your mommy's place, and she's right. We're not married so we can't live together."

Haley buried her face against his shoulder. "Ashley's mommy and her boyfriend live together, and they aren't married."

He wouldn't touch the moral dilemma with a suspension line on a parachute, and he could pack one of those in his sleep. Life was so complicated.

Emma's eyebrows created creases in her forehead. "Haley. You are going to go to bed and go to sleep. Your daddy is going to his house, and that's just the way it is. He'll visit when he can."

Haley started to cry.

Emma disentangled the little girl's arms from his neck. "Here, let me take her. I'll need to settle her down or she won't sleep tonight."

Justin had no choice but to do as she asked. If he was a real parent, he would be part of the settling down, but for now, he'd leave. "Bye, sweetie." He kissed Haley's wet cheek. "I'll be back tomorrow, promise."

Haley shrieked and tried to keep her grip on him.

"Go." Emma was stone-faced and impenetrable.

He left.

CHAPTER 7

$\mathscr{F}$or two months, Justin had been patient with Emma. His patience was at an end. Emma could decipher his irritation in his stance as he waited for her to accompany him and Haley to the movie theater. He'd been nothing but a loving father, attentive and dependable. The miles he was putting on his truck had to be adding up. He could be alone with Haley. Since she couldn't bring herself to really talk to him, these outings weren't any fun for her—her fault. She was the third wheel. She had no good reason to go.

"Justin," Emma said his name even as she dropped her purse on the table. "I think."

"Yes?" His green eyes against that tan would make most women's hearts flutter. Her heart had been mired in Lowcountry plough mud for a very long time. "What do you think, Emma?"

Hope shone in his eyes. She didn't know what he hoped for, though, and she didn't have the energy to hazard a guess. "I think you and Haley should go, just the two of you, without me. Some daddy-daughter time."

Justin's whole body relaxed, and his smile was slow and pleased. "Thank you. I'll text you when the movie is done and bring her back right after dinner."

"I appreciate that."

He put a hand on Haley's shoulder as if to keep the jumping bean tethered to the ground. "I know to get her the kids pack and, wait, should she go to the bathroom before we leave?"

Emma found herself smiling. "She already went. She doesn't have any allergies or anything to worry about. You just have fun. I'll be here when you get back."

"Great." Justin wiped his hands on his jeans. His nervousness was sweet and reassuring. "Well, then. We'll be going. Are you ready, Haley?"

"Yes, sir." Haley hopped her way to the door, like the bunnies she so loved. "Can I have popcorn and a cherry slushie? Do you like slushies, Daddy? I know you like vanilla ice cream with hot fudge, but what about slushies?"

"Are you kidding?" Justin opened the door and ushered Haley out. "Who doesn't love slushies? I like the cola kind best. Old school, that's me. What's your favorite?"

Emma couldn't make out Haley's answer. They'd gone far enough away from the door and out of hearing distance. Her daughter liked whatever flavor she hadn't tried before and cherry. Emma strained to hear the diesel engine firing up. She refused to allow herself to look out the window and watch them drive away.

They'd only be gone for a few hours, no different than when Tiffany took Haley for the weekend. In fact, if anyone was losing out on the deal, Tiffany was. Emma's stomach burned at the thought that she'd told Tiffany that she was keeping Haley at home for the weekend because she was getting fewer shifts at work.

One of the many half-truths she'd told her sister these last few weeks. Part of her couldn't believe Haley hadn't spilled the beans, but Tiffany hadn't said anything to indicate she had.

Emma walked over to open the curtains now that the danger of wallowing was past. She needed the sunlight to see every little speck of dirt.

First, she needed to change her nice casual clothes for her ratty cleaning-the-apartment clothes. She rushed back to the bedroom and scrounged through her dresser. The bedroom was dark. She always kept the blinds closed in here since the window overlooked the complex's swimming pool.

A T-shirt with the iron-on decal of a country music band hanging half off lay folded at the bottom of the drawer. Justin had bought the shirt for her, back when they were dating. He had been her everything. They'd started talking a few months before her father died. She'd been excited about cheerleading, full of life. Then, after her father had been murdered, she'd stopped talking to everyone, even him. When she finally returned to school, she'd walked the halls, eyes down, not watching where she was going, needing every bit of mental energy to put one foot in front of the other.

"Hey, watch out." Two strong arms grasped her shoulders.

She made eye contact with someone not in her family for the first time since her father's death. "Oh, sorry. It's you."

"Yeah, it's me." Justin leaned over her, his broad back shielding her from curious classmates. "I've missed you."

"Sorry." She acted like an idiot, repeating the same word like a parrot, but she couldn't do any better.

"Don't apologize." The tenderness in his eyes made her want to cry, and she'd done enough of that to last a lifetime. "Just talk to me, please. I tried calling. I was there at the funeral. You've shut me out. Can we meet after school?"

The only thing she wanted was for him to leave her alone, and agreeing had seemed the best way to accomplish that feat. Then, they met after school, and he held her when she cried. He made her laugh for the first time in months.

She clutched the shirt to her chest and sank to the floor. The concert had been one of the best nights of her life. They'd had so much fun, singing at the top of their lungs, sneaking beer with their fake IDs, making out in his truck afterward.

Then, with her grades in the toilet because of those months of grieving and not recovering, she'd gone to community college instead of a four year university with all her friends. He'd rebelled against his family tradition of attending the state military college and enlisted instead. He'd had no room for a girlfriend in his new life.

He had left her behind with everything else about this town.

She had been pregnant with his baby, and he'd left her.

He'd been the one solid thing in her life after her father's death, and he left her.

The fingers of her empty hand dug into the carpet. Everyone in her life left her. Her father. Justin. Her mother might as well have left them. She'd remarried so fast, not able to function alone. Then, when Emma turned up pregnant out of wedlock, well, her mother had barely spoken to her since then. She'd looked at her with disgust in the corner of her eyes ever since. She hadn't even come to Haley's birth, since hospitals made her nervous.

Tiffany had been there, the voice of reason tried to interrupt the rising swirl of darkness, but the other voices had more weight.

Her father, Justin, and now Haley.

They would all leave her.

They didn't need her.

The dark in the corner came at her.

CHAPTER 8

$\mathcal{H}$aley ran down the hall. Emma heard her coming but couldn't react fast enough to hide her weakness. Somewhere, maybe still in his crate after all this time, Jimbo whimpered.

"Mama, why are you on the floor?"

Emma pushed to a sitting position just as someone flipped the switch, and the light blared.

"Emma? Are you okay?" Justin's voice came from a distance, but in reality, he was only a few judgmental feet away.

Her brain struggled to invent a response they would accept. "I'm fine. I was just cleaning and dropped something under the dresser."

"In the dark?"

"We rang the doorbell lots of times." Haley danced back and forth like a child juiced up on sugar and the orange popcorn salt only found in theaters. "You didn't answer."

"The door was unlocked." Justin's voice stayed even, but accusations punched every syllable. A responsible mother did not leave the door unlocked where criminals could just waltz inside. "Did you find what you were looking for?"

"What?" Emma couldn't comprehend the question but then

remembered her excuse of just seconds earlier. "Oh, yes. This old shirt. It's my favorite."

Justin glanced down, and Emma stuffed the shirt behind her back. "Emma." He chuckled. "How old are you? Show me the shirt."

"Why not, Mommy?" Haley thought they were playing a game. She darted around her back and tried to grab the shirt. "What is it?"

"Haley, stop," Emma and Justin commanded in unison.

"If your mother doesn't want us to see the shirt, we need to respect her wishes, Haley." Justin turned to leave the room. "I'm sorry, Emma, I shouldn't even be here. I didn't mean to invade your privacy. I was honestly worried about you, or I wouldn't have come into your room. Again, I apologize."

Emma forgot about the shirt and followed him. "Justin, wait. How did it go? The movie. Did she behave?"

Justin kept walking. She wasn't going to chase after him, but there was also no rational reason to have this conversation in the hall.

Haley inserted herself into the lack of conversation. "Mama, it was so much fun. We wore funny glasses, and it was like we were inside the movie. It was called 3D. Have you heard of 3D?" Haley somehow always filled the quiet spaces.

"Yes, hon, I've heard of it. Did you keep the glasses on the whole time?"

"Yes, ma'am. I did, and I didn't spill my drink or my popcorn."

Justin stood in the middle of her small living room, waiting. "She leaves out the fact that she spilled the candy that came with the kids' pack, but that's okay. The important thing is we had a wonderful time and made a memory."

"Would you like to sit for a few minutes? I can get you a drink," Emma said, desperate to appear normal and not the woman they'd found on the floor in a heap.

"Um, sure." Justin's eyes about crossed. So, now she

appeared plain desperate. Every other time, she'd kicked him out as fast as she could get him to leave. "I would love some ice water, if you don't mind. The sugar from that slushie may have caused my teeth to rot."

Emma smiled because that was an obvious attempt at humor. "Water coming up."

As she turned past the bar separating the kitchen from the living area, she noticed the stupid shirt was still in her hand. Hoping no one would notice, she dropped it on a chair next to the table.

"So, the movie was 3D," Emma started, unwilling to let go of the conversation thread, just in case anyone asked more questions about what she'd been doing while they'd been gone for hours. "Was it a good movie?"

"It was beautiful." Haley must have found the candy and mainlined it. She held up her arms and twirled like a ballerina. "There was a girl in a tower with very long hair, and it was yellow like mine." She leaned back and shook her hair so it was as long as possible.

Since Emma procrastinated trying to get the busy preschooler to sit in a stylists' chair, Haley's hair brushed her little bottom.

"Is my hair long enough?"

"I'd say." Justin laughed, his side grin catching Emma off guard.

That grin had always stopped her in her tracks, and this was no exception. Her hand hovered over the cabinet where she kept the glasses.

"I'm thirsty, too, Mama." Haley distracted her. "Can I have some water, too?"

"Of course, baby." Just saying the words and the normalcy of her daughter's hyperactive antics had Emma calming down. She grabbed a couple of glasses and filled them with ice and cold water from the refrigerator door. "So, when are you going to be back this way, Justin?"

At some point, he'd wandered in her direction. He leaned

against the kitchen bar, his shoulders taking up half its length. "I honestly don't know. I'm scheduled to deploy in January, but I've put in a request for family leave. I just can't see disappearing for six months after I just came into Haley's life."

Emma shivered at the reminder that he was only here because of their daughter. He'd been the love of her life, and no one else had come even close to replacing him. For her. He obviously didn't feel the same. "Do you think they'll give it to you?"

He took the glass she offered and drank half the water in one gulp. The veins on his forearms stood out. She found even his hands attractive, which wasn't right given the animosity between them. He was also talking, and she needed to concentrate.

"Yes," he said. "Yeah, I do. I told my sergeant the whole story, about how I hadn't known I was a father and had missed out on so much."

Emma bristled at the thought of complete strangers knowing what she'd done and judging her. "Listen, Justin, there's more to the story than what I told you."

He held up a hand and gave a slight nod toward Haley. "You don't have to explain. I decided to forgive you no matter what. It's the only way to move forward."

This was an abrupt change. She wanted to challenge him, to find out what had brought about this transformation, but she took the hint. Now wasn't the time or place to get into a discussion of her faults and his magnanimous gesture.

"Thank you but some time." She handed Haley her water and watched while the little girl drank a few sips. Then, Haley grew bored and wandered over to the stack of presents Justin had brought earlier.

When she looked back at the man sitting across from her at the counter, she found him watching her. "So, what did you do while we were gone? I hope me being here is giving you a break."

Emma grimaced. She'd relaxed, thinking maybe she had escaped an explanation. "I did rest. Thank you."

Her brief answers must seem like she was barricading herself, putting up more blocks in the wall she'd erected between them. For the first time since Boone Hall and the mangled strawberry picking, she didn't want him to think that.

"Really, Justin, I'm happy that you're doing things with Haley. My best memories of my dad are when he took us girls places, and we just had fun. With Mom, it was always about being on our best behavior."

"Haley." Sensing the irony even as she spoke, she caught Haley in mid-jump. "Don't you dare, little girl. Get off that stool."

Haley froze in place, her hands on either side of the stool, straddling the thing, ready to play leapfrog into the living room.

"Down."

Haley puffed up her bottom lip but obeyed. She plopped her bottom on the stool and placed the coloring book she was carrying on the counter. The danger past, Emma looked up at Justin, startled. She'd just spoken of her father without tearing up.

Justin must not have noticed. "Well, I'm glad you didn't spend the time cleaning." He lifted his chin in the direction of the sink and its pile of dirty dishes. "My gut instinct tells me you don't often allow yourself to relax."

Was that what she called her complete meltdown on her bedroom floor? Emma concentrated on retrieving a pitcher of sweet tea from the refrigerator. She needed caffeine. "You're right. I don't. If I sit, I'll pretty much always see something that needs to be done."

"Mama works two jobs." Haley seemed to be mimicking what someone else had said, maybe her. "She's very busy."

Emma winced, her daughter's words on the side of a paper cut for pain. "I'm not that busy."

Haley's water sloshed when she dropped the glass on the counter.

"Okay, maybe I am." Emma took a deep breath. "I still make time for you, Haley. Didn't we just...?" She paused because the last fun thing they'd done had been with Justin and the time before that. "I do my best."

She sounded defensive, even to her own ears. Annoyed, she walked over to the sink and considered doing the dishes with the both of them sitting there.

Scrawny arms circled her waist. "It's okay, Mama. I love you best."

Emma inhaled that love like fresh air after being submerged in the ocean. She wiped off her hands and scooted around to face her daughter, careful not to break her hold. "I love you best, too, Haley girl."

Justin coughed. "Listen. I think this whole thing started with my hoping you got a break when I was here. I know you work hard, and I want to help with that. That's all."

He finished his water and stood, jammed his hands into his pockets. He sidestepped the kitchen table, bumping into a chair. The T-shirt fell to the floor. He reached down to pick it up, maybe without thinking, and the shirt unfurled in his grasp, the band name emblazoned on the front now visible.

"Ooh, Daddy." Haley shrieked like he was in trouble.

Justin's green eyes clouded. "This is your favorite shirt?"

"Uh," Emma stammered. The shirt wasn't her favorite by a long shot. That had been her babbling in the bedroom, caught in the aftermath of one of her episodes. At the same time, the shirt represented one of the best memories of her life.

Justin fluttered the shirt at Haley. "I bought this shirt for your mom the summer after we graduated from high school. That was some concert."

Emma made an unidentifiable noise.

"I'm just saying." Justin had this one dimple that flashed only every now and then, a well-guarded secret between him and the beneficiary. "Your mama used to dance and sing, Haley, everywhere she went. She'd make me forget where I was going. She was so loud."

"Really?" Haley leaned forward on the bar stool, looking at the T-shirt like it was an artifact from a lost civilization. "I don't believe you."

Justin held the shirt out to Emma. "Maybe it's the magic shirt. Have you ever seen her wear it?"

"No, sir." Haley shook her head very slowly.

"I think she should model it for us," Justin challenged her. "In fact, I dare her."

Emma marched across the kitchen and grabbed the shirt. "You had to go there."

For the first time since Boone Hall, there was something in his eyes when he looked at her rather than Haley.

"I'll be right back." She couldn't resist that look, never could. "You owe me, Justin Lee."

He saluted. "Bring it on, baby girl." As soon as the words were out there, the old nickname from a previous lifetime, he backtracked. "Sorry, that just slipped out. Old habits."

"Uh-uh, you're not distracting me." She waved the shirt in his face. "I'm thinking about a night out, babysitting on the house." She faltered. She didn't want any of that.

Turning, she cycled her old self and sashayed down the hall. Her body could project fearlessness even if she was jelly underneath. In the bedroom, she flipped on the lights and stared at a shirt she hadn't stuck her head through for five years. It would serve her right if she couldn't even fit.

She had given birth between now and then.

But a dare was a dare. She sucked in her gut and shimmied into the shirt with a glittery, "Country Music Nation," across the chest. The fit was a little snug. "Yeah, a little tight, but looking good there, Emma," she said to the woman in the beveled glass mirror.

As she walked down the hall, she contemplated going whole

hog and dancing her way into the living room. Instead, she posed, borrowing a page from Haley's songbook, so to speak. One foot and hip jutted forward, hands on her hips, chest out, she framed herself in the doorway.

Justin was in the middle of a question about Haley's preschool teacher's name. He stopped mid-inquiry, leaned back on his bar stool, and rubbed his upper lip with his thumb. His gaze roamed up and down, as if he'd met her somewhere but couldn't remember the details.

Haley sensed the change in him, whirled around, and clapped. "Mama, you're doing a me!"

Emma surrendered and broke character, laughing. "Yes, Haley, I believe I am. What do you think?"

"It's not pink." The question hadn't been meant for Haley.

"What do I think?" Justin hesitated.

Haley flew off her stool and ran over to stand beside her, copying the pose that Emma had copied from her. "Are we twins, Daddy?"

Justin rubbed his face. "I wouldn't say you're twins, sweetheart, but I would say you're beautiful like your mama."

Haley giggled and went from pose to pose. Emma met Justin's eyes and couldn't break the connection.

Justin stood and patted his pockets, pulled out his keys. "I have to go. Thanks for the water."

Emma took a step backward as if he'd pushed her away physically. "You're welcome."

"Okay, well, bye." Justin rushed out the door.

Haley's bottom lip quivered. "Did I do something wrong? He didn't kiss me goodbye."

Emma reeled Haley in for a hug. "No, baby. You didn't do anything wrong. I think your daddy had to get back to work."

The vague phrase seemed to comfort Haley.

In her head, though, Emma had the start of a crazy idea. Big, strong Army guy Justin had just run scared.

Of her.

CHAPTER 9

*J*ustin sat in his truck, fiddling with the radio, searching for whiny country music. He wasn't quite geared up to start the hours-long trek back to North Carolina. Modern country with its driving beat was letting him down.

No part of him wanted to leave this spot. His daughter and the woman he'd just discovered he might still have feelings for were inside that building, and that's where he belonged.

Shock waves reverberated through him from the blow his heart had taken when the shirt Emma had hidden from him turned his memories inside out. That concert had been one of the best memories of his life. Emma had been so full of light and life, her golden hair a halo around her as she twirled and danced. The devil might have gone down to Georgia, but the angel had been with him in Charleston, South Carolina.

Attraction he could have sworn was dead, or maybe this was brand new, surged through him. He'd been the one to break off their relationship. Years had passed with only the rare thought of her, and lately, since discovering she'd kept his daughter from him, the thoughts hadn't been good.

Slender fingers tugged at her curtains.

He panicked. She couldn't catch him sitting here like a love-struck idiot. He shoved at the gas pedal, blanking on the fact that he drove a stick shift.

The engine stalled, screeching gears bouncing him around.

"In the name of all that's holy." His whole body heated with humiliation. He didn't even check to see if his misery had been witnessed. It had. There was no way he'd earn a pass on that one. Taking a deep breath, he focused on the clutch as if trying to pass his driver's test.

A few stoplights down, he turned on to Summer Creek's historic Main Street. One thing he couldn't get anywhere else was a Tasty Express Big Bubba burger. Yeah, he'd had popcorn and a slushie with Haley, but a man needed meat. He needed sustenance if he was going to face hours of trying to figure out why he'd left Emma behind in the first place. Right now, his logic was a little fuzzy.

Five minutes came and passed before the speaker crackled and a perky female voice asked for his order. He ordered the burger, fries, and yet more caffeine. The large drink had to be crunched to fit in the drink holder, but he was determined. He spread napkins over his lap to protect his best pair of jeans. One thing he didn't possess was a lot of civilian clothes.

Of course, mayo and a chunk of tomato plopped on to his lap as soon as he hit the interstate. Grateful for the blanket of napkins, he caught the tomato and ignored the mayo.

He'd been the one to leave Emma. He hadn't really wanted to leave *her* behind, but his old self. He'd been rebelling so hard that his mother had locked him out of the house one night. His lack of a college decision had grieved his father to no end, and he'd only graduated high school because his coach had also been his Chemistry teacher and boosted him to passing.

Even if he'd known about Haley, there was no guarantee the old him would have stepped up and done the right thing.

The realization had him running off the road long enough to produce the grating sound of tires going over rumble strips.

Steeling himself not to jerk the wheel, he eased back on the road. For a few minutes, he focused on driving. Then, he cranked up the volume on a song he didn't recognize and didn't even like. The music drowned out his wayward thoughts for the length of one measly chorus.

The online calling system in his truck buzzed, and a phone number flashed across the screen. "Hallelujah. Cody. Hey, buddy. What's up?"

"Justin, my man." Cody was stationed at Ft. Bragg, his division, different units. They were both stupid enough to jump out of perfectly good airplanes. "I was just wondering when you were getting back."

"On my way now. What's up?"

"I wanted to bounce some ideas off you for training this week. I also wanted to make sure you were going to have your guys running in the morning for PT."

"You want to combine forces?" This was all normal stuff and could wait until they were both on base. Something didn't add up.

"Yeah, me and my guys."

They were both sergeants. The only difference was that Justin had been accepted for Officer Candidate School, and Cody hadn't. Any other man might have a beef with him, but so far, they'd been good, from what he could tell.

"So I was wondering." Cody paused, then raced through the words like he was deadlifting his body weight, heavy breathing and all. "Kristi was over here this weekend, hanging with the guys, playing poker like we always do. Except you weren't here. And I was wondering…"

Justin swerved a bit but somehow kept his truck between the lines. Kristi had been so far from his mind lately that she might as well have been on the moon. "What were you wondering, Cody?"

"I mean, I wouldn't want to dog on another guy's girl, especially when that man is a friend. Like we're buddies, you know?"

"Yeah, we are. I'd trust you with my life." He had before and would probably do so again.

"So, we're cool?"

His caffeine-soaked brain chugged through the message behind the words. "You and Kristi, huh?"

"I mean, not if you and her are still a thing."

Justin looked for an exit, for his and everybody else's safety. There was nothing for miles. Cody was waiting. Thing was, if his friend was thinking along those lines, Lord knew what the woman in question was thinking. "Listen, man. I haven't made it official. I can't believe I haven't, but let me talk to her."

"Sure. You got some things unresolved. No hard feelings, right?"

Justin shook his head where no one could see. "No hard feelings. I'm glad you talked to me. I guess I needed a wakeup call."

"Good one. See you tomorrow."

"Yeah. See you then." Justin drove, took a bite of his lukewarm burger, and almost choked.

Where was his head? How could he have left her hanging? When had he decided they were through? He'd thought the new and improved Justin was better than this.

Showed how wrong he could be—just in case he ever thought he didn't need Jesus.

Justin was halfway home before he worked up the nerve to make the call. The clock on the dashboard glowed in the dark, midnight.

Even still, she answered on the first ring. "Hey, babe, what's up?"

"Kristi." His voice was strained, and he took a sip of his very watered-down drink. He hadn't even considered he could be waking her up. "I'm sorry for calling so late. Is it too late?"

He shouldn't have called so late when they both had to be up at five in the morning. He kept messing up.

Still, she answered in a sweet voice. "No, not at all. What's on your mind?"

"It is too late. I just couldn't wait. I wasn't thinking." He didn't even sound like himself to himself.

"I don't understand." She sounded groggy. She must have been asleep. "You weren't thinking about what?"

"About us." He groaned. "I'm sorry. I haven't treated you right. I should have set things straight sooner."

Her tone got even sweeter, if that was possible. "That's okay. I forgive you. Why don't we talk tomorrow? Things will look better in the morning."

He maneuvered around a tractor trailer that was half on, half off the road, the wheels grinding against the bumper strips. He hoped the driver didn't wreck, but he sure wasn't going to follow behind and let the man take him with him. "Listen, Kristi, I just don't want another day to go by without us talking. I know we were getting close, but I've got so much going on right now."

"Justin, I can wait for you to figure all this out. I mean, I don't want us to give up."

"No, I can't ask that of you. My whole focus right now is my daughter. I don't really have time or head space for anyone else. It's not fair to you."

"Justin, why don't you let me decide what's fair for me?" Her voice rose a pitch. "And what I think isn't fair is for you to drop me like a hot stick without giving me a chance. We're good together, Justin, you can't deny that."

"I'm sorry." If he apologized one more time, he'd slap his own face. Might help keep him awake. "Sometimes, things just don't work out. I hope we'll be alright at work. Anyway, you'll be deploying after the first of the year, and I'm hoping to stay stateside. You'll be fine."

"No, sir." Her voice was clipped as if she were saluting him, and not in the military way. "You don't get to tell me how to react. We'll be fine at work because we're professionals, but that's as far as it goes."

"You're right, you're right." Justin's voice deepened when he was tired, and he'd driven past exhausted to bleary-eyed. "I didn't mean to do this tonight. I was going to talk to you in person."

"It wouldn't make it any better." She sounded like she was crying.

He'd swear he hadn't made a woman cry for years, and now he seemed to be the culprit every few days or so.

A tractor trailer slowed in front of him. Driving at night reminded him of war. Bored out of his skull half the time, worried sick for his life the other half. "Well, I guess I'll see you tomorrow. Hope you get a good night's sleep anyway."

"Are you kidding?" If he'd hoped she would be the cool girlfriend who handled being dumped like it didn't matter, he'd been fooling himself. "I'm not going back to sleep. I was going to say I hope you're not driving and talking on the phone, but I don't lie. Bye, Justin. I'll pray for you." He didn't want to know what those prayers might contain.

"Bye. Take care, Kristi."

The call ended.

Justin focused on staying between the lines for a few minutes.

"God." He said the word out loud. Alone and in the dark, he could get by with talking to the Lord. "Could you help me not mess up tomorrow? I mean, just give me a minute?"

The Lord didn't answer, but a song did come on the radio about a man praying for his ex.

God help him.

CHAPTER 10

*E*mma needed sugar and caffeine and sleep, in that order. She reached over to sneak a swallow of Haley's blue raspberry slushie. "Ugh. Disgusting. Why did I even?"

Haley giggled. Emma relished the light sound and wanted more. So, she leaned forward and placed a wet, smooshy raspberry on her child's neck.

Haley jumped and squealed.

They were home, in their cozy little apartment. Several weeks had passed since Justin had been able to visit. He'd been out in the field, training, and unable to get away. With each day that ticked by without his presence, she relaxed more and more. She wasn't threatened by him anymore, he wasn't going to steal Haley away, but she did feel more comfortable without the burning questions as to where the two of them fit.

Haley grabbed her drink and made for the couch.

Emma squealed. "Haley, no. Bring that back over here. If you spill on that couch." The threat hung out there, with Haley's butt hanging out to dry. Emma didn't like to punish, but if Haley disobeyed as blatantly as she had earlier that day, well, consequences would happen.

The 'look' worked. Haley clung to her cup with two hands and crept back to the kitchen table.

"Thank you," Emma said, relieved. In half an hour, Tiffany would drop by and pick up her niece, on schedule. Emma needed to get dressed in her uniform, which consisted of a pair of black slacks and black top, but there was a bit of a hassle in keeping an all-black outfit clean and free from lint. "I have to get ready."

"Is it time?" Haley chugged and then slapped her palm against her forehead. "Ugh. Brain freeze."

"Sorry to hear that." Emma brushed a kiss across the top of her daughter's head. "Slow down. You have time. I need to get dressed, but you're fine the way you are."

Haley shook her head. "No, ma'am. I need to pack a bag. Sunday is the first day of Vacation Bible School. I have to pack an extra cute outfit."

Emma squinted at her child. "Pretty sure God doesn't care how cute you are. He just wants you to be there and to have fun."

Haley squinted right back, jutting out her little chin. "You never go to church."

They'd had this argument before—her four-year old taking on the role of the adult and she the rebellious teenager. "You know that I'm too busy to go to church. I have to work."

"I thought Daddy sent us money." Haley slurped.

Emma tried to blink. "I didn't know you knew that."

Haley bounced out of the chair, leaving her precious slushie behind. "I heard you when you got the mail. Besides, you don't work every weekend. You could go to church the other weekends. Aunt Tiffy says you're mad at God."

Emma sat back down, her mind blank, and her mouth wide open. A few precious moments passed while she tried to relocate her equilibrium. Her sister couldn't have been discussing her argument with God with Haley. Tiffany knew better than that. Haley had to overhear an adult conversation.

"Mama, where are my gold flip flops?" Haley's muffled question catapulted Emma out of her confusion.

"In the shoe bag hanging from your door." Emma ran down the hallway, peeking in Haley's door to get a glimpse of the girl dancing with the shoes. "Okay, great."

Emma threw on her clothes, dusted on some blush, brushed on some mascara, and called her face done. She twisted her hair up in a messy bun and stuck a fork in it. Not actually a fork but one of those thingamabobs that held long curly hair in place with a wing and a prayer. There were the non-skid black shoes and hidden socks. "Apron, apron."

"It's hanging up in the bathroom," Haley said from the doorway, turnabout fair play, startling her. "You said you wanted to cook it."

"Yeah, right." Emma grinned. "Steam, cook, what's the difference?"

"Huh?" Haley crowded in the small space with her. "I need my mermaid toothbrush."

"Here you go." Emma reached under the cabinet for the toiletry bag she kept ready to go for these three out of four weekends a month. Now that Justin was sending child support, they didn't need to go through this madness. If only her heart would trust that he wasn't going to disappear again.

The doorbell chimed. They both shrieked, startled because Tiffany was early, as usual, so it shouldn't have been a surprise, but it was.

"I'm not ready!" Haley fled the bathroom, the soles of her little feet flashing white.

"Neither am I," Emma called over the din of the malfunctioning doorbell. Yet another thing she needed to put in a work order request for in the needy apartment. One quick scrub of her teeth and she hip-hopped to the door as she tied her shoes on the way. "I'm coming, I'm coming."

Tiffany stood on the other side of the door, flyaway sprigs of hair on the right side as if she'd been struck by lightning on one side and not the other. Her glasses were pushed up on the same side as if she'd poked at the frames one too many times. Dark circles under her eyes completed the picture of a worn-out, frazzled aunt who shouldn't be taking her niece for the weekend.

"Tiffany, you look awful."

"Thanks." Tiffany huffed out a breath, sending the baby hairs framing her face in a million different directions. "I needed that."

Emma motioned for her to come in, moved to the side. "I'm sorry. But it's summer. Shouldn't all teachers be bright-eyed and bushy-tailed?"

Tiffany's yawn showed the back of her throat, and wasn't that a pretty sight?

"Shouldn't you at least be awake?" Emma closed the door and checked her watch. She had a window of five minutes before she needed to leave, maybe enough to act like a loving sibling.

Tiffany waved a hand in front of her face. "I'm fine, nothing a little sleep won't cure." The second yawn outdid the first by a mile. "Excuse me. I know you're going to ask so I'll just tell. You know I always liked to play with clay as a kid?"

Emma would never admit that she hadn't paid much attention to what her sisters liked or didn't like growing up. They each had their own room, their own circle of friends, and even her position as middle child didn't make her closer to one or the other. Her world had revolved around her. "Sure. And?"

Even as she listened with half an ear, she searched through her purse for her car keys and a pen. Pens were guarded treasures in the server business, and hers had a pink feather rubber banded on so nobody would walk off with it.

"And I stayed up for half the night filling orders. It's going great." Tiffany had been talking, and Emma had only heard a third. "The last batch sold out in five minutes. Most teachers have side jobs in the summer."

She sounded defensive, and there wasn't any reason. Emma was the one who barely spent time with her own daughter, so much so that she'd been terrified a stranger might have a better relationship with her than she did. "Good for you, Tiffany," she said. "I'd like to see them sometime."

"I'll make you a pair for your birthday." Tiffany fought back yet another yawn.

Emma had no clue what she'd be getting as a gift and would pray to God to keep her little secret, when she got around to praying. The idea of praying bumping around in her brain was enough of a surprise. "Haley, I've got to go."

"You go on." Tiffany gave her a little shove. "I can lock a door as well as the next gal, even in my sleep-deprived state."

"Are you sure?" Emma teased. "You don't look like you should be driving a car."

Tiffany sobered. She pressed her lips together until her mouth became a narrow, first-grade teacher line of frustration. "And if I couldn't? You'd still leave me in charge of Haley, wouldn't you?"

Emma was out of time. "What? Tiffany, I trust you. Take a nap in my bed, for all I care. Why this sudden attack?"

Her sister's shoulders drooped. "I'm sorry. Thank you for trusting me. I don't know, maybe sometimes."

Emma panicked. She counted on Tiffany, desperately needed her free babysitting. "No, I'm the one who's sorry. I know I take you for granted. Maybe, someday soon, I can afford to pay you."

Even better, she could afford to pay for a babysitter now. If she would just take Justin at his word, she could quit Jasmine's and give both her and Tiffany a break.

Tiffany waved at her with both hands. "No, don't worry about it. Please. I love taking care of Haley. She's the daughter I'll never have. Hurry and go, or you'll be late."

Emma hugged her sister. They'd been going on like this for years, since Haley was a baby. There was no one else in her life she could count on, not their mother, not her long-lost friends. "Thank you again, Tiff. We'll talk soon. When I have more time, about this arrangement, if it's not working for you."

"Go, Emma." Tiffany shooed her out of the apartment. "There's no problem. I'm just tired and dumb. Good night."

Emma looked down the hallway. "Bye, Haley. Mama loves you."

"Bye, Mama," Haley yelled from the back of the apartment.

Emma gave Tiffany a grim smile and left.

Her fear affected more people than just her.

CHAPTER 11

*I*n a few minutes, Justin would arrive to pick up Haley and take her to his parents' house for dinner. He had called a few nights earlier to ask if he could start introducing Haley to his side of the family. At no point did she feel like she had a choice, so she'd said yes.

This time, she had done a better job of preparing for his visit. No more collapsing in a heap in her own bedroom just because her daughter was getting to know her father. She was a good mother. There was nothing to fear. He wouldn't take Haley from her. He hadn't even shown any inclination toward undermining her in any way.

To combat her tendency to descend into darkness when left alone, she had asked for and received an extra shift at Jasmine's. At no time would she have time to obsess or worry.

The doorbell rang, still broken. Emma flinched, despite her best intentions. Her heart thumped against her ribs, and she tossed her lemon furniture-polish infused wipe in the air. Jimbo ran past her, yapping at the door, his Yorkie glossy brown fur dotted with pink and polka dot bows.

"Haley, what did you do?" Emma was torn between the ruckus at her door and glaring back in the direction of the bedrooms. "Oh, good grief, Jimbo, hush up. It's not as if she hasn't done this to you before." She jerked open the door, maybe too aggravated with her daughter and the incessant barking. "Hello."

Justin retreated at the violence of his greeting.

He held flowers, again. This time, they were pale pink roses, sending a different message than the innocent daisies of before.

"Oh, they're beautiful." Emma's gaze dropped to what she was wearing—a ratty old T-shirt with no sentimental strings and shorts meant for cleaning and not greeting exes at the door. "Jimbo won't shut up today. I don't know what's wrong."

She made a fast attempt to grab the beast, but he scooted between Justin's legs and out the door. The two humans looked at each other, wide-eyed. Justin tossed her the flowers and took off in pursuit, shouting the dog's name. Emma wheeled around just far enough to lay them on the kitchen table, teeth pushing her lips out in dismay at the potential damage.

If something happened to that runt of a little dog, Haley would be devastated. She herself might be glad to get rid of the extra responsibility, and she squelched that thought. Shame on her. She loved the stupid dog.

"Jimbo, where are you?" Her side stretched as she rounded the end of the building. "Oh, wow. Justin?"

From her vantage point, Justin ran in circles with his hands down, grasping at thin air every once in a while. He looked like he'd lost his mind. Emma covered her mouth and stifled giggles. Justin was wearing his camo pants and a drab olive T-shirt, and his chest stretched the fabric. There weren't any cars coming or going, so she allowed herself a few seconds of appreciation. The man looked fine.

"Emma, have mercy," Justin called out, aggravation and humor interlaced in his deep voice. "Get this dog before I lose my temper."

Emma inched forward. Jimbo was juking and jiving, barely evading Justin's lunges. The dog was only three years old, in the prime of his doggie life, and quick as water pouring through his fingers. "You'll never catch him that way."

"Then, how?" Justin froze, possibly thinking he'd psych the dog into stopping his frantic figure eights. Jimbo did pause, a few feet away, but outsmarted the human when Justin tried to grab him real fast.

"Jimbo, come here." Emma leaned down and held out her hands. She jingled the leash she'd grabbed off the doorknob on her way out. "Want to go for a walk?"

Her brain-challenged dog obediently trotted over and jumped up with two paws on her knees, begging to go out.

"Doesn't he know he's already out?" Justin grumped but stayed where he was in the middle of the parking lot until she clipped the leash on the Yorkie's collar. "Guess not." He wiped sweat off his forehead with his forearm. "Now, someone tell me, why did I do PT this morning?" That was clearly a rhetorical question because it was followed immediately by a different question. "Does he do that often?"

"Never." Emma didn't know where her sass came from, but there it was. Maybe she inherited it from her daughter. She reached down and scooped up her dog, giggling. "Okay, maybe every other day. Let's go in."

Somebody beeped their horn behind them. Emma glanced back, smiled when she saw her neighbor. "Hey, Brad. How are you?"

"Fine. You need to put a shock collar on that puppy." Brad stuck his head out the window of his little electric car. "I'd hate to see him get hurt."

Emma frowned. "I don't want him to get hurt, either, but a shock collar on this little thing? No way."

"Well, don't say I didn't warn you." He nodded, tight-lipped in Justin's direction. "You Army?"

"Yes, sir." Justin barely tipped his chin in the other man's direction. "You?"

Brad jerked his steering wheel. "What? Nah, I'm a lover, not a fighter. Anyway, glad Jimbo's okay. See you around, Emma. Tell Haley hi for me."

"Sure." Emma watched him go. The man had implied there was more of a relationship between them than there was, never had been, and she had to wonder why. "Oh, wow, I left Haley alone."

Justin's stiff posture made her hesitate.

She turned back around. "What's wrong?"

His shoulders relaxed one at a time, and he rolled his neck. "Guys like that just burn my hide. I'm a lover, not a fighter. How about, I'm a protector?"

"He's an idiot. You sacrifice so much for your country. He should be thanking you." Emma lifted Jimbo up in the air. "Come inside and let me get you a drink. This precious baby," said in that little girl voice created for babies and cute puppies, "got you all hot and sweaty."

Justin caught up with her, his boots pounding on the concrete. "How well do you know that guy?"

Emma jerked to a stop, and he ended up with his face against her back. Shocked by the heat of his breath on her neck, she rushed to move forward. "Not well. He lives right there," a nod of her chin to the apartment two doors down from hers, "and we speak when we see each other. Never been inside each other's apartments. Why?"

Justin was acting like a jealous boyfriend. He didn't want her, but no one else could have her, either. Anger surged through her.

Jimbo yelped.

"Sorry," she murmured against the silky fur. "Not your fault, not this time."

"What?" Justin held the door for her. "You asked why I asked how well you know him. I don't know. I just don't trust his type."

Emma placed her puppy on the floor gently and removed his leash. "Skedaddle, brat."

Stub of a tail wagging, the dog wandered around the room until he put himself in his crate and settled down.

"You know he didn't actually take care of business outside, right?" Justin picked up the flowers and held them out in her direction. "Let's start over. These are for you."

Emma's heart stopped. Like some heroine in an old-timey drama, her hand went to her chest, but she wasn't being dramatic. His words held danger. Start over what? This day? These last five years? "Thank you. They're beautiful."

"So." Justin rubbed the back of his neck, a tell-tale sign of nervousness, and that was an old memory surfacing from too long ago. "Change of plans. Mama isn't feeling well and asked to postpone having Haley over until tomorrow. Are you free?"

Any hint of romantic bygones evaporated. Second place was okay if there were medals, but not so great in life. "No, I have work." Her cell phone was in her right pocket, and she checked the time. "In about an hour."

For the first time since he'd rang the doorbell and Jimbo had come between them, she looked him in the eye. "Why? What did you have in mind?"

His one shoulder shrug emphasized the bulk there. The man had muscles on top of muscles. "I was going to ask you and Haley to dinner. The three of us."

Now that Emma was fixed on those green eyes, she couldn't tear her gaze away. "Why?"

He grinned, and his one dimple made her realize what she'd said.

She shook her head, broke free. "Okay, I sound like a toddler. Sorry. But I can't go. I'm working. Thank you for asking anyway."

"Another time?" He pushed the flowers in her direction, more of a shove this time. "The flowers are still for you."

Her hands circled the stems. They were roses, the soft pink Haley's favorite color. There was a simple ribbon, yellow, her favorite color, back when she allowed color into her life. Now, her apartment resembled a goth teenagers' wardrobe—black and white and neutral because it was cheapest if she didn't commit to a color. She buried her nose in the small blooms. "You remembered that I love...?"

"Yellow? Baby roses?" He gave a low chuckle. "That you always said flowers aren't worth much unless they smell?"

This time, when their eyes met, there was a connection of good memories and not just that he'd left. He could always leave again. There was no way she would let her guard down. "Thank you. I'll just find a vase."

Which would be a mighty feat, since she hadn't dated since before Haley, and flowers were another extravagance that she'd never indulged in—so, even though she made a show of opening and closing cabinet doors, it wasn't going to happen.

"Hey, Daddy." Haley came running into the living room. "When did you get here?"

Emma's limp fingers let the cabinet door under the sink slam shut. They'd been so absorbed in each other that they'd forgotten Haley.

"Right before Jimbo ran out into the parking lot," Justin answered, scooping the little girl into his arms and off her feet. "I rang the doorbell. Didn't you hear me?"

Haley wrapped her arms around her daddy's neck and leaned back so she could see him better, not a second of mistrust that this man she'd known for two months would keep her safe. "I heard, but I thought you'd come find me. I want to show you my room."

Emma filled a glass pitcher with water and arranged the branches in it, turning her back on the tableau. They should have had this all along, but her fear had robbed them all. So, there was guilt. Also, there was envy. She'd had that kind of relationship with her dad, and she missed the man every single day.

"Is it okay?"

"What?" Emma squeezed her eyes shut, staving off the tears, maybe. "I'm sorry, I didn't hear you."

"I didn't want to overstep." Justin faced her, still holding Haley, an earnest look on his face. "Last time I was here, I went in your bedroom because I was worried. But I want to respect your authority."

Emma felt a stab of something like thawing in her chest. She might be softening toward the man, but reawakening hurt like thawing fingers and toes after being in the snow. "No, you're fine. If she wants to show you her room, go right ahead. Is there something special you want to show him, Haley?"

Haley winked at her. When had she learned how to do that? "Yes, ma'am."

"Go, you silly girl, go."

Justin grinned and bucked like a horse, lifted Haley up and around, positioned her on his back. He galloped down the short hallway. For a few seconds, Emma stood there and listened, fiddling with the flowers.

Then, she called herself an idiot and walked around the kitchen bar. She centered the flowers on the table and then sneaked in her own apartment. Hovering outside her daughter's door, she eavesdropped and would deal with being caught, if that happened. Right now, with only five minutes before she needed to get dressed and head out, her heart ached to be part of every part of her daughter's life.

"So, this is my bunny rabbit, FooFoo. I named him after my Aunt Tiffy's real rabbit." Haley had every single one of her toys lined up on her bed—dolls, stuffed animals, stacks of puzzles. "This is Sally 1 and that's Sally 2. I didn't give them their own names, because they're Sallies and it is what it is."

Emma's hand flew to her mouth to stifle a snort. Justin looked her way. *Busted.*

Jimbo came out of nowhere and danced around her legs, snuffling.

"Mama." Haley ran to her side. "Don't you have to go to work?"

Emma coughed. "Um, yes, I was just on my way to my room."

"Okay. You better hurry."

Did the child have to parrot everything she'd ever said? Emma shook her head and crossed the hall. In her peripheral vision, she caught Justin watching her.

The smile he gave her had not one iota of humor. Instead, it was the slow, sexy smile of a man who had noticed a woman.

"Yes, ma'am." Emma stammered over the words. "I'll hurry."

Dressing for work and touching up her makeup had never been so beside the point. She wanted to be in the other room and listen to Haley. Her daughter made her smile like nobody else ever had or could. Plus, at some point, she might just look Justin Lee in the eye and ask him what his intentions were.

Yeah, right.

"I'm off." Emma hesitated in the hall. "Are y'all going to stay here all night or go out for something to eat?"

"We're going to go," Haley winked at her again, and giggled even as she spoke, "out somewhere to eat. Aren't we, Daddy?"

"Yes." Justin looked at the child like she was having a seizure. "What are you doing?"

"Nothing." Haley giggled. "Bye, Mama. See you later."

Emma tilted her head, got no response, even from her best Mama look. "Okay, then, I'll be going now."

"Love you!" Haley chirped and then picked up a dinosaur figurine. "This is Fred."

Emma walked out of her own apartment, not feeling exactly shut out, but rather feeling on the outside looking in.

Justin fingered the collar of his shirt. He'd planned on changing clothes all along. A man didn't take a lady on a date dressed in his Army uniform. Still, the danged shirt was uncomfortable. His GPS spoke to him, directing him to turn left into what looked like a private dirt and gravel driveway to the right of a house replete with front porch and wooden steps.

If there hadn't been the sign out front and the line of people waiting for admission, he would not have guessed this was a restaurant. The dark green exterior and red shutters fit perfectly with the Italian theme. He followed the drive to the back of the building and inched his oversized truck into a parking space. His passenger door might or might not block the next person over from slipping behind the steering wheel.

"Mama never brought me here," Haley said the words in a stage whisper. "I have to behave very good."

Justin glanced at her reflection in the rearview mirror. His impulse to surprise Emma at work hadn't taken into consideration that his four-year-old daughter might not want to eat at a fancy restaurant. On the other hand, he realized that she hadn't misbehaved yet. "You know, Haley, I believe in you. We'll have a daddy-daughter date, and it'll be fun."

All she did was nod, completely out of character for the little chatterbox.

Justin watched as, from all appearances, a sweet elderly couple walked behind his truck bed and approached the car on his right. He had to fight his soldier's instinct to duck and cover.

He exhaled in relief when the man in the relationship turned out to be thin as a rail and had no problem squeezing between the vehicles. One bullet dodged, but the other concern needed addressing. "Tell you what, Haley. If you don't want to eat here, we can say hi to your mama and go somewhere else. This is not a have to, so you can say no."

Haley rested her chin on her fist and her elbow on the arm of her car seat. "What's a have to?"

"A have to is something you must do, like brushing your teeth and washing your hands before you eat." He made a show of disgust. "Ew, gross, just think about not brushing your teeth. They'd get so dirty, and your teeth would fall out."

He was joking, but he hoped he hadn't just planted the seeds of future bad dreams. Oh well, he hadn't made any claims to be good at this fatherhood stuff yet.

Haley laughed. "No, they won't. I brush my teeth every day. Teeth don't just fall out."

Justin gave her the side eye. "Girl, haven't you heard of the tooth fairy?"

"Yes, sir." Haley made a move to unbuckle her own car seat, and he realized just how long he'd procrastinated exiting the vehicle and going inside. The elderly couple had already exited the parking lot.

"Okay, then. Let's go find something delicious to eat." Justin checked himself out in the mirror. He didn't have any cuts from shaving or hair sticking straight out so he'd have to do. "What do you like to eat that's Italian?"

"Is pasgetti Italian?" Her cute little lisp came out of nowhere.

"Yes, it is and a wonderful dish." He got out of the car and held the door for his girl. "I personally prefer pasgetti and meat-balls. Do you prefer those or eels?"

"Eels?" Haley catapulted herself into his arms, and he caught her. He thanked the Lord for that bit of grace. His egging on her silliness might get one of them hurt.

Justin set her feet on the ground next to him. "Okay, we're going to hold hands in the parking lot, and I need to behave better."

"Yes, sir." Haley stuck her little paw in his hand, holding on to his pinky finger. They'd only known each other for a few months, and they already had a thing.

Justin sucked in a deep breath, and his chest filled with oxygen and emotion. Then, a car came around the building, and he focused on keeping them from being run over since the corner was a blind spot and the path led right into oncoming traffic.

There was a short line waiting for attention from the maître d'. Haley buried her head against his waist, the shyness so uncharacteristic that he stopped to stare before giving the host his name.

"Would you like a table inside or outside?"

Justin hesitated. He looked down at Haley in her pretty sundress and slippers, all dressed up for a fancy night as a princess with her daddy. "Actually, can we sit in Emma's section?"

"Wait." The host did a double-take. "Is that Haley? Sweetheart, you had to have grown a foot taller than the last time I saw you."

Haley jerked her head out from the hem of his shirt. "I did not grow a foot. I still only have two."

The host and several bystanders all burst out laughing.

Haley reddened and glanced up at him. "Why are they laughing?"

"Because he didn't mean you grew another foot, baby, but that you grew that much taller." Justin rubbed her back. "And you're precious. Sometimes, people laugh because they like something or somebody."

"Haley, we don't just like you, we love you, baby girl." The host stuck out a hand. "I'm Fred, by the way. And you are?"

Emma rounded the corner and spoke before Justin even touched the outstretched hand. She stopped in her tracks, eyes going wide and her mouth dropping open. For a few seconds, she glanced around like she suspected she was being pranked, and there were hidden cameras somewhere. "Justin, Haley girl, what are y'all doing here?"

At the sight of her mother, Haley shed some of her shyness and flung out her arms. "Surprise!"

Of course, a waiter walked by with a tray laden full of drinks. Justin's stomach flipped over in his gut with anticipated disaster.

The young man smiled and did a little side-step, avoiding disaster. Justin might send a tip his way, in addition to whatever he gave Emma.

Emma's eyes got even wider if that was possible. "Thank the Lord," she mouthed in his direction. Then, she skirted another passerby and came over to grab her daughter in a one-armed hug, since she carried a big pitcher of sweet tea in the other hand. "What a wonderful surprise it is. And you look so pretty. You're all dressed up."

Justin leaned forward to answer, but Haley got there first. "Yes, it's a daddy-daughter date, and I'm a princess."

The host handed Emma two menus. "You can show them to G4, and that will be it for your section for a while."

Emma nodded, took the menus, and pivoted. "Y'all can follow me."

"Doesn't Daddy look handsome in his special shirt, Mommy?" Haley said so the whole world could hear.

Emma looked over her shoulder. "Yes. Yes, he does, sweetheart."

Any doubts Justin harbored about whether coming here had been a good idea went the way of the dinosaur. The appreciation in her eyes made him wonder what younger him had been thinking. No sane man would have dumped her, but he'd been a teenager, and the species wasn't well-known for its rational thought.

Emma led them to the end booth, farthest away from the dining room door. The booths had high dividing walls so even his head wasn't visible. Across from him, Haley was swallowed by the large bench seat, her head barely topping the wooden tabletop.

"I'll bring you a booster seat, baby girl," Emma said, a smile bigger than he'd seen her wear stretching her cheeks. "And a drink with a little umbrella in it."

Haley did a little dance in her seat. "Really? What do you do with a little umbrella?"

Justin and Emma shared another one of those proud parent glances that were growing more common by the second.

"What can I get you?" Emma asked.

Justin stared, not comprehending for a minute. "I'm sorry. What?"

"To drink? What can I get you to drink?"

He had no answer. He hadn't got that far.

"Justin, are you okay?"

"Fine. I'm doing wine." He jerked at his mistake. "I mean, maybe a glass of wine?"

The corner of her so-blue eyes crinkled. "You're doing wine. I love it. White, red? We have a house special tonight, a Nero D'avolo from Sicily."

"Huh?" He shook his head and failed to get past her beautiful Southern accent mangling the name of the Italian wine. "You know, on second thought, I'll have a sweet tea. Unless you want to drive us home?" He aimed that last at Haley, grinning.

"I can't drive." Haley giggled. "I'm only four, silly."

"Oh," he deadpanned. "I forgot. So, make it a sweet tea for me, please."

The warmth in the waitress' eyes probably wasn't professional, but he wasn't complaining.

"I'll be right back with those drinks." No sooner did she turn to go than she turned right back around. "Specials. I'm supposed to tell you about the specials."

"Our good looks and charm have distracted the waitress. Stop it, Haley." Justin didn't know where this humor was coming from; he'd been a serious soldier for years.

Haley sat up straighter and gave a salute that almost poked her eyes out. "Yes, sir."

After a few seconds of staring with adoration at her daughter, Emma shook her head and got back on track. "Okay, our pasta of the day is cavatelli with veal marsala. That will be served with a side of roasted vegetables. Our fish of the day is a fresh catch from Charleston and that's a red snapper piccata served with a side of angel hair parmesan."

Justin leaned back against the headrest. "I don't know if I can handle this. I mean, besides Mama's cooking, all I've pretty much had to eat for the last five years is Army chow. I mean, what if my system goes into shock?"

Emma winked at him. "Then your designated driver will have to give you mouth-to-mouth."

"Ew." Haley made a scrunched up, disgusted face like only a little princess could do. "I'm not kissing my daddy."

Justin contemplated the child with a serious lift of his chin. "I guess that leaves you then, Miss Emma."

He'd gone too far. Emma backed up a step. "I'll just go get your drinks."

Justin turned to face Haley, wondering if the child had caught her mother's fear. Haley smiled at him. "This is fun." She patted the menu in front of her for a few pats, and then glanced up at him with a frown on her face. "What do we do with this?"

Justin's stomach took yet another turn. "You don't know about menus? The words on them tell us what choices we have. Here. Let me show you."

Haley's expression got sadder if that was possible. "I don't know how to read yet. I'm sorry."

"Sweetheart." Justin grabbed the little hand that rested on top of the plastic. "Of course, you can't read. You're not supposed to read yet. Why would you be sorry?"

"Tyler in my class can read. All the teachers think he's so smart." Haley flipped from giddy to bottom lip poking out in zero to sixty. "Makes me so mad."

"Well, okay. Tyler may be smart, but that doesn't mean you're not smart in your own way, too. Girl, you make me think you're a full-grown adult half the time." He read the first line of the children's menu. "So, do you want spaghetti with cheese?"

Her head drooped, and she shook her head slowly. "No, I don't like spaghetti anymore."

Justin took his turn of looking around and checking for cameras. "Are you kidding me? You said you loved it just half an hour ago. So, how about chicken fingers or macaroni and cheese?"

"No, sir." Haley laid her head down on the table. "I'm not hungry."

Justin watched her downward spiral and had no answers. His menu lay unopened when Emma returned with their drinks. He was about to suggest they cut bait and head to a fast-food place, maybe even hand off the child to her mother, but the clink of the glass against the gleaming wood tabletop in front of her had Haley's head up and her bouncing in her seat.

"Ooh, that's so cute." Haley reached out with both hands to pull the pink liquid toward her. "What is it?"

"It's a Shirley Temple," her mother answered. "And look, I had Mr. Bryan spear two maraschino cherries for you instead of just one."

"Because I'm a princess," Haley squealed, all traces of despondency gone with the wind.

"Yes, you are," Emma agreed and faced Justin. "So, what would you like for dinner?"

Justin floundered. "Um, I don't know. Haley was so upset and said she wasn't hungry. So, I was wondering if we should go somewhere else, maybe get her some chicken nuggets?"

Both women stared at him like he'd lost his mind, which maybe he had because the child across from him oozed sunshine and unicorns from her very pores.

Haley shook her head. "Nooo. I love spaghetti, and I want a huge meatball." She dragged out the word huge with hands spread wide. At his "are you kidding me" face, she nodded. "Mama brings me leftovers all the time. Their meatballs are the best."

Justin felt like he'd been had. "Okay, make it two—one kid's and one adult."

Emma's laugh was soft and throaty. The uniform of a black T-shirt and black pants set off her blonde hair like the dark background of an oil painting. He often thought of her as a throwback to past days when pale skin and golden hair were the ideal of beauty and her blue eyes the stuff a man dreamed of at night.

That girl was back and standing next to him.

"I'll be right back with some bread." Emma retreated.

Justin sucked in a deep breath. The woman had interrupted his normal breathing pattern, to be continued later. She had barely crossed his mind for years. He'd been the one to break things off because she'd been a drama queen. He remembered now.

"I love this little umbrella," Haley cooed.

Justin laughed. What had driven him away as a teenager entranced him right about now. "I love you, Haley girl."

His daughter looked at him and blinked fast and furious. "I love you, too, Daddy."

The declaration had been spontaneous and too-long coming. She should have been loved by him before she'd even been born. He leaned over and tweaked her nose. "Get used to hearing that. I'm going to say it a lot for, maybe the next sixty, seventy years."

"You'll be old." Her eyes rounded, and the threat of tears subsided.

"Me?" He couldn't stop the grinning. "What about you? You'll be sixty-four."

"No, I won't." She punched the last word, twirled her umbrella, and spilled cherry-infused soda all over the table.

Justin wiped it up with his cocktail napkin and was tempted to keep the wadded-up paper. This was the first time he'd cleaned up after his daughter on the night when he told her he loved her. He wanted pictures.

Emma scooted a basket of steaming French bread in front of him. The bread was followed by an empty saucer. She swirled the saucer with olive oil and ground black pepper on top of that. All of that was done without a word passing between any of them. "Your meals will be up soon, kids' menu privileges, child of an employee and all that."

"Great," Haley said in a tired voice. "I'm starving."

Justin fell back against the booth, his mouth working to form coherent thought.

Emma patted his shoulder, in solidarity he'd assume and not mockery. "And then, she'll take a few bites and be stuffed."

"Got it."

Another table flagged Emma down, and she left. Justin tore off a piece of bread and swirled the fragment in the olive oil. Haley watched his every move and then copied him swoosh for swoosh. For a little while, they ate in a happy silence. This evening was one of his best dates ever, maybe because she kept him on his toes and made him laugh. Or, maybe because he couldn't get over the wonder of having a daughter. He'd only known her for a couple of months, and most men had at least nine months to get used to the idea.

He was in the middle of his second piece of bread and trying to remember if he and Emma had done anything to prevent having this precious child when a plate the size of his head appeared in front of him.

"Wow." He gripped his fork like a teenager with the tines standing up and his stomach on high alert. "That may be the biggest meatball I've ever seen."

Emma grinned at him with a light of pride in her eyes. "Everything's made in house. The meatballs have a mixture of ground beef and pork plus fresh garlic and Romano cheese."

"If I slobber all over the plate, don't mind me."

"Ew." Haley held her throat and made a choking noise. "That's gross."

He started to take a bite when Haley interrupted him. She stuck out her hands and made a clicking noise with her tongue. "Daddy, you forgot to say grace. We ate heathen bread."

Justin's jaw dropped. He was supposed to be the role model here. "Wow, I blew it. I'm sorry. Heathen bread, huh?"

Emma held up a cheese grater. "Before you do that, do either of you want fresh cheese?"

"Yes, please." Haley held up her plate.

Justin copied his daughter this time. After all, she'd been the one to remember her manners when he'd dropped the ball. Emma covered their meals with cheese, smiled at both of them, and moved on to her next table. Their interactions were mostly shallow so far, but he was getting an insight into her life that going somewhere else would never have afforded.

"Daddy? I'm hungry over here."

"Oh, right. Sorry, I was wool-gathering." He held out his hands, and she placed her small, trusting paws in his. He bowed his head, but not before catching a glimpse of her squeezing her eyes shut. "Dear Lord, thank You for the food and this very special time with my daughter. Please let there be many, many more times like this one. In Jesus's name, Amen."

"Amen," Haley echoed and immediately stabbed a meatball the size of her fist with her fork and lifted it in the air. She started to gnaw on it like some wild beast.

"And I thought the raw recruits had no manners." He would say that her behavior put him off his appetite, but that would be a lie. He'd pretty much eat anything, anywhere, any time. "Haley, put the meatball down." Chalk that up to probably the first of many things he never pictured himself saying.

Haley lowered her gaze. "What?"

"Watch me." He dredged up from memory the precise way to hold his fork and knife.

"No, don't." Emma appeared out of nowhere to save the day. "She needs you to cut up tricky items like this. I should have told you."

Justin took a deep breath, visualized the gigantic meatball flying across the room if Emma hadn't intervened. "Thanks. I didn't think."

"Why would you?" Emma looked harried where before she'd looked more than happy that they'd come to the restaurant. "You haven't been around."

Whatever he'd been feeling must have shown on his face.

"I mean, you're new to this parenting gig," she stammered. "Here, Haley. I'll get that."

Justin looked at the far wall. "Emergency avoided. Good thing you were here."

"Yeah," Haley talked with her mouth full. "Mommy's good at being a mommy."

Which implied he sucked as a dad. Point taken.

"I'll be back to check on you in a bit."

He enjoyed the rest of the meal with Haley talking non-stop, food in and out of her mouth, and him listening. He was glad to be quiet for a while—for one thing, the food was out of this world and for another, he didn't know what in the world he was thinking. The rational part of the brain reassured him that no one was judging him, that Haley was having a great time, and he would improve with time. The irrational, Army grunt part of him wanted to go blow something up. He had a lot of frustration right now, with himself and the situation.

This parenting gig should not be new to him. Bottom line.

"So, how was your meal?" Emma had a smile that was all light and joy. A memory of how rare that smile had seemed when they were dating flashed past him. "I see you need a box. How about dessert?"

Haley had eaten half of the meatball before dropping her fork on the plate and declaring she was so full she might die. Now, her head popped up, and she held up a hand. "No, ma'am. We're going to go get ice cream, right, Daddy?"

Emma jerked. "Well, then, I'll be putting these leftovers in a box for your lunch tomorrow. Are you sure you know what you're getting into, Justin?"

He stacked his silverware on his plate. "By feeding her sugar, you mean? Yeah, I think the slushies last time gave me a hint."

Emma grinned. "A hint, maybe."

Justin contemplated the small child across from him. "You just said you were too full to eat another bite. Are you sure you want ice cream?"

Haley's head bobbed. "Oh, I'm never too full for ice cream. I have two stomachs, you know. One for food and one for ice cream."

His emotional upheaval got left in the dust in face of the joy of this child and her sass. "Two stomachs, huh?" Justin tried to keep his laughter down to a low roar. "Girl, you're something else."

Emma didn't join him in his uproar, but she smiled. "I'll just bring you your check, then."

"Thank you," Justin said, distracted by the warmth of that smile.

He left a generous tip, even though Emma protested the entire time he was calculating the math that he didn't need to leave her anything since he was paying for Haley. He had a vision of yelling at her that Haley was just as much his responsibility as hers, but he pushed it back. She'd had years of being a single parent, and the tendency to hover and hold tight wasn't going away in a few months, or even fewer visits on his part.

"I'll be home around ten, if you could keep her busy until then," Emma said, repeating what she'd told him earlier, maybe she thought he'd forget.

"Got it." He was proud of himself, for his calm tone and the way he hadn't called her on anything all evening. "You're good at this, Emma."

Her mouth twisted. "Thanks. It's not exactly what I planned, but it keeps food on the table." She nodded at Haley's to-go box. "Speaking of which."

"Bye, Mommy." Haley jumped up and hugged Emma as if they were parting forever instead of for a couple of hours. Haley grabbed her leftovers. "Let's go to Ye Ole Fashioned."

Justin slid to the end of the booth and found his way blocked by Emma's slender form. She caught him in a lightning-fast hug as soon as he found his feet.

"Thank you. I'm sorry. You're a good daddy." Then, she almost ran to the kitchen, leaving him standing there with his mouth open and Haley taking off to parts unknown.

He only had one choice—follow his daughter.

But a big chunk of his heart had fled to the back of the restaurant.

CHAPTER 12

*E*mma's back hurt, and her legs stopped at the point her feet started. Still, she was riding on a high from Justin and Emma's visit. So, when Mr. Fred seated a couple in her section an hour before closing time, she didn't think anything of it given turnaround time so they should be in and out with minutes to spare.

They weren't.

She wasn't going to get home in time to let Justin and Haley into the apartment before her girl's bedtime, not even with weekend hours.

"Miss." The lady's voice carried across the mostly empty dining room. "Can we see a dessert menu?"

Her husband grimaced behind his hand, out of his wife's line of sight, when Emma scurried over with the tray of samples. "I'm so sorry. We'll just take them to go, hate to keep you late like this, but it's our anniversary, and we're taking advantage of my mother watching the kids."

"That's fine." Emma lied, then pointed to the items on the tray in succession. "This is our Huguenot torte, this is humming-bird cake, and we also have chocolate cheesecake."

"I thought this was an Italian restaurant." The middle-aged

woman had been unhappy with everything, all night, and Emma had to guess she'd lost a bet. Her choice would have been some-where fancier, downtown Charleston, and she wasn't about to allow her husband to forget that this dump had been his choice. "Don't you have cannolis?"

The groan inside her head stayed silent, she hoped. The kitchen staff would kill her—they had already cleaned up and were waiting for this couple's dishes to clear out. "Yes, we do. Would you like plain or with chocolate chips?"

"Chocolate, always chocolate." The wife perked up. "Please."

"Make that two. Donna usually eats some of mine anyway." The husband held out his credit card. "Plus, you can go ahead and run the check. Make things faster."

Donna gifted Emma with a close-mouthed smile. "Here, I know we're keeping you late. Here's our dishes so the kitchen staff can pack up. I know how it is; I used to be a waitress."

Emma forced a smile and murmured, "Thank you." She started to walk away before her expressive face revealed what she was really feeling. "I'll be right back with those cannolis and the check."

Inside, she fumed. If the woman had indeed been a waitress at some point in her life, it had to have been decades earlier. Either that, or her memory was failing her at a relatively young age. Just sending in the meal dishes would do nothing if they were getting dessert and still nursing their sweet tea. She couldn't leave until the table was completely cleared and candles blown out.

Her exhale blew her bangs up in a straight line. The door swung behind her, and she met the eyes of the cook and Wyatt standing at the sink, at the ready. They all had family waiting for them on a Saturday night. Not that any of them were complaining because they were grateful to have jobs, but they groaned when she tore off the ticket and hung it on the line.

"You've got to be kidding me." Drew read the ticket. "They

couldn't have picked a dessert off the tray, ready to go? I mean, since we closed half an hour ago."

Emma swayed where she stood. She had no idea that much time had passed. "Are you kidding me?"

Wyatt deadpanned, "There's a whole lot of kidding that ain't kidding going around. Hand me those dishes."

Emma pushed at the panic rising in her chest. She didn't even have access to her phone while she was working. Since this was an unusual occurrence, maybe it would be permissible. One glance at the corner cubby where Rena processed the night's cash register made her hesitate. The boss was generous on most things, but making the customers wait while you played around on your phone wasn't one of them. Emma rushed to run the credit card while Drew said inappropriate things about customers wanting cannolis last thing at night.

"Here you go," Drew said, sifting confectioners sugar over the pastry. "I didn't spit on it, so I've earned my heaven points for the night."

The ticket spit out of the machine. Emma tore it off and checked her pocket for a pen. "Yes, you have. And I'll also not spit on it so there we go."

"Hey," Wyatt complained. "If I had the opportunity... never mind. No points for me no matter what. Send them on their way and be quick about it, woman."

Their teasing nudged the terror to the side for a few seconds. Emma grabbed the to-go box and arranged the pastries in what she hoped was an artistic manner. So many years had passed since she'd sketched that she was rusty.

"Here you go." She placed the box in front of Donna and the credit card slip in front of the husband, whose name was on the credit card that she hadn't read.

"Thank you," he said. "The food was delicious."

"You're welcome. I'm glad you enjoyed it." Emma found a smile despite every second ticking in her pulse. Justin and Haley had to be sitting in his truck, all this time, wondering what had happened to her. He would worry that there had been an accident. Or worse, that she'd abandoned her daughter.

The couple slid out of the booth.

"Y'all have a good rest of the evening." Emma forced her best Southern drawl.

"You, too."

As soon as they rounded the corner, she swiped up the credit card receipt, slammed it in her pocket, and swept up the dishes. She still needed to bus the table, but her feet flew with this first step toward freedom.

Storming into the kitchen, she almost ran Wyatt over. "Here's their dishes. I just need to clean off the table, sweep, and mop."

Of course this as her night to close, which meant doing the many little chores that needed to be done before the doors could be locked. "I know it's not approved, but I need to text my..." What did she call Justin anyway? "Ex. He's got Haley, and they can't get in my apartment."

"He doesn't have a key?" Drew was elbow-deep in suds. No sense in throwing the last few dishes in the professional-sized dishwasher. "No, of course your ex doesn't have a key."

"Maybe he should," Emma said, chewing on her lip. "Just in case, for times like this."

Drew shook his head. "When was the last time we ended up stuck like this? It's been forever."

"True." Emma twirled the lock on the safe where they stowed their purses and valuables while on shift. There was no telling who might walk into the back and take what they wanted. "Oh, wow. He's texted five times."

"Nagging?"

"No, worried." The rush of heat in her chest had to be acid reflux, not warm fuzzies because Justin cared if she was lying dead on the road somewhere like any decent human being would.

"Really." Drew wiped his hands on the paper towel roll. "Sounds like your ex wants to be in your present."

"He is." Emma blinked at how fast those two brief words sped out of her mouth. "I mean, he's Haley's father so he'll always be part of my life."

"That's not what I meant, and you know it." Drew had his wallet and car keys in his hand while she stood there, not texting Justin back. "Anyway, I'm out of here. See you tomorrow."

"Bye."

Wyatt tapped his foot on the tile floor, which was some feat since no-skid shoes made no sound.

"I know, I know. You can't leave until I do." Emma texted. *Stuck at work.*

She rushed. The faster she moved, the further the darkness moved to the side of her vision, maybe leaving her alone for the night, despite the fact that she was a terrible mother whose daughter was stuck in a truck, in a parking lot, with no way to go to the bathroom or get a drink or even go to bed.

"Stop it."

"Hey, I'm not doing anything." Wyatt stopped tapping, and his hands went up in the air. "Promise."

Mortification had her ducking her head and mumbling an apology. She grabbed the vacuum and headed for the dining room. This was the last thing before she could leave. Justin was an adult. He'd figure something out, take Haley to whatever restaurant that stayed open late if she needed to go to the bathroom. But he was a guy, how could he take her into the bathroom?

"Let me do that."

"What?"

"Emma, you're crying." Wyatt was head cook. He shouldn't be vacuuming. He held out a hand, a silent order for her to obey. "Emma, go home to your child. I'm not an ogre, you know."

"I know, but it's not your job to vacuum."

"No, but it's not your job to stay this late, either. We do what's needed. Now, go."

Emma could either argue, or give in and accept the gift. "Thank you. I owe you."

She was in the kitchen before he could get his, "you're welcome," out. The hurry was in her to the point that she almost forgot to clock out, but not quite. Forcing herself to slow down and think, she glanced around the kitchen to make sure she didn't forget anything, shouldered her purse and left.

The key was in the ignition, the engine running, when she tried to start the engine all over again. She was losing her mind. She needed to pray.

She had no time. "Go, go, go."

Drew was locking up as she drove around the corner of the building. The gravel drive turned to asphalt. Traffic on Main Street was always iffy this time of night, tons of people pouring out of the movie theaters, going home after dinner with friends, and who knew what else. There was no way she was going to make the left turn but taking the right and circling back would eat up precious time.

A small voice in the back of her head warned better late than dead.

Her night vision wasn't the best, either. Every headlight dragged out at the corners like distant stars, scaring her that she might misjudge the gap between vehicles.

She whipped her little SUV right and circled back at the next light rather than risk going against traffic. Every stoplight caught her. The car in front of her seemed married to the speed limit as if it was actual law rather than a suggested guideline.

"What's the worst that can happen?" There was no one in the car to remind her that talking to yourself was a sign of insanity, and the pitch black exterior meant other drivers in other cars couldn't see inside. "Justin is a grown man. He's responsible enough to take care of a child in the case of me being late. Nothing bad will happen."

But she was late. When people were late, they got fired.

And sometimes, they never came home.

"I'm fine. As long as I don't lose my stuff and have a wreck, I'm fine." Her right thumb tapped on the steering wheel in a staccato jitter. "Haley is fine. She doesn't know enough to worry."

What would Justin think of her?

By the time she pulled into the complex parking lot, tears seeped into her hair and ears. She had long stopped talking to herself. All she could manage was staring straight ahead at the road in front of her.

Justin's truck sat in the visitor's parking space, as expected. She let out a breath. Her right shoulder relaxed, maybe because some secret part of her had thought he'd take Haley to his mother's, away from her. She pulled into an empty resident's spot and turned off the ignition.

Before she exited the vehicle, Emma rested her hands on her thighs and spread out the palms. Experience had taught her that she'd fall on her face, her legs too iffy to hold her up, after one of these episodes. If she wasn't careful, Justin would start to understand just how messed up she was.

She didn't know what she'd do if he took Haley away from her.

Knuckles rapped against the driver's side window, and she screamed.

"Hey, it's me." Justin's voice sounded far away against the background of her anxiety.

She had to get a hold of herself. He couldn't know how close she'd been to blacking out. While driving. Fingers trembling, she pushed the button to open the window. "Hey. I'm sorry."

"No need to apologize. The important thing is, are you okay? What happened?"

Emma blinked back a fresh set of tears in the face of his concern. "What? Oh, I'm fine. Customers just kept us late, and I was set to close. I don't have access to my phone during work so I couldn't."

"Hey, slow down. I really do understand. I mean, heck, I'm in the Army. Half the time, I don't even get to say when I go to the bathroom." Justin made a move to open the door, and she hurried to unlock it for him. "Here, take a few seconds. Haley's completely asleep and completely safe. The ice cream put her in a food coma so she was fine with sitting in the truck and singing stupid songs I found on the music app."

"I'm sorry." The words tumbled out again, despite his reassurances. "Just let me get my stuff, and I'll come get her."

"Slow down. I'll carry her inside, put her to bed. I bet you're exhausted after such a long day."

Emma's breath returned to normal. His calmness was as contagious as her coworkers' impatience had been. "Thank you. I needed that. I thought, I don't know what I thought. That you'd be mad?"

Justin pulled the door wider so she could exit and looked at her sideways. "Why would I be angry? Either you were late because of work or because you'd been in a car accident. The first one is out of your control and the second one inspires worry, not anger. I hope you know me better than that, Emma."

She shouldered her purse and stepped to the side so he could close the door. Guilt on top of all the other emotions galloping through her had her tripping over her own two feet.

"Hey, I got you." Justin was there, hand at her elbow, helping her recover. Where had this man been when she'd been a pregnant teenager?

"I'm okay." She didn't shake him off, but she stepped to the side. Then, she felt guilty for being so rude. "I'm sorry. I must be more tired than I thought. You're being extremely kind, and I'm, well, I'm a mess."

"No problems." Justin shoved his hands in his pockets like a child told not to touch anything in a china shop. "So, tomorrow is Saturday. The plan was for me to drop by and pick Haley up, take her to my mom's for lunch. Is that still okay?"

He couldn't have picked a better time to ask. "Yeah, sure. What time should I have her ready?"

"Not too early." They were standing next to his truck. "I want you to be able to sleep in, take care of yourself. Maybe eleven?"

Emma pinched the bridge of her nose to keep from crying again. She really was in bad shape if tears threatened at every little act of kindness. "That sounds good." She managed to sound like an average idiot, rather than an extreme. "I have to work tomorrow night, though. How long can you keep her? I can get a babysitter."

Justin reached into his truck and unbuckled a dead-to-the-world Haley. "No need. I'll keep her as long as possible. I've got time to make up." He held up a hand like a traffic cop. "Not that I'm bringing that up to make you feel bad. It's just the truth." He scooped up Haley and hip-butted the door closed. "Lead the way. Let's get this princess, and you, to bed. I don't know which one needs it more."

"Thanks," Emma replied with a dry, dead-leaf tone. "You're right, but thanks."

Justin's grin reflected in the streetlight. Emma hurried to catch up since she'd been standing there staring at him despite the fact he'd moved on. Her fingers fumbled for the keys as soon as she started walking.

She opened the door, flicked on the lights, and started to give him directions to Haley's bedroom. "But you already know that," she fumbled. "It's so strange. Nobody besides Tiffany's been in this apartment, except Haley and me, of course."

"I feel honored." Justin was halfway down the hall, Haley's long hair fluttering down his broad back.

The solution had occurred to her earlier before she'd lost her mind. "You should be," she teased. "I could give you a key, just for emergencies like tonight."

He lowered the limp Haley on top of her covers. "Do you want to try to put her in pajamas or anything?"

"No." Emma unearthed a blanket from Haley's closet and spread it over her child. "She's a kid, and they can sleep anywhere, anytime, in any clothes."

Justin tucked the blanket against Haley's back. "Yeah, they can. She's beautiful, Emma, inside and out. You've done good, real good."

Those stupid tears threatened to appear again. "Thank you," she squeaked out. "Do you, um, want some coffee or something?"

He shook his head. "No, you're exhausted. Hey, do you want to come to my house with us tomorrow? See my mom again?"

Emma felt her right eye twitch. "Um, do you think that's a good idea?" She led the way out of the bedroom, tugging the door almost closed behind them.

Justin didn't stop until he reached the door to the outside. Hand on the knob, he glanced back at her. "Sure, why not?"

He wasn't that naïve, was he? She was a walking zombie right now, and even she knew her being in the same room as his mother was a bad idea. The woman hadn't liked her when they'd been dating in high school, the typical prejudice against cheerleaders and Emma in particular, the woman certainly wouldn't like her more now that she'd kept her grandchild from her for years. On the other hand, there was no use putting off the inevitable.

"No reason. I just wanted to be sure."

Justin touched her hand and withdrew before she could react. "I want her to get to know you again, Emma. I want, well, get a good night's rest. Tomorrow's a new day."

"Um, you too?"

He left, closing the door behind him securely.

She backed up two feet and sat on a bar stool.

He'd been about to say more, that he'd wanted something from her, and even a vague something put her back to code terror.

CHAPTER 13

*J*ustin leaned against a kitchen cabinet, cup of hot coffee in his hand, and watched his mother lose her mind. "Mom, it's just Emma, who will be so nervous she'll trip over her own two feet, and Haley, a small child."

"Hush." His mother waved a cloth napkin at his face. "You haven't panic cleaned for a long time, son, and it shows. You think they won't notice, but dirt shows."

He sipped his coffee and slid farther out of her reach. "Mom, not only is there no dirt to be found in this house, I don't know if you're going to end up with much granite countertop left with the way you're scrubbing."

She just gave him, "the look," and he hushed. The designer kitchen had seventy-two cabinet doors and drawers total—his father reminded his mother of the investment they'd put into the space whenever she started to complain about his boat needing constant repairs. The apartment he shared with a couple of buddies could fit into the space with some room left over.

Emma had always been uncomfortable with his parents' wealth.

"Hey, son." His father walked into the room, buttoning his sailing shirt. "Does this look all right?"

Warmth spread up from his chest and had him smiling. "Yeah, Dad. You look great. I wish you could give me some of your tan."

"Well, if I could get you out on the boat sometime." His dad slapped him on the arm, the old man's version of a hug. "But all you want to do is spend time with some chick named Haley."

"Yeah, that I do." His voice was a bit hoarse. The last thing he expected was complete acceptance from his parents. He had a child that he hadn't even known about—one of the worst things a man could do in his father's book. He had been a rebellious teenager, enlisted when he should have followed in his father's footsteps and enrolled in the local military college like three generations before him. "You'll love her, Dad. I'm trying to make things right, I promise."

His father got really interested in the homemade alphabet soup bubbling on the stove. "I know you will, son. Sarah, is that soup supposed to boil?"

His mother dropped the fork on the table, abandoned measuring an inch from the edge, and rushed to the stove. "No, it's not. Thank you. I'm just frazzled."

Justin took the scorched soup as his cue. "Okay, I'm heading out. We'll be back in half an hour at the most." He kissed his mama's cheek. "Mom, you're Haley's grandma. She'll be so excited you could feed her sawdust and she'd bounce out of her chair."

His words didn't take the attention away from the pot, but his mother did lean in his direction. "Thank you, son. I don't know for sure that I'll want to be called Grandma. I was thinking of Granny Sarah. It's homier, don't you think?"

The last term to describe his mother was homey. "Whatever you want, Mama."

"I want you to get going."

He made a show of hurrying his fool self out of the house. The distance wasn't far and that had been part of their problem in high school. His parents had given him a curfew, but they had never considered he could make the drive in fifteen if he hit the lights just right. There was always time to get in trouble. And Emma had been the most beautiful thing he'd ever seen. She still was.

Except maybe Haley now that she was in the picture.

He parked in the same visitor's spot he'd become so familiar with the night before. He'd driven away before he'd fully absorbed just how upset Emma had been. Her mascara had been racing down her cheeks when he'd knocked on her door, before she'd swiped the mess away. Then, there'd been that time a few weeks ago, when he and Haley had found Emma in a heap on the floor. Back in high school, he'd called her a drama queen. Now, he might have just enough perspective to know better.

He cut the radio and shut down the ignition. He was wasting time, and there were two beautiful females inside waiting on him. Plus, lunch. He stretched his legs on the way, taking several steps at a time. The door swung open before his fist made contact.

"What took you so long?" Haley hopped on the other side. "I saw your truck through the window, and then you sat there and sat there."

Justin laughed, picked her up, and twirled her as much as the small space would allow. "I did not. I barely arrived."

Emma emerged from the back of the apartment, her blonde hair pulled back in a chic and professional-looking bun. She wore a silky white blouse and gray slacks. So, his mother still intimidated her after half a decade of distance. He carried Haley across the room.

"Justin, don't you dare," Emma said, backed up, hands averting contact with her pristine outfit. "I can't tell you how long it took me to get ready."

He wanted to kiss her and that hadn't changed over the years, either. He wanted to take her nervousness and change it to the confidence she should be wearing.

"You didn't need to go to all that trouble," he started and

then got left in the dust when she disappeared back in the restroom. "It's just lunch."

"Lunch with your mother is not just lunch. I was never good enough then, and I sure haven't improved with age." Emma sounded resigned, if anything, and returned to grab her purse. "Anyway, let's get this over with."

He shifted Haley to his other side and bench pressed her to the ceiling, anything to lighten the mood. "We're going to have lunch with your Granny Sara and your PawPaw Johnny, Haley. You're going to like them very much, and they're going to spoil. You. Rotten."

The last three words were punctuated with lift, release, lift, release. Haley squealed every time she went up.

Emma's face softened a bit from the grim resignation of a few minutes earlier. "She already has grandparents."

"And?" Justin set a now dizzy Haley on the floor, kept a hand on her shoulder until she stopped wobbling. "I don't think anyone can have too many grandparents."

"I don't like Grandma." Haley slipped out from under his hand and stumbled her way over to the couch and grabbed her backpack. "And Grampa Jim is weird."

Justin lifted one eyebrow in Emma's direction, but she avoided his gaze. He searched for a way to get the information he needed without saying anything disrespectful about Emma's family. He had always loved her sisters, but something had snapped in her mother when her father had been killed. Not that anyone could blame her.

"Well, I think we're ready." Emma came to stand in front of him where he blocked the door. If he didn't move, she'd get even closer.

"I'm not that girl anymore, Justin." Emma took a deep breath and released it.

He waited.

"All right. Aargh." Emma took a step closer and lifted her

chin, her entire face a challenge. "Justin Lee, are you going to move?"

They'd played this game when they were younger. He thought he'd forgotten everything about their relationship, that he'd moved on and had left her in the past, but wow, this was fun. "I don't know. Who's going to make me?"

She got in his face like the best drill sergeant the armed forces could serve up. "I will, you just watch me."

This was the part where he was supposed to kiss her into submission. The memory must have come back to her, too, because she froze like a scared rabbit and leaned her upper body back slowly, inch by inch, as if she were trying to avoid enemy capture.

"Not today, Emma, not today." Sometimes, he didn't know what he was going to say before he said it. "But soon."

"Promise?" And with that flashback of her sassy younger self, she slipped around him and opened the door.

He grabbed Haley's hand, followed behind Emma like an obedient child, and stuttered. "Emma Grace, you should know better than to challenge someone like that. They might just take you up on that promise."

"That's what I hoped." Emma walked around to the passenger side and waited.

"Here you go," he said to Emma while squeezing Haley's hand. "Here's the thing, Haley. You're important to me, but your mama will always come first."

Emma swallowed hard, several times in succession. Her eyes glistened, and she lifted a hand to cover her mouth. "Justin, I don't know what to say."

"Nothing to say." He winked at her, hoping against the odds that he could stave off her tears. "Just believe it when you hear it."

"Okay." Emma looked shaken, but she slid into the seat and tucked her body inside so he could shut the passenger door.

Justin glanced down to see Haley staring up at him with a

big smile on her face. His little girl was pretty and smart, if she realized him respecting her mama was a good thing. A feeling of well-being swept over him, and he swung their arms as far as her little arm could go as they circled around the truck bed.

"What are we going to eat for lunch?" Haley climbed into her car seat.

He paid careful attention to buckling her in, given the last thing he'd ever want was to let his normal hurry up and get it done attitude cause his baby harm. He focused so much that he lost track of her question. "What?"

"Lunch, silly." Nothing like being chided by a child. "What are we eating? I'm starving."

"Of course you are." Justin threw a glance Emma's way as he took his seat. "Is she always like this, or could it be a growth spurt?"

"What do you know about growth spurts?" Emma popped open the lighted mirror behind the passenger side visor. "Anyway, I think you're right, but let's pretend that I'm not going to have to buy her all new clothes before she's even worn the last ones I bought."

"Pretend?" He shrugged. "Okay, denial works for me." He glanced at Haley through the rearview mirror. "By the way, I don't know what we're eating. Mom was in the process of burning the soup when I left."

Haley twisted her lips in disgust. "That's good. I don't like soup."

Emma turned toward him. "She loves chicken noodle and alphabet."

Justin concentrated on pulling out into traffic without getting hit by crazy out-of-town drivers. At least, he liked to blame the onslaught of traffic on the waves of northerners moving down to escape the snow and taxes.

"Ooh, I do like affabet soup." Haley kicked the back of his seat.

"But you said it was burned?" Emma continued to face him,

and he was very much aware of her scent and her closeness. "So what was option number two?"

Justin tried to focus on the road and not her unique mixture of jasmine and honeysuckle. "Um, what was the question?"

He could feel her eyes on him, and he forbade himself from pulling the car to the side of the road and pulling her into his arms. He really didn't know how he'd gotten to this point. A few weeks ago, a month ago maybe, he'd been filled with so much anger toward her. He still didn't completely understand how she could have done that to him, but he was getting an inkling of her insecurities and fears.

"The question was, what's for lunch?" She rolled her eyes.

"I have no idea." His answer produced uproarious laughter from both his ladies.

He was jumping the gun. He had no claim whatsoever on Emma. They hadn't even gone on a date in this new era of their lives. If today went as well as he hoped, he'd have to rectify that error very soon.

"Really?" Emma finally pivoted and faced front. "Maybe Haley is my daughter because anticipating what I'm going to eat is half the fun for me."

Justin gave a loud, mock sigh. "I bet you're one of those people who has to look at the menu online before you go to a restaurant."

"Has to?" Emma shook her head. "Don't you know how to do life? The key is, I get to look at the menu before I go to a restaurant. It's a privilege for which I'm grateful."

He laughed, low and amazed. This woman had more sense of humor in one dimple than Kristi had possessed in her whole body. A ping of guilt hit him in the gut for how he'd broken things off with her and the fact that she even entered his mind now. Comparing wasn't fair to either woman, but he couldn't help feeling that he'd made a narrow escape.

Emma felt like coming home.

Speaking of which, he made the turn into his parents' rather long driveway.

"I hate to admit it, but I'm scared," Emma whispered.

Justin flicked a glance at the rearview mirror. Haley stared at her mother, always watching, always picking up on cues as to what to say and what to do.

"It's only natural," he forced his voice to be so calm that it was almost monotone, "but I'd keep it to yourself. Little pitchers, big ears, and so on."

Emma nodded, her entire body stiff and elbows at an awkward angle, frozen that way. "You're right."

"So, Haley." Justin raised his voice as if to blot out Emma's fears from her daughter's conscious awareness. "This is my parents' house, your grandparents, Granny and Grandpa Lee. It's where I grew up."

"Okay," Haley said.

Disappointment made him quiet. He hoped for more of a reaction to his parents' Victorian-style house with the ginger-bread wrap-around front porch and gazebo. For some reason, he pictured them having a girly tea party out there. He no longer really fit on the ornate black iron seats, but he relished the idea of sacrificing for his child and sipping out of minuscule cups.

"Do you think they'll like me?" Haley's whisper was almost too small to hear.

Justin stepped on the brake, instinct setting him toward fighting the enemy wherever they popped up their nasty little heads.

Emma fell forward at his abrupt stop, caught herself with a hand on the dashboard. "Justin, what in the world?"

"Daddy," Haley whined. "You don't drive too well."

Somehow, the focus ended up on him. Putting the truck in park, he twisted around, but not before noticing Emma rubbing her hands across her lap. Haley had inherited her insecurity—the child had her knees up in front of her face. "Sweetheart," he said to his daughter and wished he could contort himself into a group hug. "They will like you. No, they will love you. They love you already. You belong to them, to me. You're family, and that means something."

Haley watched him for a minute from between knobby knees. "Okay." The hem of her dress came down, and she started swinging her feet. "Your house is pretty."

He grinned and turned back around, feeling like he doused a forest fire before it got really going. "That's my girl. That front porch has a table, and we're going to have a tea party there someday. I can see it."

"Huh." Haley kicked the back of his seat, again. He smiled. Now that he realized getting pummeled in the back meant things were right in her world, he'd grin and bear it. "Can I have little cakes with the tea?"

Emma's laugh came out as a snort. "You should know by now. She's all about the sweets."

"Aren't we all?" Justin parked in his usual spot, behind his mother's luxury sedan. Not for the first time, he cringed at the contrast between his family's lifestyle and the hard life Emma experienced after her father's death. "We're here."

Emma's hands shook as she picked up her purse where it had fallen to the floorboards. They had a lot of things to talk about, once this visit was over. First, he needed to reassure her to the point she survived this reunion. "Emma, relax. You are going to be fine. If nothing else, you're bringing them Haley, who's the only child of their only son. Chin up."

She stuck her chin toward the ceiling in a caricature of his words, but the trembling in her body didn't ease. Her hand tugged at the door handle.

His manners jerked him out of his stupor. "Hey, you're supposed to wait and let me do that."

"Why?" Emma scoffed. "I've been opening my own car door for years now and haven't experienced any recent memory loss."

Haley laughed at her mama. Justin growled. The woman

kept teaching her daughter bad ideas. "Think of it this way, Emma. You want her to say yes ma'ams and no sirs, right?"

Whatever she said in reply was muffled by the gentle slamming of her door, and yes, that was an oxymoron. The woman was full of contradictions.

He scrambled to catch up.

Emma had Haley unbuckled before he pulled the keys out of the ignition and came to stand by her side. When she reached across the car seat and pulled out a shopping bag, he lurched backward. He'd not seen her place anything in his truck and was a little freaked out he'd been so unobservant.

Emma must have caught his surprise. "Just a bottle of wine, a hostess gift. I couldn't come empty-handed."

"Okay." He wouldn't tell her that she hadn't needed to bring anything, that Haley was the gift because the truth was anything she could do to mollify his mother was a step in the right direction. "That's a great idea."

The wine bottle in one hand and her purse in the other, Emma stared at her daughter, looked from hand to hand and then dropped the wine in the cavern she called a purse. Problem solved. Justin pocketed his keys and took a few steps down the sidewalk.

For some reason, he felt the need to play tour guide. "Haley, see that big gate over there? That leads to the backyard. There's a pool and a swing set and a hammock. You'll have to fight me for the hammock because that's my favorite place in the world."

Haley caught up with him and grabbed his hand. "No, I wouldn't because I'm your princess, and you'd let me have it."

He whistled. "Wow. How did you get so smart?"

Emma laughed behind them. She sounded lighter, as if her tension might have loosened its grip. That could just be wishful thinking on his part, though.

When they reached the front door, he hesitated. Not because he couldn't just walk right in, which he could, because this was still his home even though he technically lived in North Carolina at the moment, but because he couldn't decide if his parents would want some warning.

"Are we going in?" Emma's voice was full of dread and impatience, an interesting combination. "I thought I was the one who was nervous."

Justin shook his head at her, clicking his tongue. "You mistake me. Entering my own home doesn't make me nervous. Not much does. But I'm trying to figure out if I should ring the doorbell just to let them know we're here or barge in."

"I'm hungry," Haley said, cutting any further discussion off at the ankles.

"Fine," Justin grouched, opening the door. "Mom, Dad." He projected his voice to reach the back of the house. "We're here."

He took off his shoes in the front hall, put them in the basket his mother kept just for that purpose, and then motioned for the ladies to do the same. Emma balked for just a second, and then complied. Good girl. A few years ago, everything had been a battle between her and his mother's fancy ways. They crossed the foyer and entered the living room with its two story high vaulted ceilings and floor to ceiling wall of windows. The view of the backyard always took guests by surprise, with not only the gleaming water of the pool but a fountain and palm trees beyond that.

"It's a fairy land," Haley whispered. She released his hand and walked, spellbound, to the nearest window. "Is it real?"

Justin sent a questioning glance toward Emma.

Emma stared at her hands. "We don't get out much."

Justin watched his daughter for a minute, emotions warring between sadness at what she'd missed and his brain racing to plan possible trips, starting with a backyard swim as soon as possible. "The pool is heated," was all he said.

"I don't think any of her swimsuits fit her." Emma spoke in a monotone. "She's gone through a growth spurt."

"Got ya." Justin pointed to the right with his chin. "The kitchen is through there."

"I remember." Emma braced herself, reminding him of nothing more than a downtrodden first year at his father's precious military school.

Still, she didn't move, and he relented. He needed to lead the way, not fall back on tradition and put the woman in front of him when, to her mind, they were about to engage with the enemy.

"Hey, Mom. Hey, Dad." Justin rounded the corner.

His parents both stood on the other side of the marble island, glasses of tea in their hands. Like puppets on unseen strings handled by the same master, both heads popped up in unison. "Son."

His mama's hand convulsed, and Dad took the cup from her hand without either of them saying a word. His mother looked conspicuously at the door frame as if willing her granddaughter to appear.

His troops had abandoned him. "Um, Haley?"

"Yes, Daddy?" Haley pranced into the room, skidding to a halt when she saw the other people in the room. "What do, oh."

His mother walked around the island, but she stopped at the corner.

Haley hid her face against his side.

"Haley," he started. "This is my mother, Granny Sarah." He heard some muffled sounds, but he couldn't decipher a syllable. Leaning down, he placed his hands as gently on her shoulders as he could. "Sweetheart, won't you look at her? She won't bite."

"I promise." His mother's voice quivered. "Haley, I burned the alphabet soup. I was that distracted by your coming. So, we have chicken nuggets and mac and cheese for lunch. Is that okay with you?"

Haley didn't even flick an eyelash toward his mother, but she nodded.

"Why don't you come sit on one of these bar stools?" Leave it to his dad to take charge in any situation, clumsy or not. "I bet your feet won't even touch the floor."

Haley shoved her blonde hair back behind her shoulders and the tips almost touched her waist. "I bet they will. I'm going through a growth spurt."

Justin gave his mother a side grin. His daughter saw everything as a challenge, and he wondered where that came from.

"What do you like to drink, Haley?" His mother was never happier than when she was feeding someone. "I have milk, apple juice, ginger ale, sweet tea, but I don't suppose your mother would want you to have that." She gave Justin a confused look. "I thought you said Emma…"

Justin concentrated on giving Haley a boost up on to the middle bar stool at the kitchen island. Then, he glanced behind him. "I'll be right back."

Haley squeaked. "Daddy, don't leave me."

"Shh." He put a finger to his lips. "I'm just going to go find your mama. Do you think she's lost?"

Haley shook her head and pressed her lips together in a tight, thin line.

"Right. I'll be back in a minute."

He touched his mother on the arm, maybe to reassure her, maybe to encourage her to take things slow. Haley, and clearly Emma, needed time.

Emma hadn't budged. Justin stood in the doorway to the kitchen and shoved his hands in his pockets. He'd not thought this through when he'd invited her last night. There should have been more prep time, more of the two of them getting to know each other again. Maybe she wouldn't look so haggard right about now.

"Hey, Emma." He took her arm, and she let him lead her to the couch. "Will you sit with me?"

"Yes, of course." Once there, she distanced herself and sat as far away as she could. "I'll be okay, Justin. I just needed a few minutes. I was giving them time to get acquainted without me in the way."

He drew his eyebrows together, tried to see behind her

words. He failed. "Your daughter is only four and was walking into a strange place with strange people. I might be her father, but she hasn't known me very long. She needed her mother."

Emma couldn't be more closed off. She clutched the bottle of wine in front of her, and her shoulder bag was another line of defense stacked in front of that. "Haley is fine. She's always fine. She doesn't need me."

Justin relaxed his elbows on his thighs, his hands hanging loose. He adopted the posture to make other people feel more at ease when he was getting too intense. "Yes, she does. Don't ever doubt that. Now, what's really wrong?"

Emma's eyes darted back and forth, as if searching out an escape route.

"Emma? I don't know about you, but I'm hungry."

If she held the wine bottle any tighter, there would be shattered glass and merlot on his mother's pristine living room carpet. "It was a mistake, me coming here."

Justin took a deep breath. He was an idiot or had been when he'd ignored the skeletons rattling in the closet. "Maybe. But we're here now. So, maybe it was too soon, bringing you here, but let's get this over with, Emma. You know my parents are going to love Haley."

"But me. Your parents, your mother hates me. They can see Haley any time they want. That's only right, but I should go."

For once, Justin didn't think past wanting to hold her. "Emma." He closed the distance between them and pulled her against him. She resisted for a few seconds, but then leaned her head forward, the rest of her body rigid. "Emma, you're human. You made a mistake. It's not as if I wasn't an idiot for breaking up with you the way I did."

Her shoulder shot up, and she broke contact. "I had no idea. You regret...?"

Justin brushed a tear from her cheek with his thumb. "Yes and no. I regret breaking up with you. I keep trying to remember why I did it, and I keep coming back to dumb kid. At the same time, I think I needed to grow up a lot. Rebellion for the sake of rebellion is pretty much always stupid."

He looked toward the kitchen where his parents were laughing at something Haley had said or done. The kid spread light and laughter like fairy dust. His father's deep chuckle sounded unused and creaky. "In more ways than one."

Emma grabbed his chin and forced him to look at her. "I did call your mother, once."

"You did?"

His mother had never mentioned any phone call, not even with the most recent developments. Not even a, oh that's why she called. He had to wonder if she'd kept it from him or if she had just repressed that awful year from her mind. The tension between him and his father had put her square in the middle and that couldn't have been a ton of fun.

"Yes." Emma let him go. "I wasn't clear. I didn't get that far. I just asked if she could tell me where you were, maybe give me your address."

Justin's empty stomach clenched tight. "What did she say?"

Emma picked at the paper bag holding the bottle of wine. "She said that I needed to move on, forget you, that you had decided you didn't want to be in a relationship."

"All this time." He bolted to his feet, took a step toward the kitchen. "I can't believe."

Emma stopped him with a pale, outstretched hand. "She was right, as far as she knew."

"Knowing her, she didn't let you get a word in edgewise." Justin gritted his teeth. "I can't believe all these years."

Emma's hand crept up his arm. "You can't blame her. I could have called again. I could have made her listen. It was just easier. I wasn't in any shape to fight anyone, to stand up for myself."

He examined her face, tried to figure out what she meant.

Haley ran in from the other room. "Mama, Daddy. We're waiting for you to say grace."

Justin reached over and took the bottle of wine, motioned for Emma to precede him. When she shook her head, he shook his back. Childish, yes, but it got the woman deep breathing and walking.

Haley was either oblivious or a very young child, or both. She skipped forward and backward, with the net result she ended up in the kitchen. "We have honey mustard and ketchup for your chicken nuggets. You get to choose."

Justin gave a short laugh. "That actually sounds good. Which one are you going to choose?"

"Both." Her tone implied he was silly, and maybe he was. Who would give up one or the other when they could have both?

Emma was silent. She followed behind him, meek and mild, and he had to wonder who this woman was. As a teenager, she'd been bold in the face of her discomfort around his parents and in his house.

He realized he was the one left holding the hot potato wine bottle, so he handed it to his mother. "Here, Mom. Emma brought you this as a thank you gift."

His mother perched on a bar stool, obviously having taken the seat to be next to the granddaughter who jumped around like a bean. "Thank you?" She turned the bottle over as if she'd never seen a hostess gift before.

Justin stepped to the side, removing himself as the go-between. The two grown women could talk to each other.

Emma cringed. "For having us over for lunch. Haley and me."

His mother bristled, glanced at him as if asking him to witness how good she was being when she kept quiet, and walked around the island to the refrigerator. She stashed the bottle inside when he knew good and well that the proper thing to do, and his mother always did what was proper, was to open it for the guest. "Thank you, but there was no need. You and Haley aren't guests. Haley's my grandchild."

"Yes, yes, she is." Emma crossed her arms in front of her. "Um, is there anything I can do to help get lunch ready?"

"What?" His mother pulled out a white oven glove to go with the quartz countertop. "Oh, no, just have a seat. Everything's ready."

There were three bar stools and four chairs at the kitchen table. Haley sitting at the island meant that their little group would be split up, and there was no good answer as to who went where. Justin hadn't planned further than getting the parts of his world together, but now that he was here, the goal was clear. His mother and Emma needed to mend fences, if at all possible. Which meant that he and his dad would be the audience, the onlookers, even if they normally failed to speak to each other without his mother as a go-between.

"Guess that means you and I get the table, Pops." He'd picked up the nickname after hanging with a fellow soldier from up north. Calling him that irritated his dad, and he knew better, but the name slipped out at the most random times. "Take your pick."

"This is my seat." His father came over and stood by his chair, at the head of the table, farthest away from the workspace. "Your mom usually sits there," he nodded to the opposing head, "and I guess I'm a creature of habit."

That sum total was more words than they'd spoken to each other for years. Justin nodded in response, as if he'd used up his quota.

"Wait," his mother called out, setting a large pan of home fries on hot pads even though the counter was stone. A holdover habit from the past when they had struggled financially. "Let's say grace before anyone accidentally eats unprayed for food."

The corner of Emma's mouth twitched. Justin would have missed the possibility of a smile if he hadn't been zeroed in on her reactions. His sudden re-obsession with the woman after all these years might scare him once they survived this day.

"Honey, won't you say the prayer?"

"I'd be glad to," his father said. The older man gripped the back of his chair and bowed his head. Everyone followed suit. "Dear Jesus, thank You, Jesus, for allowing us to come to You in prayer. Thank You for all our blessings. May this food be to the nourishment of our bodies and our bodies dedicated to Your service. Amen."

"Amen," Justin echoed, then turned to face the women.

"So, there's nothing fancy." His mother fluttered around the pans of frozen kid's food. "I'd made soup, but well, got distracted. How many chicken tenders would you like, Haley?"

Haley held up a hand. "Five because I'm almost five."

A feeling of awe swept through Justin. Every word that seemed to come out of her mouth was so darned cute. She wouldn't charm him this much forever; he wasn't perfect, she was human and a kid. She'd smart mouth him at some point, maybe lie to him when she was a teenager, but right now, his knees were about to give out thinking she belonged to him.

"And I want five onion rings." Haley stood up on the bar stool, her feet on the top rail and her palms planted on the countertop. "I've never had onion rings. Are they hard?"

The group consensus was to squelch the natural laughter. Smiles happened, though.

"No, they're not hard." Emma reached over and squeezed ketchup on her daughter's plate. "I'm not a fan so I've never served you any. Got any fruit, Mrs. Lee?"

The question was innocent, just a mother doing a good job and watching after her child's nutrition, but his mother's eyes widened in shock. His mother read books on etiquette for pleasure. And according to those books, the guest didn't ask for anything that wasn't offered. Justin knew because he'd been trained from birth. His first instinct was to jump in and cover for Emma, to smooth things over before they got too rough, but he needed to start the way he meant to go on.

Emma didn't register anything was wrong, and his mother's eyebrows subsided. When she'd recovered sufficiently, his mother fluttered back to the refrigerator. "Yes, I'm sure. What does she like?"

"I like bananas and strawberries and blueberries. Blackberries have bad seeds, and they get stuck in my teeth." Haley dunked a chicken nugget in ketchup and followed it up with a honey mustard splatter. "Do you have watermelon?"

His mother hadn't been around a child for too long. Helpless against the onslaught of Haley's stream of consciousness chatter, she stood frozen with her hand on the door handle, undecided. "I have bananas and strawberries. Which?"

"Whatever's easiest," Emma stuttered.

"I can have both for dessert." Haley was four, but she was smart.

Justin decided to stop worrying at everyone else and grabbed a plate. He started scooping out some chicken fingers and onion rings when his mother stopped him. "Son. I have some chicken salad for the grownups."

He almost blurted out, "Well, why didn't you say so?" He stuffed food in his mouth instead. "I'm good with this." He knew better than to go against any of his mother's plans, but he was hungry. All this emotion swirling around the room made him want steak, but that wasn't going to happen.

"Justin, really, you could wait," Emma said, then slapped her hand over her mouth. "I'm sorry. Who am I to say what you should or shouldn't do?"

He grinned at her and winked. "You can tell me whatever you'd like, darling. I just can't promise I'll listen, as evidenced by my continuing to eat these yummy chicken nuggets."

Haley giggled. "Stop. Those are mine!"

"All these?" His mother had heated up a sheet pan full, no wonder he was confused.

Haley nodded, her hair falling forward and blocking her face. Emma produced a hair tie out of nowhere—actually, she'd been wearing it as what he'd assumed was a bracelet. The teenage drama queen he remembered was now a caring, organized mother.

Chicken salad on a croissant appeared on a plate in front of him, along with a fruit salad that his mother could have very well offered Haley. He glanced at her, she shook her head, and he settled for a, "Thank you, Mom."

He took his plate to his seat and watched as his mother placed a plate on the table in front of his father. His parents wrote the book on old-fashioned. For a few minutes, they all ate in semi-silence, given that quiet didn't exist in Haley's little girl-limited vocabulary yet.

"So, Emma, what have you been up to lately?" His mother's question was nothing unusual, but it might not have been the best conversation starter given the two women's history.

Justin scooped up fruit salad despite his normal distaste for anything remotely resembling healthy. He wouldn't die if he ate something that wasn't fried, but it might cause damage if he intruded in the conversation.

"I didn't finish college," Emma said defensively. "But I've worked my way to being an office manager. I also waitress on the weekends." She glanced at her watch and then at Justin. "I have a shift tonight starting at four."

"Oh, wow, that's a lot." Again, everything his mother said could be taken two ways. She could be impressed by Emma's work ethic, or she could be remarking on how little time the mother had to spend with the child. "Who watches Haley when you're at work?"

"I go to school, and then Aunt Tiffy watches me. I'm going over to her house tonight, aren't I, Mama?" Haley was right there in the middle. Both women would do well to remember little pitchers, big ears, etc.

"Yes, sweetie. Right after lunch, we'll go home and get you packed."

Justin checked his watch—barely noon so they had plenty of time. Not that he thought Emma wanted hours with his mother.

"Sarah, bring me a soda." His father had two legs so they must be broken.

"I'll be right there, honey." Her mother put down the bite she'd just speared with her fork, got up, and fixed his father a drink.

Justin stood and went over to the glasses. "Emma, I just realized. What can I get you?" He wasn't doing it to make a point, but if the point got made, so be it.

"Caffeine. I don't care what form it takes." She blinked several times in his direction, and he tried to decode the message, decided 'rescue me' was as good as any.

"Got it." He filled the glasses with ice and poured them each half of a soda.

"I want soda," Haley complained.

"Only when you go out to eat." Emma looked around at the confused faces. "We don't go out often, and it's a clear rule."

His mother made some humming sound, and then returned to where she'd been leading the conversation earlier. "You know, I could watch Haley for you. It's got to be a lot for your sister. That's Tiffany, right? She's your sister."

"Yes, ma'am." Emma had eaten maybe two bites of chicken salad. "Tiffany is my older sister. It might seem like a lot for her to watch Haley almost every weekend, but she loves doing it."

"I'm sure that's what she says, dear, but it has to be a burden, given that she also works. Don't I remember hearing that she became a teacher?"

Emma squeezed her eyes open and shut. "Yes, she's a first-grade teacher. She just loves kids."

"I'm not a burden." Haley stood on the rail of her chair. "Aunt Tiffy loves me. She takes me to church."

His mother came around to do something about Haley's safety, but Emma was there, her hands on Haley's waist tugging her to sit. "Haley, Aunt Tiffy does love you. So does everyone here. Your grandmother is just trying to figure out when she can have you stay the night. Would you like to stay with her and Pawpaw some time?"

Haley's mood switched like a circuit breaker, completely up and then completely down. "I don't know." She hung her head, and the bottom lip came out.

"Oh." His mother covered up disappointment with forced hospitality. "Well, I hope you'll think about it. We'd have a wonderful time. You could swim in the pool and watch a movie."

"Sarah," his father interrupted. "Did you say something about dessert to go with this lunch?"

The man still ran miles every morning, which was about the only excuse for the hole in his leg and an absence of concern for whatever else was going on around him.

"Yes, yes, of course." His mother hadn't managed to eat very much, either, given the demands on her time. "Brownies. Do you like brownies, Haley?"

Up came the little blonde head, and her mouth fell open. "You made brownies? How do you know how to do that?" Haley's head jerked toward her mother. "Do you know how to make brownies, Mama?"

Emma huffed out a short laugh. "From a box, sweetheart. You know I don't cook much."

Haley went back to her plate and nodded, serious. "Yeah, you're too busy." There was no accusation in the little girl's voice. She was just stating facts.

Emma's whole face dropped, and she looked away from her daughter. Justin crammed the last bite of chicken salad in his mouth and jumped up to try to salvage the day yet again. According to the untouched food on her plate, tension wrecked Emma's appetite. From the way he was eyeing those brownies, he subscribed to his father's line of coping.

"Well, I'm a lot older." Bless his mother, she was trying. "And I don't have to work because Pawpaw does." And failing. "I mean, we're married so he makes the money, and I stay at home.

It's an old-fashioned way of doing things." She wound down, like somebody should have taken a pin to her balloon before she started. "I just like to cook. Would you like some ice cream with your brownie, since it's a special occasion?"

She glanced at Emma for permission, but it was too little, too late. The offer was out there, and Haley was chomping at the bit.

"Sure," Emma ground out the word through clenched teeth.

Justin brought his plate over to get his serving, anything to hurry up the rest of the meal, drop the ladies off at home, and cower in a corner somewhere.

Emma pushed her chicken to the side. "I always have room for chocolate."

His mother didn't bother to fake a smile. She wasn't stupid, even if her mouth tended to runneth over when she was nervous.

Haley bounced in her seat. "I've never had dessert for lunch. You said there was a special auction? What did you say?"

His mother's expression softened. "It is a special occasion, dear. That means today is an important day to me, to us," she glanced at her husband who hadn't really spoken for most of the visit, "because we finally get to meet you." His mother got teary eyed. "After all these years."

Emma's spoon clattered on her plate. "I told you." She glared at Justin, as if he'd done something to make her uncomfortable.

He held up flat palms in surrender. "Hey, I didn't argue with you. But just hang in there, okay?"

Haley looked back and forth between the two of them, face scrunched up in suspicion. "What are you talking about?"

His father scraped his chair back. "That's what I want to know. What did you think would happen, young lady? You've robbed us of precious memories of our grandchild that we'll never get back."

His father was so often in the background that when he did impose his will, it added a twinge of fear. He had never been violent, never raised his voice, but there was also no need. Justin marveled that he'd ever had the heart to rebel the way he had, or maybe that was why he'd made the biggest mistake of his life when he'd enlisted rather than go to college. Make that two of the biggest mistakes since wrapped up in that had been leaving Emma.

Emma gathered her purse close to her body. "Haley, sweetie. You finish your brownie. I'm going to go outside for some fresh air. Justin, whenever you two are ready, I'll be waiting."

His father's face twisted with a half sneer, as if he fought to gain back some semblance of kindness. "You don't need to leave. Sit and enjoy the chocolate. Just don't act like my wife doesn't have a right to be upset."

"Goodbye." Points for Emma, whether in the plus or minus column was debatable. She'd never backed down to his parents, but she'd never stood up to them, either.

"Wait." Then again, Emma wasn't the one to stand up to his parents. "Emma, you had your reasons. We're all going to have to accept that and move on." Justin straightened so the couple of inches he had on his father became more than evident. Then, he softened his voice. "Emma, sit, please? You're our guest, and I'd love it if you could enjoy your lunch."

"Mama?" Haley's lower lip trembled. The last thing, the very last thing he wanted, was for his little girl to cry. "I'm not hungry anymore."

"Baby," Emma said, the word coming on an exhale. "Of course you are. You're always hungry. Us grownups are just making you a little nuts. Here, I'll share with you."

Which accomplished her goal of getting out of there faster.

Justin took a depth breath and gave both his parents a look. He'd be giving them a talking to later, even if he was the son and their roles were about to be reversed. Sensing defeat as far as Emma was concerned, he put his plate in the sink. The brownies and ice cream would be here when he got back from dropping Emma and Haley off at her apartment. He wished he could have assuaged his parents' hurt feelings, or prepared Emma better, or something. Or maybe this was just a step they had to walk through to get to the other side.

"I'm done." Haley jumped off the bar stool.

"Manners," Emma hissed a reminder.

"Thank you." Haley ran to his mother and father and gave each of them a fast hug, her arms around their legs more than anything else. "I loved the brownies and ice cream. Mama, do you think you could learn how to make them?"

"She doesn't have to, sweetie. I can make them any time you like." His mother seemed subdued, the fight gone out of her. Her grandchild was about to leave. They had no rights as far as she was concerned. He didn't even have any legal standing as her father.

As far as the courts knew, he'd abandoned them both.

"Thank you." Emma had her purse on her shoulder and her torso turned toward the door. "It was, um, nice seeing you again."

The woman was a terrible liar, which was probably a good thing.

"Any time." His mother wrung her hands with the help of a dish towel. "I'm sorry if we said anything to upset you. If you could, we just need time."

Emma looked anywhere but at the rest of the people in the room. "For what it's worth, I'm sorry. I truly believed Justin didn't want me in his life, and you told me to leave him in the past."

His mother gasped, dropped the dish towel to the floor. "I didn't mean. I didn't know."

"About Haley." Emma's shoulders dropped. "I know that now, but then. Well, anyway, I need to get home and rest before work. I don't have much time."

She'd already told him that she'd slept late that morning. A picture was forming here that scared him. Emma was in her early twenties. How much sleep did she need?

"Sure," he said. "Let me just..." He patted his pockets. He

was more unsettled that he'd realized. "Never mind, my wallet's in my pocket and so are my keys. Ready, Haley bean?"

"Yes, sir." Haley stumbled a bit toward him and put her hand on her belly. "Oh. I think I ate too much."

"Goodbye." His mother looked like she might cry, and his father was about to explode in defense of his wife, again. "Can we plan for her to come over in the next couple of weeks?"

"We'll see." Emma wasn't giving an inch, and that wasn't fair.

Justin shook his head at his father when the man moved forward and prayed to God he'd see reason. They needed to give her time, no matter how right or wrong their objections or wrongdoing on one side or the other. "I'll be back in a bit," he said, attempting a smile. "Don't eat all those brownies while I'm gone."

His mother waved a hand at him, shooing him out.

Justin took the few steps needed to put a hand to Emma's back and lead with his chin. "Ladies first."

Emma's shoulders went up, but she didn't need to be told a second time. Haley followed along like a puppy tethered on a string, going from one side of the living room to another as they went. "That's a nice picture. Who is that? Is that you when you were a baby? Do you have any brothers and sisters?"

"Yes." Justin answered them one at a time since there were short gaps, and he didn't know whether there was more coming or not. "That's me. I don't have any brothers or sisters. I'm an only child, like you."

"Only child?" Haley ran ahead and blocked the front door. "Can I come back next week, Mama? They asked me to. Can I tell Aunt Tiffy about their pool?"

"We'll see." Emma seemed stuck on that one phrase. Her distance grated on his last nerve.

He reached around his daughter's little sturdy body and pulled at the knob. "That's not really an answer, Emma."

If life was a cartoon, there would have been steam coming

out of her ears. "Well, that's the only answer you're going to get."

Justin pressed his lips together and ushered her out the door. She could have the last word for as long as it took for the both of them to calm down.

The drive was quiet until Emma's phone insisted on buzzing its way out of her purse. She glanced at the screen, flicked her eyes in his direction, which he only knew because they were at a stoplight, and then shoved the offending technology back in its pocket.

"Who was it?" Nothing stopped Haley from blurting out what was on her mind. They might need to teach her to curb her enthusiasm, but not today. He wanted to know what had caused that little flicker, and he wasn't above using his kid's innocence if that was the only weapon in his pack.

"Nobody."

The phone thought differently, buzzed again, insistent, not to be ignored.

"You can answer the phone, Emma." He didn't know that much about her life right now, she might be involved with someone, and he'd barged right in as if he owned the place. "I won't listen in."

He'd been joking, badly, but he didn't deserve the crumpled frown and snort he received.

"I'll just text." Emma's fingers flew for a few seconds, then she closed her eyes and leaned her head against the headrest. "Wow, I'm exhausted."

"Do I have to take a nap?" Haley was always paying attention.

"No. You can watch TV." Emma's neck fell forward, and she rubbed at the crook between shoulder and long, graceful neck with slender fingers. "Or read in your room. Just be quiet."

"Yes, ma'am." Haley sat back and plopped her thumb in her mouth.

Justin's own mouth dropped open. He hadn't seen her do

that before now, and he wished he hadn't. His first sergeant talked about having to pay for an appliance to keep his son from sucking his thumb, or there would be braces to pay for later.

The light switched to green, and he focused on the miniature car running a red light before making his turn. "Wait." He was slow on the uptake sometimes. "Why did Haley ask if she could tell Tiffany about the pool? Shouldn't she just do it?"

Out popped the thumb. "You're a secret, Daddy."

He slammed on the brakes to keep from hitting the car stopped at yet another stop sign. "I'm a what?"

"You're a secret," Emma answered, but she sat, stone-faced, looking straight ahead. "I haven't told my family about you being back, not yet."

The Lord was very good. The next turn emptied into the apartment parking lot and "his" visitor's spot stood empty. He parked with as much care as if he was taking a driver's test.

He did not turn off the engine and did not release the child locks. He waited until his hands stopped gripping the steering wheel like it was Emma's neck and released a cleansing breath. "Can you tell me why?"

"I'm not ready." That seemed to be all the answer he was going to get since Emma was opening the door and swinging her long legs to the ground.

He shut off the engine and got to Haley's door before she did. "Whatever is going through your head, Emma, stop. I'm not abandoning the two of you. I'm not going anywhere, and I plan on being part of at least Haley's life for years to come."

"Not in public," Emma hissed and almost pushed him out of the way to get to Haley.

Justin shoved his hands in his pockets and backed up a step. He'd not come this close to shaking a woman since, well, Kristi. He hadn't touched either one of them violently, and he never would, but the woman was driving him right over the edge. "I've been nothing but patient and kind to the both of you, Emma. What do you think I'm going to do?"

"We're going inside." She made a move as if to pick Haley up, but the girl was much too heavy.

"Mama, I want to walk," Haley protested. The little girl looked scared, glancing back and forth between the two of them. "You're hurting me."

Emma paled, which was hard to do since the woman looked like she hadn't seen the sun for years. "I'm sorry. I'll put you down, but you have to hold my hand."

Since the sidewalk was only a few feet away, she might be overreacting. Haley didn't protest and neither did he. When he fell in step behind the two of them, pressing the clicker to lock the truck behind them, Emma glared at him. He ignored her.

The apartment door was shut behind them before Emma spoke again. The parking lot and the hallway had been deserted, but he guessed there were always neighbors at windows and doors with nothing better to do. "Haley, go to your room."

Haley's spunk had faded between his parents' house and here. She silently obeyed, and her demeanor burned his hide.

As soon as the little girl's door shut, he turned on Emma. "What are you doing? She was so happy and now..."

"Now, she's tired and so am I." Emma pointed at the door. "You need to leave."

Justin debated. They stood in her apartment. She had all the power, but this was one battle he couldn't afford to lose. "I will, I promise. But I need some answers. What does your family know about me?"

"Nothing." She crossed her arms in front of her stomach, toe tapping like a clock winding down on how long he had before she kicked his butt to the curb. "They don't know anything. I didn't want to bring you up only to have you disappear again."

Justin gave a low growl. "How many times do I have to tell you? I am going to be a father to Haley. I am not going anywhere."

She shook her head. How could she deny him when everything he'd done since they'd reunited backed him up? He was a good guy.

"What?"

"It's not just that." She sat down on a bar stool, looking like a woman two or three times her age. "They think you didn't want Haley to start with."

"What?" Justin needed to find a seat himself. "Why would they think that?" He wasn't stupid. "Because you told them so. Because it was easier than saying you hadn't told me about being a father." He dropped to the arm of the sofa, shoved his hand through his hair. "Emma, I really need to understand you on this. Help me out here."

She started to sob. "I know I was wrong. It was just easier, like you said. I'd tried calling your mother. I was pregnant. I was a teenager. I can't."

He was helpless in the face of her tears. "Emma, don't. I didn't mean to make you upset." Okay, maybe that hadn't been his intention, but he wasn't exactly happy with her. He shoved his fingers at his head one more time, pretty sure his hair was standing on end by now. "Please don't cry. I just need..."

What he needed didn't seem to matter now. She'd gone past the point of no return to deep wrenching sobs.

Haley came running out of her room. "Mama."

The little girl comforted the older woman, and he lingered, useless.

"Okay, then, I'll just get going." Justin pushed himself toward the door. "I'll call in a couple of days. I want to talk about the holidays." He kept going despite the resistance on the child's face and the wreck that was Emma. "I want to spend as much time as possible with Haley." He sighed. "Goodbye, for now."

CHAPTER 14

*J*ustin guzzled the gas station coffee as if he was the one with a 52-gallon fuel tank sitting empty instead of his truck. His weekend back home, his attempts at calming Emma down followed by his wailing mother, and the six-hour drive back fighting holiday traffic, had worn him down to a nub.

Getting up at 4:30 so he could get back on base and run with his troops sounded like blunt force torture. He had to do it, there was no choice, but every cell in his body rebelled.

He had no sooner parked when the sergeant from B company knuckled the window, startling the crazy out of him. "What the...? Cody, you mad man, I could have run you over."

"Naw." The jarhead, even though they were all Army and not Marines, shook back and forth. "I can find my way around a parked vehicle. Anyway, I want to give you a head's up about the hornet's nest you're about to walk into."

Justin reached over and chugged the last of the scorching hot coffee before it was too late. "I don't know what you're talking about, but shoot."

Cody wrapped an arm around his shoulders and led him to the back of the truck, motioned to the bed. "Have a seat."

Justin wanted to point out that time was a 'ticking, and he wasn't in the mood to get yelled at or written up for being late when he'd started out being early. He did as he was told instead.

Cody took his silence and ran with it. "So, if I ever needed proof that dating another soldier is a bad idea, here you go. Your ex has been spreading rumors. We all know that you just found out you got a kid a few months ago. Now, she's saying your baby mama kept it from you all these years, and she's real messed up."

Justin gripped the cold metal of the tailgate and kept his mouth shut. So far, Kristi wasn't spreading rumors; she was sharing facts. "Yeah, anything else?"

"You mean it's true?"

Justin kept his own counsel, not wanting to throw Emma under the bus just in case things turned around for the two of them. He didn't see much hope right at the moment, but she was still beautiful, and he still cared.

Cody took the silence for agreement. "Man, I'm sorry. That sucks. Anyway, Kristi is also saying that woman is messing with your head, and you might not stay in the Army. That you're not able to keep up with your work. One of your guys got in trouble in town this weekend, and you were nowhere to be found."

The early morning cadence of men shouting stupid songs to keep time while running could be heard over the rapid-fire beating of his heart. PT had started without him. If he hadn't been falling out on his duties before, the both of them had just stepped in trouble right about now.

"We need to get out there before we get written up."

Cody slapped his shoulder. "Keeping it close to the chest, are you? I get it. I would if I were in your shoes. I just wanted you to know what was going on. I tried to tell Kristi that she should keep her stuff to herself, but she said she was just concerned about you, as a friend."

Justin gave a short laugh. "Yeah, we all need friends like

that." He checked the lock on the truck. "Thing is, she's half right. I'll talk to her. Thanks, man."

They both hustled to get in line. Experience had taught him where to park, otherwise, he would have been in big trouble.

After a few hundred yards, his lieutenant fell back and ran alongside him. "You were late, sergeant."

"Yes, sir."

"Is there anything I need to know about, Lee?"

"No, sir." If Justin had issues, he'd solve them himself. The code was ingrained in his growing up, in his buddies, passed down from his father, modern therapeutic interventions weren't going to undo what had been drilled into him for some time to come. Men were supposed to be tough. "I heard there was an issue with a Joe this weekend?"

"Yeah, I'll brief you on that after I finish grinding you into the ground." Many sergeants looked down on their lieutenants as fresh-faced college boys who didn't know their head from a hole in the ground, but Justin knew better. This boy was his age and had played rugby in college.

"Thank you, sir. I'm looking forward to it." Justin smart-mouthed, but he'd rather be in bed any day. Being a soldier was in his blood, but sleep sounded pretty good right about then.

"Yeah, right." Lt. Curtsinger grinned his backwoods-from-Kentucky grin that fooled so many people into underestimating him and picked up the pace.

When the man was out of ear shot, Justin allowed himself a deep, heartfelt groan.

The next hour was an excruciating form of torture disguised as a workout. They ran their normal five miles followed by short sprints and jumping jacks like they were a bunch of overgrown kids. After eating like a horse over the weekend, Justin felt every extra ounce going up and coming back down.

By the time they got the go-ahead to hit the showers, his legs were crying for mercy, but he had to act like he wasn't worn to a stub before his day had really started.

"Hey, Justin." Kristi came over to where he leaned over his feet thinking he might not see the sky again for days.

If he was a betting man, he'd have placed good money on her avoiding him as much as possible. He'd have been wrong, but the odds would have been in his favor. "Hey, Kristi. What are you up to?"

He'd given a normal greeting, not meant to imply anything for the simple reason that he didn't want to get into their business with her this early in the morning and especially not in front of their fellow troops. Too bad she turned red in the emerging sunrise and stiffened in response. "What is that supposed to mean?"

He took a deep breath. "It was only a way of asking how you're doing, nothing more, nothing less."

She planted her feet wide, and she narrowed her eyes at him so very little color was visible. "Okay. I'm fine. How are you?"

"I'm fine, thank you." He'd always wondered why breakups were like this, as if the person who changed their mind metamorphosed into the devil incarnate no matter how respectfully they declined the offer. "Anything else on your mind?"

"Yes," she hissed. "I'd like us to have lunch, or coffee later, something. I want to talk to you."

"Since you asked so prettily," he started, then stopped himself. His Christian self should refrain from cruel sarcasm, no matter how great the temptation. "I'm sorry, Kristi. How about after work, we meet at the Java Hut?"

Java Hut was a coffee shop right across from the base's main gates and was usually packed with soldiers trying to get their caffeine fix after early rising and few breaks. The very busyness of the place should prevent any ugly scenes. He could only hope.

Kristi's stance loosened, and she gave him the ghost of a smile. "Sure, that sounds great. I'll see you then. Don't forget."

He had never forgotten a date or a meeting in his life. "I won't. Have a good day."

Her expression softened even more. She gave a short nod and walked away.

He threw a glance toward the morning sky and pled for some extra credit points. One thing he could say for his day, the shower was hot. After that, his day went downhill and worse. His raw recruit had gone over the bend Saturday and sat in jail. Normally, even though it had been a weekend, Justin would have been his one call, and he'd have dropped everything, no matter what awful time of the night, and gone to help the dude. Instead, he'd been hours away with his ex and his daughter. Not that people expected him to ignore his family, but somehow, he should have been in two places at once.

Then, he walked into the rigger shed to get to work only to find that while the lieutenant briefed him in his office, every soldier under him grabbed the opportunity to get behind in his or her duties. The job they did was so important he couldn't sleep some nights, and these idiots didn't take packing a parachute seriously?

Hours later, on his way to meet Kristi, his throat hurt from yelling so much. He was looking forward to the coffee, if not the company. He swallowed hard against his dry mouth. A few months ago, he'd enjoyed the woman's company, and now, he dreaded walking into the charming little shop. Life was weird.

Kristi had taken the time to change. He hadn't. She hovered around the entrance, black beret in her hand as if she'd kept one thing from her uniform to hold on to, like a talisman.

"Hey." He attempted to keep his voice friendly yet not interested. He hated how aware he'd been of the tone of his voice these last few days, trying to placate one woman and not give yet another woman the wrong idea. "Have you ordered yet?"

"What?" She flinched. "No, not yet. I thought we'd order together, sit on the bench for a while. I want us to be friends."

"Sure." He reached around her and held the door. Fewer soldiers than normal crowded the little shop, maybe because

Monday meant catching up on work after a weekend of relaxation. "Friends are good."

They got in line, and he studied the menu, even though he always got the same thing because, to him, coffee meant caffeine and there was no use fooling around. He always got the high octane, with one sugar and one cream. It was almost as good as the Army made it.

"I saw Cody come over to talk to you this morning after PT." Kristi didn't let them get through the line before starting. That made him sad. "I wanted to make sure he wasn't telling you things about me without a chance to defend myself."

In reality, why did she care? They might both be in the Army, but they had completely different job descriptions. She worked in admin, and he oversaw men packing parachutes. They would rarely see each other. "Don't worry," he said. "I don't buy into gossip."

Even though if Cody had heard it directly from her, the man hadn't been gossiping but acting like a true friend. Coming to him with what he'd heard as more of he was danged if he did and danged if he didn't.

Kristi's shoulders went back. "I'm not saying your best bud was gossiping. I just wanted you to know my side."

"Okay. That's what this talk is for." He stepped up toward the cashier. "Large plain coffee, please. I'll add the sugar myself."

"Yes, sir. Can I have a name for the order?"

Justin glanced at Kristi, and she shook her head. He wasn't paying for hers. This wasn't a date. "Justin. How much?"

The girl looked between the two of them, a wrinkle in the middle of her forehead, but she pushed the buttons anyway. "Two-fifty."

He handed her cash, which turned the wrinkle into a furrow of 'please don't make her do the math.' "Just keep the change."

Kristi bumped into him on her way over to place her order when he didn't move to the side fast enough. She often did things like that; now that he thought about it, the woman was wound too tight. He'd put money down that she'd end up standing rather than sitting on the bench the whole time.

"Justin, your coffee's ready." The young man at the counter was too young to enlist, and he had stars in his eyes at the stripes. "Thank you for your service, sir."

Justin laughed. "I'm not a sir. I work for a living." He grinned at the kid and moved out of the way before he got run over by the next customer.

"You ready?" Kristi stood at his elbow, fancy cold coffee with swirls on the top in her hand.

"Uh, sure. What is that?"

"This." Kristi held the drink up in the air. "It's the special. Pumpkin spice coffee chiller."

She might as well have said she was going to drink kale. "Pumpkin and coffee? No way."

"Yeah, way." She bumped shoulders like she was one of the guys, which she had to be most of the time. "It's delicious. You should try it sometime."

Her acting like just any other soldier made the walk over toward the bench more comfortable. "No, thanks. The only way I can stomach pumpkin is in a pie with lots of sugar and eggs and other things that cover up the actual pumpkin."

Kristi's laugh was deeper than the average woman's, and what was wrong with him? He kept picking the woman apart. "I bet I could get you to like it. There's this pumpkin stir fry I made last week. Yum."

He cringed. One flaw he'd own was his pickiness when dealing with food. Maybe just another thing he'd inherited from his father. "That's okay. I'll take your word for it."

They sat on opposite ends of the bench, which barely gave them a few inches between them. Justin took a sip, regretted it, waited for his tongue to cool down from the fire he'd just imbibed. Kristi took a sip, put the coffee down between them, and then jumped to her feet.

"Here's the thing, Justin." Her hands started flying, Italian without a drop of the heritage. "I know it's not my business. You're an adult. You decided to move on. But that doesn't mean I stop caring."

He flicked a glance around the open area surrounding the restaurant. The place wasn't crowded, but there was a steady flow. If he thought she'd stay down, he'd ask her to sit but there was little chance. "I understand," he said. "I don't wish bad things for you. Heck, I wish good things for you, Kristi. I've just got a daughter now, and I'm not sure, but Emma and I are working things out."

Her hands dropped to her sides, and she fell back to the bench. Her coffee almost toppled over. "Are you sure that's a good idea?"

The audacity of her question had him almost spilling his coffee, which would have probably caused third degree burns. He didn't relish the thought of the pain. He already had scars on his thigh from landing too close to a bush last year during a night jump. "Um, I think that falls under the category of not your business, Kristi."

"I know, I know." She waved a hand in front of her face, as if it had suddenly got hot outside, in October. "But as a concerned friend, I mean, she dumped you, didn't even bother telling you that you had a daughter. I mean, what other kinds of secrets might she be keeping from you?"

Justin's temper was getting about as hot as his coffee. "For your information, I dumped her. And she called my house to tell me about Haley, after I'd left for boot camp, and my mother shut her down."

The fact that Emma had only called once and could have located him some other way if she'd tried, well, all those and other tidbits also fell under the category of not Kristi's business.

"Sure, sure." Kristi did more gesturing with her drink than she drank. "I knew that you'd been the one to break up with her, but it wouldn't have been that hard."

"Regardless," he started. Anything he said would fall into the category of too much, but he had the urge to defend Emma. Difficult, really, since she'd been a basket case on Saturday. "Emma is a wonderful mother and has experienced a lot of hardships in her life. I'd appreciate it if you'd express your concerns to me and not anyone else in the unit."

Kristi's eyes widened. "I only spoke to your friends. They're concerned about you, too. You've been gone a lot, missed a lot."

Justin's belly grumbled. He didn't want coffee. He wanted a greasy burger and fries. "Well, then they can come to me with their concerns as well. I doubt they will, given that they're guys, but tell them to come to the source. I'd appreciate your help on this matter, Kristi." He willed her to do the right thing.

"Sure, sure." She jumped to her feet, taking her drink with her. This probably meant the interlude was over. "Just know, I'm here for you, as a friend, in case."

All the patience was gone. "In case what?"

"In case she fights you over custody. In case you end up hurt because she keeps you from your daughter." Kristi made a chopping motion with one hand. "Just in case. I'll see you around." Her face was closed off, and she strode away as if she were late for an appointment.

Justin leaned forward, elbows resting on his knees. There might be a just in case in his future, but he wouldn't turn to Kristi. Dating her might be in the running now for worst mistake of his life.

Too bad there were a lot of contenders for the role.

CHAPTER 15

*E*mma tucked Haley into bed the Thursday after the terrible, no good Saturday and almost closed the door. Her daughter insisted on the hall light being left on and a slit of light seeping into her room, just in case there were monsters. She believed Jesus protected her and that her guardian angel was busy watching over her, but she also needed to see.

Emma only hoped she hadn't instilled that extra caution.

She walked down the hall, ears pierced for the sound of a little girl begging for a drink of water or feet slipping across the floor sneaking one last peek at tonight's book, but there was nothing. Haley had been extra tired this week, maybe also catching the contagion from her mother.

Emma had been going to bed as soon as she could after putting Haley down. She knew she was sliding down a long hill to an abyss, but there was nothing to hold on to except her job and her child. Somehow, those two things didn't give her the energy to stay awake at night. They got her up in the morning, and through the day, but the shadows crept forward at night, when she was all alone.

Tiffany had noticed the dark circles beneath her eyes on

Sunday when she'd brought Haley home, but Emma had just said she was having trouble sleeping.

Emma still hadn't told Tiffany, or anyone else for that matter, about Justin being back in their lives.

He might not be after her performance on Saturday.

She hadn't heard from him since, which might mean nothing. He might just be busy, or he might be cutting his losses.

Her pajamas called her name, and she slipped into the soft cotton T-shirt and three quarters length pants. She brushed her teeth. She put on eye cream but stared at the cabinet where her hand lotion sat untouched. She played a game with herself, what must be done and what could she get away with not doing.

Her phone vibrated on the counter.

If she closed her eyes this early, just after eight, nightmares would wake her in the wee hours of the morning. Tomorrow was a big day at the office, payroll day, and she needed her wits about her. Sinking on to the bed, she took the phone and answered without registering who was calling, not really.

"Hey, Emma." Justin's voice ran through her like warm water. "Did I miss Haley's bedtime?"

The hurt that followed his words surprised her. She must have fooled even herself into believing she didn't care what he thought of her. "Yeah," she said softly. "Not by much, but she tends to hit the pillow and be out like a light."

"Okay." He sounded as worn out as she felt, but she had a hunch he had a better excuse. Their focus had been on Haley and their reunion and old, calcified bitterness. She didn't have a clue as to what he did on a day-to-day basis. "That's good. Not that I don't want to talk to my girl, but I really wanted to talk to you."

Emma cracked her head on the headboard. "Ow. Wow, that hurts. You wanted to talk to me?"

"Are you okay?"

"Yeah, don't mind me. Clumsy as usual. So, did you call to talk to me or Haley?"

His laugh was short and rich. "Yeah, you. I know last

weekend was a bust. I'm sorry for my part in not smoothing things over better, planning, smacking my parents upside the head, whatever else I should have done. I wish it had gone better."

Emma snorted, rubbed the crown of her head. "I can't believe I'm laughing."

"Sometimes laughing is the better option. You know, instead of crying."

If he kept stunning her, she'd have a lump on the back of her head from rearing back in surprise. "When did you get so smart, Justin Lee?"

"Emma, can we video chat?"

Ouch. She reached for a pillow to cushion the blow. He'd shocked her yet again. She also had an idea that she looked about her worst and didn't know what to do with his request. "I don't know, Justin. I had a long day, little sleep, not my best."

"I don't care." His voice had a rough edge to it, like she mattered in his life, and he wanted to see her face. "It doesn't matter what you look like because you'll always be beautiful."

Emma shivered, hugged another pillow against her chest. "Okay, but don't say I didn't warn you."

"Duly noted." There was a shuffling sound on his side of the phone. "Let me just…"

Her phone buzzed, and she shoved her hair out of her face and pinched her cheeks. Trying to find some color in her face was old-fashioned and stupid, but she knew her face hadn't seen the sun for any appreciable time lately. The buzzing grew insistent. She swiped. "Hey."

"Hey." The phone distorted his face, and she tried to ignore her own reflection on the small screen. "Told you. You look beautiful."

"Uh-huh. And you want me to trust you?" She mourned his buttering her up, with an undercurrent of stunned that she had found the energy to tease. "What's on your mind, Justin?"

He started to answer, but she interrupted him, realizing she had been rude. "You look good, too, Justin, by the way. Tired, but good."

She'd always been too honest for her own good. His eyebrows shot halfway up his forehead, waggled there for a few seconds, and then settled back down. "Emma, I'll never get a big head around you, will I?"

A strand of hair twisted between her fingers, and she looked at the phone sideways. "You know you're a handsome man, Justin, always have been, always will be. Now, stop fishing, and tell me what's on your mind."

He ran his free hand through his hair, and the straight blond hair stood up like a shock of corn silk. She longed to reach across the miles and touch it. "Like I said to start with, you. Before Saturday went south, I'd planned on asking you if I might take you out the next time I come down."

"What?" They'd been flirting around so she should have seen the change in their relationship coming, but still. "What about Haley?"

One pale brow quirked higher. "Um, a babysitter? Tiffany?"

Just hearing her sister's name made last weekend's argument rear its head in her memory. At the same time, nothing had changed, and she wasn't the one to bring it up. "I think that's a good idea. She always enjoys time with her favorite niece."

Justin snorted. "Favorite niece? Isn't Haley her only niece? Or did Shelby have a child I don't know about?"

There was a lot of things he didn't know about her family, but that wasn't one of them. "No. Shelby can't settle on one man long enough to…" Her voice faded. She hadn't been married when Haley had been conceived or born so there was no expectation that her younger sister would have better morals.

"It's okay. Haley would be anyone's favorite niece, no matter the competition. What was I thinking?"

"You weren't thinking, that's what." Teasing was so much better of a conversation gambit than bringing up unpleasant subjects. "I'll double check with Tiffany and let you know." Once again, her voice faded as she realized where her words were headed. "That is, were you thinking this coming weekend? You were just here."

Justin pushed at his eyelids, as if forcing himself to stay awake. "You're right. Maybe not next weekend. I've received some push back for being gone so much. Funny how the Army thinks it owns you even on your days off. How does the following Saturday look?"

Emma had no social life. She worked every single day of her life so she could take one single night off. "That sounds good."

Then, her curiosity got the best of her. "Why, Justin? I was awful last Saturday. I know you apologized for what you see as your part in the debacle that was the visit to your parents, but it was really my fault in the end. If I'd held it together, been less emotional, more mature, then things would have gone a lot better. Why aren't you angry with me?"

Across the miles, his bloodshot eyes met hers, strong and steady despite what had to have been a very long, no good day. "Because I can't stay that way. You know, back in high school, when I broke up with you? I regretted it the next day. You're part of me, Emma. You might be too emotional sometimes—your words, not mine, but you are also a loving mother and person. Heck, I can't put a label on it. I could list your characteristics, but when does that matter? You're the woman God made for me. I believe that with all that I am."

Emma hit her head again.

"Whoa." Justin's eyes went wide, and his mouth fell open so she could see down his throat. "I'm sorry. I didn't mean to scare you to death."

She groaned, rubbed her head, and turned so that her back was no longer resting against the pillows in range of the head-board. "Well, what did you expect? We haven't even gone on our first date."

Justin dropped his phone. She was treated to a picture of his messy bedroom and a barren wall before he got a good grip on his screen again. "Are you kidding? We dated for three years in high school and were good friends before then."

"We're different people now," Emma said the words, but she could only hope they were true. "At least, I think I am. I hope I've grown up."

Justin yawned. "Sorry. I know what you're saying. The things I've been through have certainly changed me, but we're the same people at our cores. I mean, I haven't even seen Tiffany, but I can tell you she's probably tripping over nothing right now, and she loves kids. Am I right?"

Emma laughed. "Yes, yes, you are. She's a first-grade teacher at Summer Creek elementary."

He yawned again, and it was contagious, or maybe she was just as exhausted as he was. He took mercy on her, or maybe himself. "Sorry again. Can I call again tomorrow night?"

She blinked, which was a decided improvement over bludgeoning her own head. "Um, sure. Are you sure?"

The wrinkles around his eyes were faint, but the laughter behind them was evident. "Emma, what happened to the confident cheerleader who could barely see me for looking down her nose?"

Her throat was suddenly parched dry, the child begging for a sip of water before bedtime. "Was I? I wasn't, not to you."

He leaned forward, and a short shock of hair fell on his forehead. "No, you weren't, but you could have been. You were the popular one, and I was a ROTC kid in that green polyester uniform."

She began the yawning this time. "I liked that uniform. You looked so buff and watching you do pull-ups?" She fanned herself with her hand. "Whew."

His grin lit up the screen. "Well, thank you, ma'am. You should see me now. Me now could whoop me then."

Her heart tripped over itself. "Okay. You are hundreds of miles away, and we're practically strangers. Behave."

"You were the one fanning yourself." His eyes twinkled, despite the drooping lids. "Good night, Emma. Dream of me."

"Well, aren't you ahead of yourself?" She almost put fingers to her face to trace the edges of her lips. Smiling wasn't foreign, Haley was part of her life, but still. "Good night, Justin. Ditto."

They let go of the connection.

Emma fell back against her mattress, the soft chenille bedspread tickling her cheek. She felt like a woman again, even if only for a little while. Justin could leave, at any time. She had to guard herself.

A prayer escaped her lips, something she rarely did. "Dear Lord, help me. Help me not succumb to the shadows. Help Justin stick around this time. If it's Your will, of course, whatever You want. But please. Amen."

CHAPTER 16

*E*mma bit her lip to keep from laughing at Haley's antics. The child was tired and hyped up on a fruit punch juice box, so she couldn't be blamed. But the last thing Emma wanted to do was reinforce her child's sassiness on a Tuesday night. Her daughter might be tired after a long day at preschool and her own refusal to succumb at naptime, but there was homework to be done.

A page of the letter T did not write itself.

"Shh, girl. Do the work and you can go watch television," Emma said and regretted the bribe as soon as the words slipped past her lips. "Forget I said that. Do the work because you love learning. Writing letters is fun because eventually you can write cool stories about unicorns and princesses."

Okay, so attempting to channel her sister Tiffany may have pushed the boundaries.

Haley's plump lower lip poked out, and her chin came down, ready to fight. "But I want to watch television. And I can't write stories yet, I can only write the stupid letter T."

Emma surrendered and laughed. Her daughter smelled weakness. She clamped her mouth shut and tried to perfect the look. "Just do it."

She'd avoided saying 'do what I say because I said so,' but the night was still young, and Haley had years of school remaining. Haley huffed and puffed, but the pencil started moving.

The doorbell rang. They looked at each other as if the big bad wolf had to be on the other side. Literally no one came to visit them without texting first. Emma had little discretionary income so she wasn't expecting a package.

Haley recognized a reprieve when she heard one. "I'll get it!"

Emma saw panic stars in her peripheral vision. Other than telling Haley not to answer the door when she was home alone, which was only when Emma ran to the complex office for their mail, she had not taught her the least bit about stranger danger and checking through the side first.

"Wait!"

Haley was adorable, but she was still a kid. She acted like she was deaf and opened the door anyway.

Ice shot through Emma's veins, a vaccine of terror. Some stranger could be at the door and grab her child right before her eyes.

Instead, her mother stood on the other side.

Which in some ways wasn't that far off. Haley took one look at her grandmother, whom she hadn't seen for months, and gave a little shriek. She ran behind Emma and peeked around her body to study the virtual stranger.

"Well, good evening to you, too, sweetheart." Her mother put a hand to her chest. "What's wrong with her? She about gave me a heart attack."

Emma managed to suppress a groan. "I'm sorry, Mama. We're just not used to having visitors." She tripped over her own words. They were used to having Justin, but he texted first. "And it's been a while since she's seen you."

Her mother looked down at the threshold and coughed.

"Oh, Mama. I'm sorry. Please come in." Emma backed up a couple of steps, hampered by a child in the way. "Haley, let go. Say hello to your grandmother."

Haley stared at the older woman and narrowed her eyes as if she doubted her identity.

"Haley Grace." Emma gripped her daughter's shoulders and turned her toward her mother. "Say hello."

"Hello." Haley did the kid thing where she dragged out the word, drew a circle on the floor with her big toe, and looked anywhere but at the person she was addressing.

Emma sent an apologetic look at her mother.

Her mother brushed past them both to walk inside and put her purse on the high-top table that really only seated two. "You need to tie a knot in that girl's tail, if you ask me. No better manners than to disobey you when you tell her something. And why didn't she look at me when she was talking?"

Emma bristled. "Maybe because she's only four?"

Her mother crossed her short arms over her big belly. "You need to start now teaching her how to behave. It doesn't get any better."

The pointed look she sent Emma's way pierced her like a barb. No, she hadn't gotten any better. She'd only disappointed and humiliated her mother beyond words, not that her mother had ever been short on words.

"Yes, ma'am," Emma said, tired.

"Do you have any coffee?" The thing was—Emma would have gotten around to offering. She just didn't have a chance.

"Yes, ma'am." Emma gave Haley another nudge toward the living room coffee table. "Finish your homework, Haley."

"Yes, ma'am." Now her child decided to display some manners. Haley acted like she was a half-animated zombie as she dragged one foot, and then the other, arms flailing, across the room.

The right corner of Emma's mouth twitched as she stifled laughter.

"What is wrong with that child?" Her mother pulled a stool out from the bar and struggled to stretch her short legs high enough to reach. Her mother was shorter by far than any of her three daughters. Even though Shelby was shortest, and Emma the tallest, there was still that gap. "I need the pink packets for my coffee, can't have any sugar."

"I knew that." Emma bustled around the small countertop and started a pot.

She thought wistfully of the fancy single serve pot she'd saved money for last Christmas, only to need tires on her jeep last minute. Coffee was cheaper this way, and she rifled through her cabinet for the packets she'd bought last year, the last time her mother had dropped by.

"So, Mom, how are you?"

She'd tried for as neutral a question as available, but the words were still pocked with land mines. Her mother fanned herself with a piece of junk mail in the stack Emma never seemed to get rid of. "Oh, I am a mess. Jim insists on cooking a big meal every evening, and I need to lose weight or my doctor said I'm going to be forced to cut out all sweets and salt. And how is that living? I have indigestion every night."

Emma poured steaming hot coffee in a mug and handed it to her mother, followed by packets of artificial sweetener and single-serving creamers. She'd learned long ago not to guess at how much of anything her mother might want. She'd get it wrong, and they'd have to start all over. "Um, I'm sorry."

"You think he'd want to do what is best for my health, but he doesn't seem to care." Her mother tore open one packet after another, and Emma turned half away so her face was in the shadows of the fast-approaching night. "I told him I was going to see my daughter tonight and would eat at your house."

Emma's eyes shot open, wider, more awake than she'd been all day. "Um, Mama. We already ate. We eat early because of Haley's bedtime."

Her mother stirred cream into her coffee until it turned the color of Haley's fading tan lines from the summer. "Well, if you don't have any food in the house, I guess I can stop by a restaurant and get a salad. I don't want much."

Emma had lost the train of the conversation, but she should have known where this was going. "Mama, of course I have food in the house. It's just that I don't have anything ready."

Her mother sipped and sighed. "This coffee is good, but I probably shouldn't drink it so late at night. I'll never sleep now."

Emma was so proud of herself when the scream stayed inside her head. "You don't have to drink it, Mom. If you'd like some water or milk, just let me know."

Her mother waved at her. "No, no, you made it for me. I'm going to drink it."

Haley seemed to forget her Meemaw was there and sidled over to Emma's side, paper limp in her hands. "Mama. I want a cookie."

Her mother did a spit-take with scalding hot coffee. "Oh. Hot, hot."

"Mama, are you okay?" Emma rushed to hand her a dish towel. "What happened? Did you choke?"

"Yes." Her mother dabbed at her chest. "It's okay. I think it had cooled down a little bit, or I'd have third degree burns."

"I'm sorry." Emma held her hands over a towel, not able to move. If she'd caused her mother to be injured, she would never live it down. "I don't understand. Was it too hot?"

Her mother had a habit of waving her hand, dismissing the unpleasant rather than saying the negative. "The coffee's fine. It's that girl. Not a please to her name. I can see that I have been remiss in my duties as a grandmother. She needs to learn her manners."

Haley had stuck to Emma's side through the whole debacle. Now, she stuck her head around Emma's body like a long-necked turtle. "I know how to say please. I just forgot. Tell her, Mama."

"Young ladies don't talk back to their elders." The steely gaze from behind weak blue eyes barely lingered on Haley long enough to recognize the child's existence and landed on Emma. "You been spanking that child?"

"I don't..." Emma started, and then faded.

"I know I didn't always do my best with you girls, working so many miserable jobs like I did to make ends meet, but you never lacked for discipline." Her mother pushed the two-thirds full cup of coffee away from her. "The girl needs a man in her life. Someone you can count on, not like that boy who left you without so much as a penny for a diaper. Pretty girl like you, Emma, surely you can find somebody."

Emma slapped a hand over Haley's mouth. The last thing she wanted was for her mother to get wind of that boy's presence back in their lives.

"Homework?" Her mother clicked her tongue. "I thought you said she was only four. Isn't that awful young to have homework?"

"Yes, ma'am. It is." Emma didn't see as how she had any choice. She had to work, thus Haley had to go to preschool. And shouldn't her mother know how old her only grandchild was?

"Well, I need to eat, and since y'all already ate, I guess I'll go through a drive-through, even though I don't see how that's any better than what I could have had at home." Her mother picked up her purse. "It's good to see you, Emma. You need to come and visit me the next time. I'll make sure there's dinner for you. And I'll teach that child of yours how to cook."

Emma blinked, not sure what to say to that since Haley was too young to be let near a stove. "I don't know when I can, Mom, with working two jobs."

Her mother shook her head. "I know it's a shame, so much time spent away from your child. I wish I could help you, but we barely make ends meet as it is." She put a hand to her side. "Well, my stomach is rumbling. I better go before my sugar gets low. Love you."

Emma leaned down for her mother's hug but made no effort to force Haley to come into the cluster. Every time these two important females got in the same room, bad things happened. She had no idea what to do about any of it. "Love you, too, Mom. Be safe."

She could have protested, pushed her mother back into her chair and force fed her the leftover lasagna she'd prepped last weekend, but she didn't. Her mother needed to go if Haley was going to get any sleep on a weeknight.

"Bye, Haley, Meemaw loves you."

"Bye."

Haley was nothing if honest. She didn't love her grandmother, barely even knew her since their visits were so infrequent on either side.

Her mother gave a long-suffering sigh and left, the steam from her coffee still floating in the air.

Emma didn't move. She couldn't move. Her own mother thought she was a terrible mother, that she didn't discipline her child, didn't spend enough time with Haley. If she hadn't been so rebellious as a teenager, if she hadn't been reeling from the loss of her father, if she hadn't distracted him so much that night, he might still be alive. *If, if, if.*

"No."

"Mama? Why did you say no?" Haley stared up at her, her eyes scrunched as if she needed glasses. "Are you okay?"

Emma shoved at a non-existent flyaway strand of hair. "Sure." She stumbled when she went to take a step. "Um, let me lock up after grandma. The door." The sound of the door clicked from far away, but she had done what was needed to keep her child safe. "The coffee. It's still hot."

"Yeah." Haley bounced around, and Emma winced when she came too close. "Why did Meemaw not drink all of it? I never do understand her."

The shadows ebbed a few inches in the face of her daughter's humor.

"I think Meemaw's stupid." Haley had gone too far.

"Don't." Emma's voice was sharp, sharper than she intended, but maybe that's what her daughter needed to hear. "You shouldn't be disrespectful."

"Yes, ma'am." Haley slumped over, then sidled over to her homework. "I think I'm done. Do you want to check it over?"

Emma dumped the coffee down the sink and a few droplets splashed on her fingers, scorching. "Um, no. I'm pretty sure you got it right." Actually, she had no idea. "I'm tired, and I think I'm going to go on to bed."

Part of her brain screamed that Haley was only four and shouldn't be left unsupervised. Part of her wondered if she'd make her way down the hall to her bed without falling. The few feet seemed like such a distance, even though she knew better. She was only in her twenties. She could walk down a hallway, but she felt like she was falling.

"Do I have to go to bed, too?" Haley recovered fast, seemingly no matter what came her way. "I'm not tired."

"No, you can watch television. It's okay." Emma stuttered over the last word, knowing full well that there were so many shows that were inappropriate for her daughter to watch.

"That's okay," Haley said. "I'm going to color you a picture so you'll feel better."

The words came from behind her since she'd crossed the threshold to her bedroom. The room was swathed in darkness now since the time crept toward her actual bedtime, and the shadows were outside her as well as inside now. She crawled on top of her bed, one knee and then the other, pulled both legs up against her chest and wrapped her arms around them.

Her eyes drifted closed.

She lay that way, mired between sleep and disappointment in herself, for who knew how long when Haley bounced into her room. "Mama. Your phone is buzzing."

Emma lifted a hand. "Just ignore it. They'll go away."

The lit screen came at her face. Justin's number. He couldn't see her like this. Couldn't realize she had these episodes. "I'll call him tomorrow, sweetie. Why don't you get ready for bed?" Her voice sounded like an old lady.

"Call him?" Haley was too smart for her own good. "Daddy? Hi, Daddy, it's Haley."

Panic shot through her like the pain of stepping on a live wire. "No, don't. Answer that."

"Ouch." Justin's disembodied voice came through loud and clear. "Good to hear from you, too. Why don't you want to talk to me? Did I screw up and not even know it?"

If he only knew just how messed up she was, he'd not only take back his words but his child. Emma shoved at the shadows and sat up. "I'm upset and tired, and I'll call you tomorrow. Is that okay?"

"I'm sorry. Sure." He backtracked fast. "Wait. Isn't being a friend all about being there for someone when they're down? I want to be here for you, Emma. What's wrong?"

They'd both forgotten Haley, and their daughter wouldn't be forgotten. "Meemaw came, and she was mean. Mama went to bed, and I'm watching television."

Emma clamped down on her lip and tasted the salty bite of blood. Her heart could have stopped while she waited for Justin's reaction, but then she would have been dead, and her weakness would no longer be an issue.

Justin whistled. Emma flinched at the cheerful sound that had no place in her darkness.

"I'm sorry, Emma. Do you want to talk about what she said?"

"No." She didn't mean to shut him out, but she couldn't just snap her fingers and everything would be okay. She needed time, sleep. "Maybe tomorrow. I just need to process."

"Which is code for butt out, Justin." He groaned. "I have a night jump tomorrow. I don't normally go with the unit now that I'm a rigger, but I need to re-up my qualifications."

Emma pushed at a forehead that was slick with sweat without reason. "I don't understand a word you just said."

"Of course you don't. My job is packing parachutes, but I'm also jump-qualified, and I need to jump every once in a while, to stay qualified. Does that make sense?"

Emma met Haley's wide eyes and knew her daughter would take her cues from her, just as she always did. What she said next could either leave Haley terrified about what her father did for a living or excited. "No, that doesn't make sense." Emma forced a teasing tone. "Why would anyone jump out of a perfectly good airplane?"

Haley's eyes barely had white showing in them at this point. "You jump out of airplanes, Daddy?"

Justin nodded several times in a row. "Yes, ma'am, I do. Have you ever wanted to fly like a bird, Haley?"

In response, Haley spread her arms like a make-believe airplane and raced around the room. "Yes, look at me."

Emma tracked her with the phone for Justin's benefit.

"Yeah." He laughed. "That's what it's like. Now, we do a lot of things to make sure we're safe. We don't just jump off things without somebody teaching us how. Got it, little girl?"

"Got it, Daddy."

"Okay." Justin drew out the word. "I feel like a dad now. Um, Emma. So, you don't want to talk?"

"No, not really. It's not you, it's me." She tried to keep her eyes open, maybe wink or flinch in reaction to her own callous words, but the shadows were heavy. "I'm just really tired."

"Ouch." He said the one word, and there was an awkward silence as he thought whatever negative thoughts were going through his mind, and she tried to see in her unlit room. Haley had flipped on the hall light and that shouldn't have been her little girl's job, but it was the only light available. "You know, that's fair. No one has to talk just because the other person calls or because it's a tradition. Do you want to call me the night after tomorrow? Make it your call, I mean choice?"

Those words, respecting her need, shone through her like a

streetlight filtering through the blinds. "Yes, yes, I'd love that. Thank you."

"You're welcome. I hope you get some rest." He hesitated. "Hey, Haley, I'm going to tell you good night, and I love you, sweetheart."

"Love you, too, Daddy."

Emma's eyes were gritty, but the happy tears could come. They were welcome here. When had Haley and Justin started saying they loved each other?

Her little girl had a real father, despite all Emma's mistakes.

"So, now you go brush your teeth, put on pjs, whatever little girls do before they go to sleep."

Haley giggled. "Yes, sir. Good night, Mama."

Emma somehow sat up, the energy coming from some hidden reserve, and she held out a hand to Haley. "I'll be there in a bit to tuck you in." She only hoped she hadn't just perjured herself.

"So, Emma. I'm going to let you go, I promise. I just wanted to say that I want you to know you can tell me anything." Justin stared at the screen straight on. "I care, okay?"

Emma nodded. She knew she should give him something in return. "I'll call the night after tomorrow, Justin. I promise."

His smile was tight, but his eyes were solid. "I'll take it. Good night, Emma. Take care of yourself."

"I will. You, too. Goodbye."

She swiped out of the call and pushed the power button off. Going off the grid was dangerous in these times of all cell phones and no land lines, but she needed that break from reality.

Haley ran in the door. "I can put myself to bed, Mommy. I know you're really tired."

Emma watched her go. A four year old shouldn't put herself to bed. Being that responsible shouldn't enter her world of expected stories and kisses and prayers.

Justin knew she'd been in bed while Haley wandered the

apartment alone. He knew what a terrible mother she was. Her own mother knew what a terrible mother she was.

She couldn't have long before they did something about it.

And Emma didn't think she'd survive that something.

The hall light flickered, and Haley called out, "Good night, Mama."

CHAPTER 17

*T*he lurches in his gut hadn't been there during the previous trips he'd made from one Carolina to another. He had been tired, yeah, not sure how Haley would take to the idea of having a father around where there had been none, but his body did its job. Now, his stomach rumbled like a C35 heading down the runway, its ancient engines telling friend or foe that the Americans were coming.

He was an idiot. He'd been an idiot all those years ago when he'd broken things off with the best thing that had ever happened to him. Now, he felt like a teenager all over again, unsure and nervous.

The Summer Creek exit came into view. He checked his blind spot and flicked on his turn signal. Some things didn't change, but some did. That kid who'd walked away from Emma and the unborn child he'd missed seeing being born hadn't known a speed limit he wouldn't break, hadn't known another pickup he wouldn't gun his engines and challenge to race.

Competition was best left to the places where he had a chance of winning and no chance of getting hurt.

The light at the end of the exit changed to green, and he waited the few seconds necessary to let the idiots run the red going in the other direction. He'd not survived the Middle East to come home and get cut down in traffic. When he made the right on to College Park, the curve was sharp enough that the flowers on the passenger seat slid down into the crevice between seat and door. He swore under his breath.

Then, out loud, he talked to the universe. "Sorry, God, I'm still in the Army. Right. No excuses for cursing. Can You at least not let the flowers be destroyed? Right. It wouldn't be more than I deserve."

He glanced around and assumed the other drivers had their own problems and were too busy to notice the crazy dude having a conversation with an unseen deity. He loved the idea of hands-free technology. This way, if someone saw him talking to himself, they wouldn't label him as a whacko but assume he was just another busy man on his cell phone.

He parked as straight as possible in his visitor's spot. "It just never mattered this much."

He almost forgot to turn the engine off before stretching across the cab to rescue the flowers. Other than one crushed pale pink rose that he tucked in the back of the bouquet, they were good. One glance in the mirror told him that he looked as good as he could, given that he still wore exhaustion like a uniform.

Once he exited the truck, though, the crisp autumn air and the smell of slightly burned, ready-to-fall-from-the-trees leaves woke him up. Anticipation replaced the anxiety, and he picked up the pace. He hadn't known but he'd been waiting for this moment for years.

The door swung open before his knuckles hit the wood. He felt a grin coming on. She just might have been watching for him through the window, and that made his day, maybe his week. He'd postpone her making the rest of the month until after the date. "Hey, there."

"Oh." Her voice was breathy, and her eyes softened when she saw the flowers. "For me?"

Which was a rhetorical question and they both knew it, so he thrust the roses forward, and she took them.

Emma whirled back into the apartment and left the door wide open. "Thank you. They're beautiful."

He followed her inside and was startled when no bouncing Haley greeted him. "Has Tiffany already picked up Haley?"

"Yesterday. The normal routine when I waitress is for her to stay over there most of the weekend."

Somehow, that hadn't computed. "Well, I'll miss seeing her," he said.

He moved over to watch her fill a vase with water and stick her whole face in the flowers, inhaling deeply. The simple appreciation made him appreciate her more.

"She didn't understand that she wasn't going to get to see you." Emma's blue eyes matched the soft blue of the silk blouse she wore. Her pale blonde hair against the blue could have made her seem cold, but instead, she lit the room like sunlight against snow. "I'll be paying for that tomorrow night, thank you very much. You owe me."

"Owe you?" Their first date had barely begun, and he wanted to move in for a kiss. He didn't like to be in anyone's debt. "As in a steak dinner? Roses? Candlelight?"

She tilted her head to one side as if considering the worth of his offer in comparison to the price she'd pay in Haley complaints. Then, with a sudden movement, she put the flowers down and jutted her chin out. "Yes, that will about do it. Where will we go, where there's candlelight?"

He glanced at his wristwatch, which was waterproof and good at high altitudes. It also let him know they were running a little behind. Okay, not them, him. He'd been the one to just arrive after driving from out of state, late because he'd changed shirts five times—the exact number of button-downs he had to his name. "Oscar's."

Her head jerked up, and her eyes flew to his. "Oh, wow. Did

you remember? I mean, did you choose the restaurant on purpose?"

There was no pretending they didn't share a past, and he didn't want to even try any more. "Yes, I remembered, and yes, I did that on purpose." He walked around the counter and took her by the arm, drew her closer. "I know there's part of our past that I regret more than I can say. I was a stupid kid. But, there was also so much good. Our prom night was magical."

"Yes, it was." Emma bent her head and leaned into his neck, her breath warm against his skin. "The food, the dancing with all our friends, the beach house on Isle of Palms where we all hung out afterward."

"I want us to recapture some of that magic, if that's okay." He kissed the top of her head. Her hair had always smelled like southern wildflowers—confederate jasmine and magnolia. "Now, we need to go, or we'll be late."

Her laughter was husky mixed with honey. "That sounds vaguely familiar, too. I'll just go grab a jacket."

Late October and the weather in the Low Country was its usual yoyo of hot and chill, no one would go as far as to say cold. "I'll wait."

She skirted around him, and he caught her glancing back when she reached the hallway, as if there was a fear that he was a figment of her imagination and that he'd bail on her, again.

He wouldn't. He wandered over to a refrigerator covered with picture magnets of Haley in all her splendor.

"I'm ready." Emma breezed back into the living room. "Oh. I'm so sorry."

"Don't apologize," he said, half meaning it. "I'm beginning to understand why you didn't tell me. None of us made it easy for you, and the whole situation was so hard already."

She hugged her jacket to her chest. "Thank you. Just you trying to understand means so much."

Something rumbled like a car going across rumble strips.

Emma's shoulders jerked, and she touched her tummy. "Oh, wow. I might be hungry."

Justin chuckled. "You might be near starvation by the sound of that. Come on, let's get you fed." He motioned for her to exit the apartment in front of him and then double-checked the lock on the door.

Emma watched him and then tsked. "I've been a big girl for several years now."

Justin put a hand to her elbow, hoping to at least arrive at the restaurant before starting an argument about feminism. "I know. You've been taking care of Haley, and you don't need a man. I'm hoping to prove to you, though, that while you don't need a man, I might be handy to have around."

"By checking the locks?"

"Two heads are better than one." He opened her door for her, tucked her dress out of the way of the closing door. "I can forget things. You can forget things. But together?" He waggled his eyebrows. He had no idea if that was an attractive look for him, but he hoped the ridiculousness of the gesture kept things light.

"That's true." She swung her skirt even higher and gave him a glorious glimpse of leg. "There are many advantages of together."

He walked around the back of the pickup, the long way around, took a deep breath of cool autumn air, got himself calmed down. She was always the most beautiful woman in the world to him, that had never changed. He hadn't been able to handle all the emotional upheaval as a kid, but he was a man now.

Justin slid behind the steering wheel and put the vehicle in reverse. Turning his head to check his blind spot, he got one more glance of Emma's slender curves and all his good intentions went out the window. "Um, Emma. Can you like push your skirt to your ankles? Maybe hide your face behind your hair or something?"

She didn't play stupid. Instead, she made things worse by

giving him another one of those laughs. "Sure thing, sweetheart."

The southern accent could be a powerful weapon in the hands of a teasing woman.

"And stop that. Talk like a Yankee or something."

This time, her laugh was young and carefree, which was as it should be, and his mood shifted to grateful that he'd been the one to get her there. "That's better," he said. "I know you're hungry so no more acting up. Don't make me pull this truck over."

"Ooh." Emma pursed her lips. "What would happen then?"

He beat a rhythm on the steering wheel, surprising himself at how strong his reactions were in this moment. "I have a feeling I'd be kissing you to the tune of making up for all this lost time."

"Oh." Emma dropped the act. "I don't think I'm ready for that yet. Need to figure us out first."

"Yeah." He agreed, and then again, he didn't.

"So, tell me more about Justin now. What do you do in the Army?"

The topic switch caught him off guard for a few seconds. That, and the traffic. "I'm a rigger. I pack parachutes and oversee the guys who are on the line."

Her stare burned a metaphorical hole in his side. "You told me that already, but Haley was around. Can I now say that I think your job would be terrifying?"

"You'd think." He turned into the restaurant parking lot and followed the signs to the parking in the back. Parking was located in another gravel lot, which didn't make sense for one of the nicer restaurants in the area, unless one was willing to drive all the way downtown Charleston and brave the historical one-way streets and the concrete garages. "But it's just like everything else in the military. Things you could never do on your own, you can do with your boys—and that includes both genders. My buddy has my back, and I have his. Always."

Emma's response had to wait while he ran around the warm engine to get her door. "It's still terrifying."

"Yeah. But somebody's got to do it."

The building was unimpressive from the outside and not particularly beautiful inside. It was a one-story, another converted house, with rooms on either side of a small foyer.

"Reservations for Lee, Justin Lee," he said and leaned toward the podium in the corner next to the pretty pine bar. "For two."

"Good evening. How are y'all tonight?"

"Fine, just fine. And you?" Justin gave the automatic answer and followed Emma following the hostess. There was candlelight but not the fancy white tablecloths of yesteryear. The food was a mix of down home southern and fancy. He had looked at the menu online and not much had changed in six years.

"How's this?" The hostess stopped at a table in a secluded corner.

"Perfect." He spoke for both of them and glanced at Emma to make sure his habit wasn't rubbing her the wrong way and that maybe she agreed with him.

"Thank you." She nodded and hooked her purse on the side of the chair even as he pulled it out for her. "This is great."

The hostess handed them menus and then placed a small clipboard between them. "That's the specials for tonight. Have you dined with us before?"

"Yes," they answered in unison, but Emma added, "It's been years."

The hostess gleamed. "I don't think much has changed. We've got the same chef, and his specialties are still fried green tomatoes and fried chicken. Pretty much fried."

Justin opened and closed his menu. "Well, I know what I want."

"Jeffrey will be your server." The hostess started to walk away then pretended to divulge a secret. "Laugh at his jokes. It makes him happy."

Emma had her nose buried in the menu, but looked up at

him, eyes wide. "You already know what you want? How could you know?"

Justin hadn't seen anything as cute as Emma with her nose above her menu and the rest of her face hidden, except maybe his daughter when she did the same thing.

Conversation took a time out as Emma studied the menu, and he drank in his fill of her beauty. After a few minutes, she lowered the menu and gave him the evil eye. "Stop staring, it's not polite."

Justin laughed, low and deep. "Sorry. I was raised better. It's just been too long."

"We've been back in each other's lives for a few months now." Emma closed the menu. "Halloween's coming up, to be followed by Thanksgiving and Christmas. I'm having a salad."

"Really?" He started to glance down at her slender figure but stopped before he really did go down the rude road. "You're beautiful the way you are, sweetheart. But the holidays are coming. What's Haley going to be for Halloween?"

"I don't really know." Emma glanced at her phone, then showed him the screen to let him know she was pressing the mute button. "Tiffany always takes her to the Trunk and Treat at church."

Justin experienced another one of those heart-stopping warning signals that he needed to clamp down on his tongue before he blurted out the obvious question. Why would a mother not take her child trick-or-treating? Why would she miss such important moments?

His silence must have said something. Emma squirmed in her seat. "You don't understand," she said. "I have no one to pay for anything but me. It costs a lot to raise a child. I work a lot."

Excuse after excuse came out of her mouth, and he still didn't get it. On the other hand, he wasn't in any position to judge. "I want to talk about that, Emma. I sent you a check, but I need to know if it's enough. I want you to be able to quit that second job."

Her eyes flew to his then flitted off to the side when the waiter popped up at their table.

"Hello. I'm Jeffery, your servant for this evening. May I answer any questions about the menu?"

Emma shook her head, her mouth squeezed shut tight.

"All right, all right, tough audience." Jeffrey unfurled Emma's silverware and placed her napkin on her lap with a flourish, not touching her, just swirling the fabric and letting it fly. "So, shall we start with drinks?"

Justin remembered the man's backstory and grinned. He had been their waiter all those years ago. He'd also been a radio personality years earlier. "Yes, I'd love whatever you have on draft." He caught Emma's face pinching even tighter, if that was possible. "On second thought, make that a sweet tea."

Jeffery didn't write anything down, just turned toward Emma. "And for the lady?"

"Water with lemon, please." Emma glanced at Justin. "And we're ready to order our meals. I'd like the Southern chopped salad with blueberry basil vinaigrette."

"Delicious choice." The waiter played it straight since Emma clearly wasn't playing. The woman seemed to want to hurry things along.

Justin almost went back to his menu, just to slow things down, but he'd already said he'd decided. "The sweet tea fried chicken and waffle, gouda cheese grits, and collards."

"Even better choice." The waiter shrugged in Emma's direction. "Hey, I'm a man. That salad is good, but the chicken and waffle? If I die, heaven better offer that meal, or I'm going to sin on my way in."

Justin laughed, he couldn't help it, and he was gratified to see Emma crack a smile.

The waiter dipped his head in a slight bow. "I'll be right back with your beverages."

They stared at each other, silent for a few minutes. Justin struggled to find a way around the impasse. He wanted to spend every holiday with his daughter, but Emma's family didn't even know of his existence, in the here and now. So, he couldn't very well invite himself to Tiffany's church, show up for Trunk or Treat. He could insist she tell, but he didn't want any conflict between them, and he wanted this night to be near perfect.

"How about Thanksgiving? Are you going to spend it with your family?"

She squinted at him, as if there was a hidden meaning behind everything he said. He stared back at her, willing her to take him at face value. He'd made one mistake, admittedly a big one, when they were younger, but that didn't mean his word wasn't good.

Finally, Emma glanced away. He wanted her to turn toward him—but it was a start. "Yes, the day of, we always go over to my mother's."

"Would you want to spend the day with us, my family, I mean?" Words often left his mouth without permission or planning. "Haley has never."

Guilt flashed across her face like a dark cloud covering the sun. "I know. I'm sorry."

He didn't repeat his earlier request that she not apologize any more. "So, what do you think? I promise my mother will behave."

Emma snorted. "You can't promise that."

"Yes, I can. After you left the last time, she was mortified. She was so worried that you wouldn't let her see Haley again." Justin refrained from pointing out that weeks had passed, and Emma had done just that. "She'll be on her best behavior without me saying a word."

Emma straightened the napkin in her lap. The waiter returned, and Justin chafed at the man's horrible timing.

"Water for the lady and sweet tea for the gentleman. And a bowl of lemons so you can squeeze to your heart's delight."

Justin mentally chided himself for looking a gift horse in the mouth. Jeffrey's humor had the side effect of lightening the tension between him and Emma. Justin would take what he could get.

"That's all I'll be squeezing," Emma said, her expression deadpan but her ire aimed at him.

Justin flinched, and then laughed maybe too loud given the stares of the other customers. "Sorry. Woman, you keep me guessing."

"That is definitely a good thing. My wife and I have been married for over thirty years, and she's never bored." Jeffery angled for a good tip, and he'd be getting it.

When Emma laughed, the whole world was a little bit lighter. Justin leaned back in the booth, happier than he had in a very long time.

After that, the meal sped by, with him asking questions about her work and Haley's preschool, anything that didn't send up a red flag as far as a potential land mine. If his own brain pinged every few minutes, he tried to ignore it, or at least turn the volume down. She was a secretary and a waitress, so very different from the animated artist of the high school version of Emma. Nothing seemed to bring excitement or passion except Haley. As far as a social life, she didn't seem to have any. Her friends had faded away over time given their very different lives, other than Scott's wife Sandra who had made some overtures. Even those with babies had more support than she did.

No wonder the woman slept more than was normal and gave every sign of battling depression. When the word popped into his mind, he flinched, for real, where she could see.

"What?" The right corner of Emma's rosy-red mouth lifted in the approximation of a smile. "I know my talking about my co-workers' practical jokes can't compare to the excitement the Army has to offer."

Justin hoped he recovered fast enough and that the traitorous word didn't appear on his forehead or something. He felt evil for thinking that this woman smiling across from him could be struggling. "Sorry. Different topic? Are you thinking about dessert? Because I am."

Suspicion flickered in the back of her eyes but faded quickly to be replaced with deliberate neutrality. "I think that might defeat the purpose of me having a salad, don't you think?"

He gave a one-shoulder shrug. "Or it could be the reward for having the salad. It's all in how you approach things."

She full out grinned at him and flipped back her long hair. "Okay. Let's see what they have and judge whether it's worth it."

Jeffrey appeared like magic, or maybe it was creepy. Justin was going to go with attentive waiter. "So, who's ready for dessert?"

Emma answered for them, which was a first. "We're going to withhold judgment until we know what you have."

Jeffrey did a little dance with his shoulders. "I am so excited to tell you. We have a vanilla bourbon bread pudding, a Kentucky pecan pie, and a Grand Marnier soufflé. Yes, indeed, the chef was feeling a little boozy today, but if you're not—there's also an apple dumpling with vanilla ice cream."

"That." Emma said it so quickly that it took the two men back. "I'm a sucker for plain vanilla ice cream, and the apple dumpling will just be a bonus."

Justin recalled her earlier shake of a head when he'd started to order a beer, but he was a sucker for a pecan pie and the alcohol cooked off. "I'll have the pecan pie."

Jeffrey gave a couple of approving nods. "You won't regret it. I forgot to mention that it's a chocolate bourbon pecan pie—that's what makes it from Kentucky. And they know their horses and their whiskey. I'll be right back with your treasures." He took two steps and then twirled back. "Do you want coffee with that?"

"Yes, please," they answered in unison. Jeffrey grinned and disappeared.

"I thought you didn't like coffee," Justin said as soon as the waiter disappeared. He really did have a lot to learn about this new version of the woman he'd loved. The feelings still seemed to be there, though, no matter the minor differences.

"I don't." Emma twitched. "I mean, I didn't. Now, I need it for survival. I can't seem to get enough sleep. It was like all those nights staying up with Haley left me with a deficit I can't make up."

The end of the meal drew near, and he hadn't gotten a firm answer on his questions earlier. So, he decided to address it now and maybe sugar could make it better if things went south. "So, back to Thanksgiving. If you don't feel comfortable spending the day with my family, I have another option in mind."

He had her full attention, but she gave no indication as to whether she was open or waiting to pounce with a no way. "So, I've pretty much used up my leave for the year. Plus, my company is having a dining out for the families the Saturday after Thanksgiving. It's our way of making sure everyone has a holiday, even the single guys who live too far away and can't afford to fly home for the weekend."

"That's nice." Emma pleated her napkin into an accordion fan. "And?"

Justin reached a hand across the empty table. "And I'd like you to come with me. I know it's over a month away. I know we're just now starting to get back into each other's lives, with and without Haley, but I figured it might take you that long to get used to the idea."

She stared at his hand for a few seconds as if the simple grasp might be a monumental commitment.

"Come on, Emma. Don't leave me hanging."

Her eyes were moist when she blinked up at him, hand hovering a few inches from his. "You hurt me so much when you left the last time."

Justin bridged the gap. If he was going to have to be the one to cross the distances, so be it. "In my defense, that was the only time I left you. I stuck by you throughout all of high school. I was there for you when your father died. And I don't plan on leaving you again."

She squeezed his fingers. "I hope not. I don't know if I could live through that again."

The harshness of her pronouncement made him swallow hard. "Not that we're going to be testing the theory, but yes, you could. You're a strong woman, Emma."

Something in his peripheral vision caught his eye. The waiter stood off to the side, hot coffee steaming on a tray, clearly waiting for an opening in the conversation. Justin shifted and gave the man the go ahead.

"Whew." The waiter placed the tray on the table. "This coffee is about as intense as whatever you two were talking about." He held up a hand. "Not that I'm prying, mind you, just explaining why I have steam dripping down my face."

The man did look a little hot around the edges. Justin almost groaned at the thought that the man had just earned a sizable, painful tip.

"Oh, you brought hazelnut cream," Emma gushed, her finger poking around the small bowl of single serves. "I could kiss you."

Jeffrey coughed. "Um, wrong man." He tilted his head toward Justin. "That young man there seems smitten."

Justin could kiss the man himself. He grinned at Emma. "We'll be addressing that later in the evening, I believe."

Emma smiled, but her face looked strained. "We'll see."

"And that's my clue to be right back with your dessert." The waiter was very good at his job.

Justin concentrated a few minutes on stirring plain cream and sugar into his coffee. "So, do I get an answer, or do you need to think about it?"

Emma counteracted her salad with the number of little creams she poured into her cup. "Why don't we see how these next few weeks go?"

Justin exhaled rather than say something that would get him

into trouble, along the lines of he'd thought so. He knew her, despite the changes. "Your call. I'd get you a hotel room for the weekend. Maybe Tiffany could watch Haley."

"She normally does," Emma answered without hesitation. "That's Black Friday weekend, and the restaurant would be super busy, all hands on deck."

Keeping his mouth shut about how little time she obviously spent with her daughter was becoming harder and harder. On the other hand, there was something he could do, rather than say. "How much, Emma? How much child support do you need to stop working the second job?"

She clenched the coffee cup, and then immediately dropped her fingers. She stared at her own hands. "I can't believe I just did that. I knew the coffee was hot. What do you mean how much?"

"A dollar figure." Justin kept shocking her, and she'd shut down, even if this had to be a pleasant shock. "You tell me how much you make waitressing. I'll look at my expenses and see if I can swing that amount. I also have some savings since I've been a bachelor all this time."

"I-I..." she stammered. "I don't know, what if?"

Bourbon chocolate pecan pie materialized in front of his face. "Wow, this looks great."

"And here's some custard pouring sauce." Jeffrey set a miniature pitcher next to the pie. "Oh, did I forget to mention that earlier? Silly me."

"Wow again." Justin reached for the small handle, and warmth emanated from the stainless steel. "Y'all are outdoing yourselves here."

Emma's eyes met his. "Do you remember the last time? We got crème brulee, and they torched it in front of us."

The woman sent him every kind of signal. The warmth in her eyes right now had him thinking long term and never letting her go. Her inability to even commit to a dinner with his family had him expecting a punch to the gut. He didn't know whether to duck or cover.

"Yes, yes, I do." He smiled at the apple dumpling placed in front of her covered with a generous scoop of vanilla ice cream. "That looks delicious, though. I guess we're starting a new tradition."

"I guess I'm going to have to taste that custard sauce. Pour it on, baby."

He obeyed, marveling at how human beings made the necessity of eating into an art. He took a bite and almost moaned out loud, but that would not be manly. "So delicious."

"Ditto." Emma twirled her spoon in the air. "This place was a good idea, Justin. Not only are we connecting with our past, but this is a wonderful meal."

He wanted to reach across the table and touch her again, but he also didn't want to push his luck. Instead, he pushed his dessert toward her. "Want to try a bite while the sauce is still warm?"

"You don't have to ask me twice." Emma's spoon was like a vulture swooping in and taking charge.

Justin laughed. Despite her ups and downs, Emma had him laughing more than he had in the whole time he'd been with Kristi. Pushing that woman out of his mind, he reached around Emma and snuck a spoonful of apple dumpling dripping with caramel sauce.

Neither of them said anything remotely serious the rest of the time they were there. After leaving a gratuity, which cut into his lunch budget for the next week, Justin found himself ushering Emma into the truck seat and not wanting the evening to end.

"Emma, when does Tiffany expect you to pick up Haley?"

She concentrated on tucking her skirt out of the way of the door. "Not until tomorrow. Why?"

His heart warmed. She questioned him, and he had no idea why that would make him happy. "Nothing nefarious. I just don't want this evening to end quite yet. What do you say to walking around Azalea Park?"

Everything about her softened. "I'd love that. I can't tell you when I've relaxed this much."

He hurried around the truck. The sun hadn't set yet, and he meant to make bank with every drop of light coming his way. The park was on the other side of the small town, and he drove down a side street rather than merging back on the busy Main Street. There were dancing water fountains on one side of the street, and farther down, one of the few surviving independent grocery stores to be found.

He parked at the tennis courts, which meant they'd have to run across Main Street when an opening presented itself. Before he got out of the car, he turned to Emma. "You know, when I was a teenager, before I ever took you out, my mom and I went for what she called date training. We went to dinner at the Greek restaurant off Central. Do you remember it?"

"Yeah," Emma said. Inches separated the two of them, and the sparks that had been there since middle school made the air crackle, at least in his head. "It's closed since then, but it was next to the antiques store."

He had to touch her, despite his vows not to break the barrier too often. He lifted a lock of her hair from her shoulder and tucked it behind her back, exposing the bare skin of her slender neck. He could see himself kissing that vulnerable spot, but he moved no closer. "Then, she said a perfect date would end here at this park. I forgot all about that when we were teenagers. There were always football games and parties to go to."

She turned toward the window. "And risks to take. I think your mother had a good idea. It's beautiful here."

"I'm moving." Justin made short work of opening her door. "Why don't you leave your purse in the cab? It'll get heavy carrying it around the park."

"Bossy." She turned and tucked her purse behind her seat. She hopped out, and he shut the door. His truck was not exactly woman and kid friendly, but he wasn't ready to give up his jacked up tires. He wasn't that old yet.

They walked side by side to the main road and waited for a break in the traffic. Him grabbing her hand and her screeching like a girl when they ran across the busy highway felt like the most natural thing in the world. The entrance to the park veered off to the side so they held on as they hurried along the shoulder to get to the entrance.

"Oh, my goodness." Emma put a hand to her chest. "I haven't run anywhere in years. Why do I suddenly feel old?"

"Maybe because you've been living old?" The words were out, and he couldn't retract them. He could only try to explain. "I mean, you've been all work and no play from what I can tell. You're still young and beautiful; I'm just throwing it out there."

The path dipped, and a row of massive azalea bushes blocked the road noise. In the spring, the bushes would be on fire with azalea blooms and the trail would be surrounded with daffodils and so much more.

"You say that a lot, you know."

"What?" He'd become so absorbed in their surroundings that he'd forgotten what came out of his mouth last.

"That I'm beautiful." Emma dropped his hand and wandered over to a pond. The chill in the air probably meant no alligators hiding among the water lilies. "I'm not, not anymore. I may have been in high school, but that was before."

An egret took flight on the opposite edge of the water with a flash of white.

"Are you kidding me?" He reclaimed her hand and reeled her in. "You might look a little tired under the eyes, but that only emphasizes how hard you work to provide for you and Haley. You are beautiful, Emma. Inside and out."

Something snapped behind them.

"Good evening," an older gentleman mumbled. He looked a little worse for wear but kept going as soon as they replied with their own, "good evenings."

Emma pulled away and walked farther down the path. "You know, I don't know that I've ever been here. It feels so secluded."

He pointed out an ibis, its curved beak distinctive. "My mom brought me here several times, and then I would come here to think. When I got back from Afghanistan, I craved the peace and quiet."

Her head jerked up. "I haven't even asked you about that, what you did. How are you?"

Justin probed at the memories, the way he'd push at a toothache to see if it still hurt, if he was still numb. "I'm fine. I won't say I didn't experience some bad stuff, but it's not something I talk about. It's also not something I avoid, so if you ever want to know something, just ask. I've had enough therapy, I'm good."

"Therapy?" Emma backed down the path. "I never saw you as someone who'd get therapy. My dad always said therapy was for the weak."

Justin snapped off the oak leaf he grazed in passing. The words hit him like a sucker punch. "Emma, your dad was a great man, but that is just wrong. If you can go to a medical doctor for a physical problem, you can go to a therapist when you need one."

The gazebo caught her attention. She spread her arms wide and twirled. "The temperature is perfect, the sun is going down, it's so good to just relax."

"What did I say?" he said more to himself than her. "Beautiful."

After a few minutes of just enjoying the view, he held out a hand, and she clasped it. They retraced their steps back to the truck. The highway was completely clear so there was no running involved, but neither let go.

Emma was quiet on the drive to her apartment, and Justin stopped pushing for the night. His questions had received no real answers. Besides, he had wanted one more push that he was saving up for.

"You don't have to walk me in," Emma said when he parked in his visitor's spot. "I'm a big girl."

Justin snorted. "If you're a big girl, you know that safety has nothing to do with why a guy walks you to the door."

"Yeah," she started, but he was out and opening her door before she could finish. "Justin."

"Shh." If that's the way she wanted to play it. He leaned down and captured her lips, and kissing her felt like coming home. The years fell away, and they were kids again, sneaking to the back door so the flashing porch light wouldn't interrupt their good night kissing.

He pulled back and rested his forehead on hers. "Now, you can walk by yourself to your apartment since you don't need no man."

"We'll see about that, Justin Lee." She rubbed noses. "We'll see."

She ran for the second time that night, this time, away from him.

CHAPTER 18

*E*mma watched Haley sleep for a few minutes, needing the reassurance that her girl was safe and sound and fully out. For some reason, she still operated under secrecy. This time, even from her daughter. She could debate with herself all day and all night, but the hard cold fact was that it was fear.

If Justin decided she wasn't worth the baggage, if he preferred the single life to a ready-made family, then she didn't want to face her family. It was better for them not to know and be surprised than to watch her constantly for the signs of her cracking along the edges.

They would find the signs, even now when things were going well, if they just looked.

Her family hadn't done more than the routine greetings yesterday at Thanksgiving and then it was off to the races with stories about her mother's health and Jim's health and how the girls don't call often enough. Shelby hadn't even lingered around for dessert.

Her phone buzzed in her pocket. She and Justin had been video chatting pretty much every night. All day, she found herself looking forward to this time. He made her laugh, he made her feel good about herself, and he was dragging her back to faith—whether that was purposeful or not.

For a few seconds, basking in the innocence of her daughter sleeping, she ignored the phone. It had been the two of them for so long. If Justin bailed, Haley would be devastated.

Her heart pinged in her chest. In sock feet, Emma ran to her room and closed the door like a spy. "Justin, hey. Sorry about that. I was watching Haley sleep."

The fact that she didn't attempt to dissemble said something good.

"Wow. I don't blame you. I wish I was there."

"I wish you were, too." As soon as the words exited her mouth, she sucked in a breath as if she could recall the admission. "I mean."

"Don't you dare take back my table scraps. Let me enjoy." Justin sat back and closed his eyes for a few seconds. "Okay. I'll be there at nine in the morning. Right? You'll have dropped Haley off at preschool and be ready to go?"

"Yes."

He must have sensed her trepidation because he started chanting. "I am not going anywhere. Repeat. I'm not going anywhere. Earth to Emma. Hear me?"

"Yes." That time, she was teasing and shocked herself that she could do so, given that her legs wouldn't stop jittering because she was nervous. "I trust you, Justin. I really do. It's just life I don't trust."

"Life or God?" Immediately after posing such a serious question, Justin yawned. He dropped his phone trying to cover his mouth. "Oh, wow. I am so sorry. It's been another long day."

Emma flirted with laughing at him but decided she wouldn't risk putting him off the day before they were going to be spending the weekend together. "I'm sorry. I know you get up early. And tomorrow it's on my account."

"No, it's on our account. Us." Justin shoved down another

yawn. "Wow. I really am sorry. Maybe I should cut it short if all I'm going to do is yawn in your face."

"And I still need to pack." Emma grinned at his startled face. "You're right. It's not a good idea to wait until the last minute, but what can I say? It's who I am. Impulsive and free-spirited."

"Yeah. That's the Emma I remember." His look could burn a hole across time and space and her cracked cell phone screen. "I just didn't know if it was the Emma now."

They referred to themselves in the third person when they explored and probed what changes the last few years had wrought.

"I'd like to say it wasn't Emma now. But I'll never be Tiffany organized, and Shelby's her own universe." One more yawn and she took matters into her hands. "Justin, go to sleep. Be safe in the morning and don't drive if you're still tired. I can always wait to come visit."

He barked a short laugh. "No way are you getting out of this. I'll be rested and revved up on caffeine and at your door at nine. That gives us time to drive back up here, check you into your hotel, and you can beautify as much or as little as needed before dining out at six. Got it?"

"Got it." She should, since they'd gone over it every night since she'd finally given into the begging and pleading. And that had been her heart. Justin had been pretty patient, given that she'd delayed and postponed and delayed some more, not giving an answer until last Friday.

"Good." His smile crinkled his eyes. "Good night, Emma. I can't wait until tomorrow."

"Me, neither."

"Wow." He saluted her. "Two encouragements in one night. I'm going to sleep like a baby."

He signed off, and Emma cradled the phone in her palm.

She didn't think she'd sleep at all.

CHAPTER 19

*E*mma sat next to the living room window in her apartment, feeling like the neighborhood busybody, watching and waiting for Justin to arrive. He was late, and she did trust him. She was packed, the apartment was as clean as it had ever been, and she couldn't focus on a book or even social media.

She started to rock back and forth. With effort, she forced herself to be still. She wiped clammy hands on her jean-clad thighs and tugged her long-sleeved blouse over her waist. Every inch of her skin alerted to the fact she'd be meeting strangers who knew what she'd done.

She and Justin would also be spending more time together than they ever had. Before, there had been curfews and school and extracurricular activities to act as buffers. Now, there would be the two of them and reality. He had emailed her a copy of the hotel reservation, as a way of reassuring her, and the privacy would be a refuge. At the same time, she never stayed in a hotel room alone.

The anxiety came at her in waves where the depression lingered in the shadows.

Fighting nausea, Emma stood and walked over to where her

purse sat, ready to depart, on the kitchen counter. When Tiffany had dropped Haley off the weekend before, she'd left behind a little devotional magazine that the church subscribed to for its parishioners. Her pushy sister had shoved it into Emma's hand as they walked from her car to the apartment door, carrying all of Haley's stuff for the weekend. The child should have her own entourage with the stuffed toys and pillow and extra stuff she took to her aunt's most weekends. So, with no free hand, Emma had shoved the little booklet into her purse.

Now, the brochure called to her.

Pacing would only cause her anxiety to skyrocket so Emma found her way back to the chair.

Still no sign of Justin.

The pages were labeled day by day, published quarterly, and it was the day after Thanksgiving. Black Friday, to be exact, but years had gone by since she'd taken the day to shop since the office was usually open, and she needed to be at the front desk to greet potential clients. Still, the devotion talked about shopping and materialism, which wasn't a problem for her since she'd been barely scraping by, and her mother before her, ever since her father had died.

The verse of the day, however, struck her like the Hallelujah chorus. "God is able to do far more than we'd ever ask or dare dream of."

The blow was soft and pushed her back in the chair. When was the last time Emma had asked for, or dreamed of, anything?

The doorbell rang.

Reading the devotional had made her miss Justin's arrival and had the poor man running to her door instead of her running to meet him.

"Sorry! Coming." She stuffed the devotional back into her dark cavern of a purse and ran across the room. "Hey."

Justin grabbed her by both arms, kissed her soundly, then jogged past her. "I have to go to the restroom. Be right back."

Emma leaned against her own front door and tried to catch

her breath. The man had her wanting to give up everything to be with him and laugh at the same time. It was a good combination.

Like a man, he was back in the living room before she could double-cross off everything on her list. She glanced down at the phone calls she should have made before leaving for the weekend and gasped. "Jimbo."

"What?" Justin had her suitcase in one hand and was in the process of hefting her overnight bag. Not that she got out much, but she liked to double up in case something got lost or left behind.

"The dog." They both looked over at the crate where the little pooch slept like a baby. "He might be a lousy guard dog, but Haley loves him. I can't just leave him behind with food like you would a cat."

"Oh." Justin glanced around as if the solution would present itself. "I'm guessing you forgot to ask someone to watch him for the weekend?"

Emma's shoulders drooped. Not only had she forgotten, but anyone she'd have asked wasn't on the list of people who knew about Justin. The list that was non-existent. Her fears were seriously handicapping her about now. "I don't suppose the hotel allows dogs?"

Justin placed the suitcase down and jerked out his phone. "There's a pet deposit."

"I'll pay it." Emma scurried into the kitchen and grabbed dog bowls, food, and a bottle of water. "Okay, what else?"

Justin came as close as he had since they'd reunited to being frustrated with her. "I hate to say this, but we're tight on time."

Emma threw one last look at the list that should have been finished, but there were still a couple of items in the middle. Her anxiety seemed to prevent her from seeing all that needed to be done. "Okay. I'm sure if it was important, it got done."

Justin picked up the bags again and headed for the door. "Bring the list with you. I'm sure you can make calls or whatever needs to be done on the drive. You'll have plenty of time once we're moving, trust me."

Emma swiped the list and crammed it into her purse, registering how she'd just performed the act a few seconds ago. Instead of wasting her time watching out the window and reading the devotional, she could have been making sure everything had gotten done. "I know I printed a computerized list of clothing and toiletries so I'm good there. It's just apartment and life stuff."

"Haley got off okay this morning?"

They reached the truck, and he placed her stuff in the back seat of the extended cab.

"Yes. For her, it was just a normal weekend off to Aunt Tiffany's."

He held her door for her, and she climbed in, focusing on the fact that she'd gone places with him before and this wasn't a big deal.

"Emma, I don't want to shut the door on your legs." Justin waited, his hands poised to shut and run. The very neutrality of his expression said that he knew she was thinking of bolting. "It will be fine. Just think of this as an extended date."

Emma let the strength in his eyes move her body in the way it was supposed to go. The door closed, and she focused on her breathing. The sun shone on one of the warmest Thanksgiving weekends in Charleston history.

Justin got in, started the engine, and then stared at her. "We forgot the dog."

Emma's anxiety evaporated in the face of humiliation. "I can't believe it. Oh, bless my heart." She jumped out of the truck and retrieved the dog, now whining and scratching at the thin bars of the crate. "Jimbo, I'm so sorry! I'll buy you extra treats, I promise."

He licked her fingers.

Justin met her halfway and reached for the carrier. "Did you lock up?"

Emma couldn't control herself. She leaned over, hands on her thighs, and started laughing. "No, I did not," she said when speech became possible again. "I may be a mess. I apologize now and ahead of time for whatever future mistakes are coming. Because they are coming."

"Yeah because you're human." Justin switched the carrier to one hand and knuckled her chin with the other. "It's part of the package. Image of God but living in a broken world kind of thing."

Emma's laughter dried up. Now, she felt teary. "That...that is an amazing thing to say, Justin. I don't know what to say."

"Say you're still going with me and that you're going to allow yourself to have a good time." His blond hair fell over his eyes, probably not regulation, probably because he hadn't had time to get a haircut with all of his traveling across the Carolinas, but he looked so good.

"I promise," she said, sounding a bit breathless, because that's what he did to her, always had.

They'd driven across the state border before the nagging at the back of her brain bore fruit. "My charger!"

Justin's hands jerked on the steering wheel. "Do you want me to have a wreck?"

Emma shook her head and looked at him, really looked at him. "No, I want you to stop for lunch, eat, maybe inhale some caffeine, and then I'll drive the rest of the way. You look exhausted."

Justin snorted. "You think? Sorry, I think I'm getting too far gone. What do you feel like for lunch? And what were you saying about your charger?"

Emma switched to staring straight ahead, recognizing that she was failing at adulthood right now. "I left it in the apartment. Right next to Jimbo's crate, which was supposed to act as a reminder."

"Except you forgot the dog until the last minute," Justin spoke over the whining, which was reaching a crescendo behind them, "and therefore didn't give the brain time to remember the charger. What kind of phone?"

"An old one that makes it hard to replace the charger." She moaned when she reached for his cell where it sat in the drink holder between them. The charger didn't match. "Aargh. My being cheap is going to be the death of me. Yours won't work."

"No worries. You can use my phone if you need to make a call."

Emma tucked herself back into her seat. "There's an exit coming up. Burgers or Mexican or...?"

"Believe it or not, and don't turn in my man card, but I'm in need of a salad." Justin patted what she perceived as a ripped abdomen. "PT's been kicking me into next week lately with all this good eating."

"All the traveling back and forth." Emma repeated her recognition of all he'd been doing to make this work. "I am impressed by this version of you, Justin. Not that I wasn't impressed by you before, but..."

"Thank you." He switched on his turn signal and exited the highway. "Mind you, I will deny it completely and look at you like you've lost your mind if you tell my buddies that was my pick."

"Sounds great." Emma tugged down the visor and checked herself in the mirror. She still looked like the tired mother of a preschooler, but there were laugh lights in her eyes in addition to the circles underneath. "That's one of my favorite places so why would I undermine future visits?"

Justin steered with one hand and caressed her cheek with the other. "I can't tell you how happy that makes me to hear the word future coming from those sweet lips."

Emma leaned into his hand then pulled away. "Eyes on the road, buster. And future, future, future."

He laughed, low and slow, and focused.

Lunch was quick and healthy, and she drove for the next couple of hours. Justin slept for maybe half that time, the rest he checked on her to make sure she was okay even though she'd gotten a normal night of sleep, and he'd been on the road at four. The man would be too good to be true if he wasn't also the boy who'd broken her heart into smithereens only a little over five years earlier.

On the other hand, in the silence of the truck cab, she finally admitted that she might have driven him to it. Her reaction to her father's death had been so bad, and no one had done anything to help. Her mother had grieved by getting in one disastrous relationship after another, going online, finding men in all the wrong places. Then, there had been the guilt. Maybe if she hadn't shown up after curfew, maybe if she'd been a well-behaved kid who didn't distract her father all the time worrying about what was going to happen to her, maybe he'd still be alive.

No one had blamed her, but the voices in her head... they drowned everything else out.

The GPS directed her to take the next exit, and the mechanical voice woke Justin. He stretched like a little kid, but the sinews in his forearms and the biceps popping in his arms were that of a man.

Emma shoved on the brakes to keep from rear-ending the car in front of her and stopped at the red light at the end of the exit.

Justin braced himself against the dashboard, emphasizing his arms even more. "Whoa. Where were you?"

Her cheeks could combust from the heat. "Um, nowhere. Where do I go from here?"

"Nowhere, huh?" Justin winked at her, which she knew was because she was looking at him and not the road. "Turn right and the hotel is just down the way. My parents stay here when they come to visit so it's pretty nice."

Emma followed his directions, interspersed by the GPS. The building wasn't a typical motel chain, but a smaller, historical-looking inn with two stories and a verandah—at least that's what they'd call the long upstairs porch in Charleston. She didn't know if the terminology held up here in North Carolina.

She didn't even know if she could expect sweet tea or if she'd be deprived for the weekend.

Justin was out and around the truck door as soon as she coasted into a parking space, or maybe she'd been distracted by her wandering thought processes. "I'll just grab your bags. It's registered under your name so you can go on in."

"Is it futile to insist on paying?" They fought this battle several times, with her coming out on the losing, or was it winning, side every time.

"Very much so." Justin seemed to move at the speed of sound. He now had both of her bags in hand while she still dilly-dallied in the driver's seat, thinking too much. "I have years of back child support and every other kind of support to catch up on."

Emma inhaled and pressed her lips shut. She was the reason he hadn't been part of their lives, so he didn't owe them anything. But she appreciated the offer.

In a matter of minutes, she was registered, and Justin carried her bags into a lovely room with a four-poster bed and chenille bedspread.

"I'll be back at five?"

Emma stood in the middle of the room, rooted to the floor. "This is beautiful, Justin. I've never stayed in such a beautiful place."

"Yeah, beautiful." That was becoming a thing with him. "Will you be ready at five, or do you need more time?"

She grinned at him, tearing her gaze away from the deep cherry furniture. "What? I thought you said I was already beautiful. Why would I need more time?"

He held up flat palms in surrender. "Don't ask me. As far as I'm concerned, we could walk right back out that door."

Without thought, Emma flung her arms around his neck. "Thank you, Justin."

His arms came around her and cradled her back. "You're so welcome, Emma. All I want to do for the rest of my life is compliment you and make your life easier and take care of you and Haley."

The rest of his life sent off warning signals, but rather than pulling away as she might have done a few weeks or months before, she nuzzled her nose against his neck for a few seconds and absorbed his scent.

Justin backed up a step. "I think I better go. That drive wore me out." He winked at her. "Plus, you might not need the time, but I need to go make myself pretty."

He left before she could contradict him. He'd never be pretty. He was too much of a man for anything besides handsome.

~

Emma touched up her eyeliner just as a knock sounded on the door. She'd managed to take a short nap, a quick shower, and get ready in the time allotted. She felt good, more energetic and alive than she had for a very long time.

Just the thought of a nap made her feel blessed, much less waking up from one.

"Whoa." Justin's eyes tracked her from head to toe. "I was wrong."

"Wrong? How were you wrong?" She shifted so one leg pointed in front of the other.

Her outfit wasn't fancy; this was a family event, and her skirt and boots were casual, but the skirt fit like it was supposed to do. Her sweater wasn't tight, but the loose deep blue emphasized her slim torso.

He coughed and shook his head. "Uh-huh. I was wrong in thinking you couldn't get more beautiful than you already were. I guess there are degrees and you keep raising the bar."

Emma felt like a soap bubble floating in the air, no sharp edges in sight. "You are too good to me," she said and grabbed her purse.

Justin shut the door behind her and motioned for her to go

ahead of him. "So, this dining out is a potluck. Most of them are. I always sign up to bring drinks—single man, can't cook, easiest thing."

"Okay." They were walking through the foyer that doubled as a lobby. The sweet older gentleman with a military haircut hurried to hold the door. "Thank you, Mr. Bobby. You're so sweet."

"Not at all, not at all. It's my privilege to serve." Then, seeing Justin, he saluted. "Thank you for your service, young man."

Justin saluted back. "Don't salute me, sir. I'm not an officer. I work for a living."

Mr. Bobby chuckled. "So did I, son, so did I."

The sun was getting ready to set, the last semi-circle gripping the edge tight. Emma reached for the visor as soon as she slid into the truck. "So, the first strike against the new girl is that I didn't cook anything for the potluck."

Justin concentrated on backing out in the suddenly busy parking lot. "Nope. I just told you that so you wouldn't worry that we didn't contribute. You're a guest."

Emma's hands drifted to her rumbling stomach, a weird combination of hunger and anxiety. "That's nice. I don't know what to do with myself if I'm not running around helping. Am I not supposed to help either?"

He pulled out on to the main road, a third lane available for a short time before he had to merge to the right. "Nope. You are supposed to relax and maybe get to know some of my buddies. I want you to be part of my life, Emma. You've met my family, and the next step is my friends."

The elephant in the room about squeezed all the air out of the truck. Emma still kept his presence in her life to herself. How Haley hadn't blabbed was a mystery beyond all mysteries, but the child seemed to think keeping a secret was the most fun ever.

He deserved a response. She needed to stop living in fear. "I'll tell them when I get home. My family, I mean. I've sort of let the friends drift away or they let me, one or the other."

He rested his hand on hers where it rested on her thigh, balled into a fist. When she let her tension show outwardly, no idea, but the touch set off sparks and soothed in one contact. "You've been very busy these last years, Emma. It's a wonder you've taken such great care of Haley, much less getting together with friends."

The man kept giving her grace. "What happened to you, Justin? You seemed to have found God."

It was blunt and more real than she'd been with him up to now. She almost took the words back, as if they were kids.

Justin waved at the guard station at the front of base and drove through. The military aura intimidated her, and she got quiet for a few minutes. There were large grassy areas and more buildings than she had pictured if she ever imagined what a modern Army facility might look like. Mostly, she survived each day and watched a romantic comedy once in a while. There might have been a WWII flick in her background, but that had only left a vague impression. Soldiers were people she felt gratitude toward and prayed for but didn't really know.

"The answer to that question is a very long story," Justin said. Her mental wanderings had almost made her forget where she'd led them. "Suffice it to say that you can't look death in the face without either accepting or rejecting a Creator. I accepted, big time."

"You looked death in the face," Emma spoke softly, again without censoring her words, which wasn't like her at all, not anymore. "I'm sorry. I don't mean to pry."

Justin backed the truck into a parking space. He shut off the ignition and turned to face her. "Part of being in my life means getting to ask questions like that. And I'll answer, later. For now, let's go have a good time. I will say," he tapped her nose, "that I feel better than I ever have about us. You asking questions is a sign you're interested, and that makes me happy."

"Good," Emma said and turned to hop out of the truck before he could move.

Sometimes, a woman needed to be full of surprises. Justin didn't move, just watched her through the windshield as she came around to his side.

"Of course, this is the time you make me look bad, in front of my boys." He leaned his head back against the seat, roaring with laughter, when she opened his door with a flourish. "What are you doing to me, Emma Marano?"

"Being nice." She affected an innocent air and smiled at a bulky African American man and his family as they exited their minivan two parking spaces over. "Good evening. How are you?"

"Doing fine, doing fine. Is that you, Justin? What are you doing, letting your woman open the car door for you?"

Emma was having fun. Opening the back door, she hefted the bags of soft drinks Justin had pointed out earlier. "Ready to go?"

"Staff Sergeant Sanderson, pay no mind to the crazy woman. This is the first time this has happened, and it won't happen again, I can promise you."

Two strong hands grabbed her by the waist, picked her up, and positioned her to the side so Justin could close both doors. He held out his hands. "Now, give me those bags."

Emma hadn't teased another adult for so long she wasn't sure where the line was, but she hoped a little further. "No, that's okay. I've got this."

"Emma." Justin threw a sideways glance to an approaching jeep. "Come on. Of course, you've got this. And of course this is the twenty-first century, but let me carry them anyway."

She handed him the bags immediately. "Thank you."

"For what?" He nodded in the direction of the building, the path obvious in the wake of the family of five leading the way. "For being a caveman?"

"No." Her jaw ached in the face of this much smiling. "For being a gentleman and for laughing at my silliness."

Staff Sergeant Sanderson held the door. "Here you go, Justin. Can't have you opening any doors now."

"Thanks," Justin growled. He threw an exasperated glance at Emma, but he took advantage of the open door since his arms were full of liter bottles. "Good to see you, Mrs. Sanderson."

"Good to see you, Sergeant Lee." The woman had her twins by the collars. "And who is your friend? I don't believe we've met."

"This is my friend, Emma Marano, from back home. We were high school sweethearts." Justin gave Emma a smirk, indicating that revenge was indeed sweet.

Emma held her hand at the ready, but the woman didn't release her children and only nodded at Justin's introduction.

"Nice to meet you." Mrs. Sanderson turned to the boy on her left. "Now, to get these recruits-in-training somewhere they can wash their hands. I don't know how you found mud between the house and the car when I was watching you the whole time."

"Nice to meet you, too." Emma blinked.

"This way," Justin said, as if nothing unusual had happened. "I'll just put these down and then start the rounds. They're a solid group of people. Sergeant Sanderson had my back over in Afghanistan more times than I want to count."

The dangers he had faced, the changes he'd undergone while she hadn't traveled any farther than when they'd known each other, overwhelmed her. "Lead on."

Justin led the way to the end of a long row of tables covered with white cotton tablecloths and deposited the drinks. Two women dipped cups into a bucket of ice and filled other cups. "Good evening, Margaret, Kieran. This is Emma Marano, my girlfriend."

"Nice to meet you," one of them said. He didn't differentiate between the two, so Emma gave a general smile.

"Nice to meet you. Can I help with anything?" He'd told her she was a guest, but watching others work didn't sit right.

The startled look on the older woman's face was quickly replaced by a closed-mouthed smile. "No, no, we've got it under control. You just relax and enjoy your visit."

The younger woman shoved straight brown hair over her shoulder and grabbed two of the sodas Justin had just deposited. "I'm going to put these in the fridge, so we don't have to use so much ice."

"Oh, good idea." The older woman grabbed more bottles, hugged them to her chest, and then hastened to follow her friend.

Justin scratched his jaw, watching them. "Okay, that was weird. Usually, you can't shut those two up no matter how hard you try." He huffed out a puff of air and glanced at her. "So, let's go introduce you to everyone."

Emma almost begged for mercy. If this was the way the evening was going to go, she'd like a return ticket to Summer Creek, please. Instead, she put on her big girl panties and grabbed the hand Justin held toward her. "So, high school sweetheart, eh?"

He brought her fingertips to his lips. "Truth is truth. As far as I'm concerned, the intervening years were just a break."

"I can't believe you just did that in public," she mumbled, shocked. Then, the tingle from her fingers made it to her brain cells. "But I like it."

Justin smirked and led her to a group of guys standing around a table, half with cups in their hands, all of them loud and raucous. "Hey, single men, this is my girl, Emma, and hands off."

Emma hadn't really spent much time with men in years, given that her co-workers in both office and restaurant were mostly female, and she had never been around soldiers. Their very size intimidated her.

"Ah, Justin. You're no fun." A blond came around and stuck out his hand. The welcome made her stomach muscles unclench. "Hey, Emma. Don't let this idiot fool you. We're all harmless, I promise."

He looked anything but harmless, but she shook his hand anyway. "You didn't say your name?"

His eyes widened, and he glanced at Justin. "I take it back. That voice is so full of Southern honey that I'm going to have to cut you out, man. Friendship only goes so far."

Emma laughed. "I still don't know your name so I can't say that Justin has competition."

Justin whacked the guy on the back, hard. "This is my best bud, Cody. We go back almost as far as you and I do."

Emma shook the hand that still held hers. "Nice to meet you, Cody." She tugged her hand out of his and patted his arm before addressing the next man. "And you are?"

"I'm not washing that hand," Cody teased behind her back. "You start to make sense now, Lee."

"Ignore him." The Hispanic took her hand and brought it to his lips as if they were on some movie set. "There is a reason he is alone in the world."

"And what's your excuse, old man?"

"Too many beautiful women in the world to choose from, but I can see what would make Justin throw all the others away." His dark eyes twinkled.

Emma grinned. "Do I have to work to get all your names? Justin?"

"That's Diego. And Robbie, Marcos, and Demetrius." One nodded, another tipped an imaginary hat, and the last one raised his cup. "There now, Emma. We were at the drink table and I didn't even think to get you a drink. What would you have, sweetheart?"

She had no idea what was available, given that she'd been leaping to conclusions about not being welcome. "Something with caffeine. A cherry cola would be good, if they have it."

Justin tapped her arm as he moved past her. "What do you think was in those two-liters?"

She watched him go. Each day they rediscovered something they had in common, or a precious memory, or maybe just how much they were attracted to each other. Or a combination of all three.

"Huh." Cody stood beside her. "You really like him, don't you?"

Something about his disbelieving tone sent chills running down her forearms, and she tucked her hands around her waist. "Yes. I really do. Why do you ask?"

"Don't know. It's just I got this impression."

Emma squeezed herself smaller. "We just met. How could you have any impression?"

They both still faced the drink table. "Well, let's say there's been talk. Plus, Justin's racing down to see you too often is interfering with his work. We've been wondering what kind of woman would do that."

Emma's hands dropped, and she twisted to face him, fists forming. "Are you kidding? I had no idea he was having trouble with his work. If I did, I would do whatever it takes to help. Not once have I done anything to force him to visit."

The big man backed up a step. For a few seconds, he looked around the room as if making sure no one had seen her overreaction. "I guess people jump to conclusions. He hasn't said anything to you?"

Emma concentrated on relaxing her fingers. "No, not at all. We mostly talk about Haley, our daughter, and our past. And getting to know each other again. I don't know much about his job, only that he helps pack parachutes."

"Yeah, he's a rigger. But that's not all a sergeant does. A sergeant is responsible for the men under him, watches out for his guys. When he's gone as much as he's been, Justin's not been there when some of the soldiers need help."

Justin was heading back their way, but he got hailed by a group of women and stopped to talk, balancing two cups.

Emma faced Cody. "Justin is a grown man and makes his own decisions. I think you should talk to him about any issues with his job. Not me. Besides, shouldn't his weekends be his?"

Cody lifted his chin to a couple passing by. "The Army is a

way of life. We don't work just weekdays or regular schedules. If you're going to be a part of his life, you should know that."

Emma's stomach churned, and the meal had not been served yet. "Thank you."

"Welcome." Cody took a sip of a drink, more amber than soda. "By the way, the reason I haven't told him my concerns is he's never around. You might want to shorten the leash a bit."

Emma had this vision of her head exploding and taking him with it. "I think I'm going to meet him halfway. Nice talking to you." She covered a cough, which emphasized the lie.

Justin held out her cup when she approached. She only avoided chugging the whole thing by a sip. "Sorry. I got waylaid. You've met Kristi before."

Emma forced a smile, although one of her eyes twitched. "Nice to see you again."

Kristi's smile was full of wattage. "So good to hear you made it. How's Haley?"

"Um, she's fine. She's with her aunt, my sister."

"Oh, does she spend a lot of time with her?" The other woman's teeth showed, and Emma was mildly interested there were no fangs. "I understand you've had to work a lot of hours to make ends meet."

The conversation seemed surreal. "Yes, she does, and I do."

"But that's going to change." Justin's arm went around her waist, and she almost leaned against him for support. "Anyway, Tiffany is wonderful. She's a teacher and great with kids."

"That's great." Kristi pointed with her cup. "Emma, this is Joanna James and that's Terry Cloud. They're both fellow admin like me, only I work in the motor pool and they're in the staff office."

Emma's hand moved of its own accord, but she got the hint faster this time—no female wanted her here. "Good to meet you. I manage a life insurance office during the week. So admin is a big part of my life."

"We're not civilians, though, so our admin is different," Kristi interrupted, if Emma had wanted to say more. "We're military, and we understand how the Army works. I was an Army brat growing up, too, so you could say it's in my blood."

Justin laughed, low and easy, but Emma felt the tension radiate from his arm to her body. In fact, if he squeezed any tighter, she might lose weight. "Come on, now," he said. "Admin is admin. Anyway, Terry here is from South Carolina, too. What part did you say, Terry?"

"Sumter." She stood taller than Emma but not by much. "Were you ever on a swim team, Emma? You look like someone I swam against in the travel league."

Emma shook her head. "No, I love to swim but was never on a team. I was a cheerleader and did gymnastics, though."

"Oh." The other women closed off even more.

Growing up, being a cheerleader had put her into the popular group. As an adult, it was like a sign around her neck that she was probably superficial or a dumb blonde, since the hair color fit. Emma smiled and then put a hand to Justin's arm. "If you don't mind, I'd like to sit. I guess the long drive wore me out."

Her labels now included weak to go along with the stupid and outsider. Shallow could be in the mix, never knew how far people took the cheerleader gig. Still, she got what she wanted.

"Of course," Justin said, letting go of her waist and taking her arm. "See you later, ladies."

The women all murmured goodbyes of some sort, and Emma gave a princess wave. That might be overdoing it, but she had gotten the lay of the land and now just wanted to get through the evening with as few scratches as possible.

"Not only do they have your soda of choice that I brought, but they have seafood lasagna. Do you remember that time at your house?"

Justin's voice came from a distance that didn't jibe with his physical nearness. Emma could have kicked something to find the shadows coming at her from the unoccupied corner where he led. She sat in the cold metal folding chair and crossed her legs, wrapping one around the other.

"Sure," she managed. "You brought me home and there was no one there, no dinner, no nothing. So, I dug through the freezer and found a frozen block labeled lasagna. We microwaved it without removing the wrap and sparked a fire."

"But somehow, the microwave wasn't destroyed, and we had a free dinner." He took her cup from her slack hand. "I didn't mean to go all poetic on you, but this could be like that." The cup danced as he talked. "Kristi, the other women, they're sparks, making noise."

She gave a short laugh that held no humor. "Or not."

Not one laugh wrinkle showed on his face. "Or not. But they signify nothing." Someone famous had said that line, and they both racked their brains. Emma gave up before Justin continued talking. "So, they're being rude to you tonight, probably put up to it by Kristi. It just proves I should never have dated, even for a little while, someone from my workplace. It says nothing about you."

A man across the room tapped a spoon against a glass pitcher. Since the rest of them held plastic cups, a few members of the audience slapped their hands on the table and others dog-whistled. The man wore a clerical collar and seemed to have a bright light behind him.

Emma blinked, and then realized the room was actually well lit and the difference was the lack of shadows. Justin had pushed them aside, for the moment, by his concern for her and no one else. This good place couldn't last forever, but her heartbeat settled.

"The ladies have asked that I bless the food in exchange for a free meal, and I personally think that sounds like a good deal." The chaplain smiled when he was rewarded with a round of chuckles. "If y'all will bow your heads. Let us pray."

Emma closed her eyes and tucked her chin, by reflex if not by practice. The devotion book was a good start, though. The prayer forced her to pay attention.

"Dear Lord, we come to You in prayer and ask that You be here with us during this time of fellowship. Bless the food to our nourishment and our hands to Your service. And please keep the men and women of this unit safe as they deploy back to the Middle East in January. You have them in your keeping and don't let them forget that fact. In Jesus's name, amen."

"Amen."

Emma's eyes snapped open and met Justin's pained ones. "I was going to tell you."

"When?" The question could pertain to when he was going to tell or when he was going to leave. Neither of which, answered, would make things any better.

"Later, and January ninth." He put the cups on the table. "I think it would be best, if we're going to salvage anything from this evening, to put both of those aside and get in line for dinner. Then, I'm going to guess that you want to eat over here by our lonesome and not deal with the rest of the people tonight?"

Emma's body could have been glued to the metal folding chair. The right answer was to keep trying, let people get to know her, push past their prejudices. "I don't know. I think I'll just sit here for a minute, catch my breath."

The line grew with every second of her procrastination.

"Okay." Justin stood like an old man, slow and with his hand on his back. "I'll go save us a place in line. You come join me when I get close. I'd love to bring you back a plate, but I don't think I'm that talented. One of us would go hungry, and there would be a cleanup in aisle five."

Emma gave him a closed-mouthed smile.

The pitiful twist of her lips was all she had to give, and she knew it wasn't enough.

He would leave her again.

Like before, her shadows would push him away.

CHAPTER 20

*C*haplain Mike waved people in front of him and waited for Justin to join him. They had become close on the last gig overseas. The man was only a few years older in calendar time but much wiser. Justin had this running joke with the man about dog years.

They grabbed each other's hands as a greeting, rather than have him slap a priest on the shoulder. "Hey, man. How are you?"

"I'm doing well, doing well." Mike grinned at Emma in the corner. "But not as well as you, I take it. So, that's the famous Emma."

"Famous?" Justin shoved his hands in his pants pockets, a good alternative to bashing Kristi in the face. "You mean, infamous? Even though no one here knows her whatsoever, and that includes my ex, who only met her a grand total of one time."

"Easy there." The chaplain took one agonizingly slow step closer to the food. "I've heard the gossip. Thank God no one sees me above all those human failings so I can keep informed. Word is that she didn't tell you that you were a father and wasn't going to let you know about your daughter ever. You've been messing up at work because you're tired from driving all that way every weekend. What else?"

Justin found Kristi across the room and wished the wrath of God on the woman, and then repented before the lightning could strike. "Fact is, all that's true. But there's more to the story."

"There always is." Mike was watching Emma even as Justin glared at Kristi. "Tell me, then. What's the rest, but keep to the short version, because we'll reach the plates in about half an hour or so."

Justin chuckled at his friend's lame humor. "Okay. Emma's father was murdered when she was a teenager. We stayed out past curfew that night, and she's convinced him being upset with her had distracted him, part of the reason he died. She would never admit it, but the guilt weighs her down. I broke it off with her our senior year because I couldn't handle what I called the drama."

"Depression." The pastor's keen eyes registered Emma's closed-off form, her eyes on the floor. "Has she ever received help?"

"Her father was a good man, but he was old-fashioned in some ways. He taught her that only the weak go to therapy." Justin waved his hand to indicate the line had moved and there was a break. "She was more than surprised when I told her that I'd sought counseling after deployment."

Mike held a master's degree in counseling in addition to his MDiv. He had been there for Justin in some terrible times. "You can't force her to go if she doesn't want to do so, but have you suggested it?"

Step by step, they approached the beginning of the serving line, and Emma still didn't move. "No, not yet. Everything seems so tenuous. I want to marry her, but she would have to uproot her whole life. I want to come home and see my daughter at night."

"Why did she not tell you about her?" Anyone else and the question might have been prying and unwelcome, but Mike's peaceful expression oozed simple concern.

"I'd dumped her, and she thought I didn't care. She called my mother and got shut down. So, it's just as much on me as anyone." He whipped out his phone for the distraction as much as anything. "Hey, have I shown you pictures?"

Mike's smile almost reached the streaks of gray at his temples. "You'd think she was a newborn."

"She is to me." Justin left it at that. He decided about a month into this thing that he could resent Emma for the rest of his life for the years he'd lost or lose the rest of Haley's life to bitterness. He was going to enjoy every minute moving forward. "Look at those blue eyes. I tell you, they light up my world."

The chaplain leaned over and laughed just as Emma walked up. "She is beautiful. How old, four, five?"

"She'll be five at the beginning of the year." Emma said the words in her soft drawl. "January seventeenth, to be exact."

The fire in Justin's gut crackled a bit. He had not known his daughter's exact birth date until that second. He found some stillness in a silent prayer for forgiveness, for himself and Emma, since they both needed it. "You know, I'm going to need to buy a lot of presents to make up for missing the last few birthdays and Christmases."

He meant the words, not the rebuke behind them, but still, Emma winced. He could have kicked himself for adding to her discomfort.

"I don't think you need to do anything but be there, my man. I can't imagine a better gift than your time," Mike said.

"Yeah, but I want to have fun," Justin protested. "It's all about me, right?"

They both laughed, and Emma's shoulders came up a notch. "What do you mean by fun?" she asked, a suspicious look on her face. "Are you planning on dressing up like Santa?"

Justin picked up a plate. "Anything. You name it, I want to do it."

"Take her to see Santa?" Emma was on a roll, and he was thrilled she'd left the despondent version of herself back in the corner. "Wrap presents?"

"They'll look like a five-year-old wrapped them, but sure." They'd just had a traditional Thanksgiving the day before so he bypassed the ham and scooped up some meatloaf. Hey, he was a traditional guy. "I haven't taken time off except for the occasional holiday so, contrary to rumor, I still have the days coming to me."

All this time he'd been standing behind Cody and Diego in line and hadn't spoken a word to either of them. He'd noticed Cody talking to Emma while he'd been sidetracked by Kristi and her minions. He had also noticed that Emma was visibly shaken. So, he aimed the words meant to squash rumors at his so-called buddy's back.

"That sounds wonderful. She'll love it." Emma gave him a soft smile. "I'll love it."

Justin would deal with his erstwhile friends later. Right now, Emma had used the word love in his vicinity. "Then, we'll set the dates. What do you think this is?" He pointed to a dish covered with what looked like corn flakes.

"Let me see." Pastor Mike was still in the conversation. "Oh, that's a cheesy potato crunch. One of my favorites."

"That looks like corn pudding next to it." Emma pointed with a serving spoon. "And this is Hoppin John. It's a little early for that, though."

"Never too early for good luck." Pastor Mike's plate was already burgeoning with food and the dessert table sat off by itself. "By the way, I'm Mike Smith, company chaplain."

"Emma Marano." Emma juggled the plate so she could shake the pastor's hand. "Nice to meet you."

"Pleasure to meet you." Mike lifted his plate. "Well, I'm full.

What if I grab us some seats, and then I'll come back for my second plate?"

The man didn't have an extra ounce on his body and didn't do PT because he wasn't an average soldier. Justin whistled. "Second plate? How do you do it? Sure, grab us some seats."

Mike lifted his eyes up piously. "Just blessed, I guess. Be right back."

Emma tapped him on his shoulder. "Can you share that salad?"

Justin jerked, dumping the tongs back into the bowl and not on the table, thankfully. "Sure. Guess I was just preoccupied."

Even her half smile did things to his whole heart. "I understand. He seems nice."

"Yeah," Justin said, knowing the judgment sold the good man short. "He and I became good friends over in Afghanistan." He lowered his voice and then thought better of it. If there was no shame, then he needed to act like it. "He acted as my counselor for a few months until I switched because we'd rather be buddies."

Emma's eyes flew to his and then veered off. Cody's back stiffened in front of him, and then the big man walked away, bypassing the macaroni and cheese that Justin knew was his favorite. Diego turned only his head and grimaced. Both men had been turning to drink instead of the shrink, and that had driven a wedge between them. Cody's hostility had gotten to the point that Justin avoided spending time with the guy who had once been his best friend.

"I think my plate is as full as I can handle." Emma filled the silence. "I see where the pastor put his plate. I'll just go ahead and sit."

"Sure." Justin glanced down at his own plate, pretty sure he didn't remember putting half the items on there. "I'm going to grab dessert now before the best stuff is gone."

Her smile brightened. "Sounds like a great idea. Bring me something chocolate?"

"Yes, ma'am."

He scraped the last of the mac and cheese on to his plate before reaching for a dessert plate and juggling.

Mike rejoined him in a matter of seconds. "So, what looks good on the dessert table?"

Diego held up a box of store-bought cookies. "Hey, I brought the good stuff."

Justin and the pastor both laughed. Then, Justin caught the label on the package. "Hey, those are red velvet. Give me."

Diego gave a slow, dancing, told-you-so nod. "Uh-huh. What I said. The good stuff."

Justin took a couple of the cookies and then searched the table for more chocolate. There was a German chocolate cake, cheesecake, and brownies to choose from and rather than stretch his brain, he selected a little of each.

When there was no space left on either plate, he checked himself against Mike. "Wow, man. This is for two people and you still got me beat."

Mike grinned. "I have a secret. As a married man whose wife is at home with the baby, I always take leftovers home. It makes her happy when she doesn't have to cook."

Justin chuckled and headed to the table. Mike had chosen the empty end of a long table on the other side from a sporadic grouping of couples. Justin knew all of the guys, but none of them well. He set the dessert plate next to Emma and noticed that she had her phone in her lap. "Anything up?"

"No." She tucked her cell back in her purse. "I just have this nagging feeling that I've forgotten something, but, of course, I can't remember what that could be."

"Other than your charger?"

She pushed her lips to the side and rolled her eyes. "Yes, other than that. How did Jimbo react when you pulled him out of his carrier?"

He sliced up the roast beef and dipped it in the cheesy potatoes. He had this thing about combining foods, the opposite of his daughter, whom he'd learned didn't like her food to touch. "He's so little that I'm not sure whether you own a dog or a rat."

"I live in an apartment," Emma said around a mouthful of turkey and stuffing. "He sleeps with Haley most nights, except when I'm waitressing."

No sooner had the words left her mouth than she dropped her fork. The clatter caught the attention of the others at the table, but they looked away quickly, as if afraid to be caught staring.

"No, no, no." Emma dropped her head into her hands. "I didn't call. How did I forget to call?"

Justin sat there, helpless, aware of people's subtle focus on Emma, but more concerned with whatever was causing her such anguish. "What?"

"My job at Jasmine's." Her whole face was strained. "I forgot to switch shifts with someone. I kept thinking about it and then something would come up. I'm fired."

Justin did a progress check on the good pastor, who'd been stopped at least twice on his way across the room. "Not to jump the gun here, Emma, but that's what I was hoping for anyway."

She pinched the bridge of her nose and faced him, which was better than succumbing to tears. "I know that's what you said, but."

"No buts," he interrupted. "I am going to set up a plan, maybe direct deposit, so you'll start getting enough support right away. I want you to work less so this just speeds up the process."

"But they would be short-handed. I can't believe I did that to them. They've been so good to me."

One of the women from the other end of the table passed by them on her way to the kitchen. Giving Emma an odd look, she bent down and retrieved the fork. "I'll just take this to be washed."

That was all, but the off-the-wall comment had Emma scrambling even more. "I'm sorry. I was going to get that. Just distracted."

"No problem. I got it." The woman hurried away. Someone must have had told people that Emma had the plague, and she was not only contagious, but a super spreader.

Mike finally made his way to the table. "Are you guys half finished? You are."

"Never mind." Justin waved at the man to sit down. "The program will be happening before you know it so we're not going anywhere."

"Ah, nothing like a captive audience," Mike joked, but only then did Justin realize how he'd sounded.

"I didn't mean."

Pastor Mike waved him off. "I know what you meant." The man had a turkey leg and waved it around like a child. "Does Emma know you're winning an award?"

Justin shook his head. His focus had been on getting Emma here and making her comfortable. Her possible reaction to his attending Officer Candidate School, to upending his whole career path, well, he pushed that to the back of his unconscious mind.

"What?" Emma's smile communicated her readiness to be proud of him.

Justin pushed the dessert plate toward her, away from him. "I put in for officer candidate school before I met you again. I'd become a second lieutenant, and follow in my dad's footsteps finally."

Emma pushed the dessert back toward him, in a silent tug of war. "I thought your enlistment was up soon. That you'd get out."

Pastor Mike stopped chewing. "Should I leave?"

"No." Justin held out a hand the way his mother would have kept him safe in the front seat of a car, completely useless but reflex. "We should talk about this later, Emma. They're about to start."

She somehow positioned her chair into the corner. "Sure," she said. Her voice was toneless, and her body as far away from his as possible.

Up until now, the enemy had been everyone but him.

Now, he'd been the one to put her in the shadows.

He only hoped he could pull her back out again.

CHAPTER 21

*E*mma should congratulate Justin on his acceptance into OCS. His father would be very proud. The fact his son had enlisted rather than attend the military college of South Carolina, just as generations had done before him, had instigated the fight that predated their own fighting that contributed to their breakup. Funny how the years between could illuminate the real causes of past events.

Being a mature adult should mean that the wasted years would pay off in time. But she still didn't know where the darkness outside the truck window ended and her own edges began.

"Are we going to talk about this?" Justin's voice held a brusque tone that it had not held before. "I know you assumed that I'd go civilian and come home to Charleston. The thing is, these things were set in motion back in the spring, before."

"Before Haley and I re-entered your life. I know," Emma said and was pleased she found the strength to speak at all. She guessed curling into a fetal position in the cab of a truck proved more difficult than doing so in the privacy of her insulating bedroom. "And I understand your wanting to advance, to follow in your dad's footsteps now that you've stopped rebelling."

"I don't know about that." His interruption was followed by

a grinning glimpse in her direction, as if he thought she'd crack a smile.

She wasn't there yet, if ever again. "But that doesn't change the fact that you'll be gone. You've just come into Haley's life—and mine—and it will really be hard to deal with you being gone for months at a time." She honestly didn't know she possessed a scrap of this courage.

Justin pulled into the inn's parking lot. The wind had picked up and smacked the old-fashioned wooden sign against the porch rails. He shifted into park but left the engine running. "I know, but I already signed a contract. I'm a man of my word, Emma. Isn't that what you want?"

Her hand rested on the door handle, her entire physiology seeking escape. "Yes, of course. But I don't know how to handle the military"—she stumbled over the natural word to follow—"life. I don't know if I'm capable of moving all over the place, to new places where I wouldn't know anyone and have no support. Not that you're asking me to, I'm just thinking about where this is going."

A small voice in her mind mocked the word salad that had just exited her mouth. If she met his eyes, there was no doubt he'd be confused and wondering what the heck she'd just said.

"I am asking." Justin ran a hand down her arm, took her hand, and interlaced their fingers. "That's what this whole weekend was about. I didn't hide my intentions. I wanted you to meet my friends, who, contrary to tonight's behavior, are generally good people. They would support you and come to love you once they got to know you."

Had he been in the same room as she had this evening? Someone or something had turned them against her, sight unseen, and her own nervousness had done nothing but cement their preconceived notions. Then, her heart stuttered a bit as her brain finally computed everything he'd said.

Abandoning the view of the parking lot, she let go of the car door and twisted in her seat. "You're asking?"

Justin brought her hand to his lips. "Technically, not now. I will do it right. But, let's just say, that one of the stops on the itinerary for tomorrow is a jewelry store. Just to watch your face and gauge your reaction to certain items that may or may not be purchased in the near future."

The streetlamp could have been the sun coming up in the morning. Emma's whole body felt like she could take off from the clouds and touch the stars with no glue in her feathers to melt her down. "Okay," she said slowly, trying to keep her feet on the floor mat. "It doesn't hurt to look."

Justin cupped her cheek. "And it doesn't hurt to believe in the future. Those people tonight will either come around, or they won't. I have signed up for another four years, but there's the rest of those years after that. Stick with me, Emma."

Her eyes fluttered closed, and she leaned forward. She wasn't making any promises, to him or to herself, but she could kiss him.

For the immediate future.

The next day was like a dream. Emma asked to sleep in until eight, and Justin had laughed his head off. She luxuriated over a hot shower with no little faces, human or canine, peering through the glass. At nine, she met Justin in the dining room of the bed and breakfast for a home-cooked brunch that she didn't have to cook.

After brunch, Justin transformed into a tour guide, showing her the base and the small town. They ate lunch at a diner on the two-lane main street, and she made up for the previous night's dinner and the morning's brunch by having a salad for lunch that had a strawberry wine vinaigrette so good it made her forget she was depriving herself.

After lunch, they walked up and down the street, stopping in a small antiques store and an updated bookstore. Main Street

Shelves had a whole children's section written by local authors. Emma took a good ten minutes trying to decide between a story about a unicorn foal and an alligator swamp.

"Get them both," Justin said, grabbing them out of her hands. "Consider it the first installation of a multi-faceted Christmas for my girl."

Emma tried to take them back. "Wait—those were my ideas. You can't take my ideas."

"Watch me." He winked and walked away.

She grabbed the Blackbeard the Pirate history that had been the third choice.

Since they'd been meandering from one shop to another, Sara's Jewelry Box had been just another stop. Justin played it cool, leading her toward the necklaces. "I want to learn every little thing about you. What do you like, what do you not like? If I play my cards right, I have at least fifty Christmases and birthdays coming up."

Emma rubbed her arms back and forth, a chill hitting her in the heated showroom where she had been more than comfortable out in the cool December air. "You overwhelm me sometimes."

In public, in front of the large bay window leading to the street, Justin pulled her into his arms and went nose to nose with her. "That's the last thing in the world I want to do. I want you to feel safe and special and good. Got it?"

"You can't force me to feel those things." She twisted her lips in a funny smile. "But this hug is a real good place to start."

"Good." He rubbed her cheek with his thumb. "Now, don't hold back. What you don't get now could be in your future."

Emma wandered a few steps, trailing her fingers over the glass case. "I'm not actually a huge jewelry person."

"Is that because you can't afford it, or is that truly your taste?" Justin's voice was low, probably to prevent the approaching salesperson from judging Emma's state of poverty.

"As far as necklaces go, according to my taste." Emma took

two steps and contemplated the first case of engagement rings. "I don't even wear turtlenecks. I don't like anything around my neck, but I do like earrings and…"

The words dried up like pluff mud after the tide went out. The rings were beautiful, there was so many to choose from, but the diversity wasn't what caused her to back up a step.

Justin didn't say anything for a few seconds, and she righted herself. If he hadn't left, if he hadn't broken up with her, in her dreams, they would have been married for years.

"Just show me what you like. Figure out your size." Justin rubbed her back. "No panic. It could be years before something happens." When she startled, his grin had her punching his shoulder. "Hey. I thought that would make you feel better. Months? Weeks? Days?"

Her head went back down.

The sales lady took that opportunity to walk closer. "Do you have a particular style or cut in mind?"

Emma hadn't dreamed of rings or wedding gowns for years. Then, last week, her social media feed had scrolled by and there had been ads for nearby bridal shops. She hadn't said a word, so the internet must have progressed to reading minds. Then, since Haley had been asleep, she'd started browsing and saving web pages, dreaming. Since no one hardly followed her, it had seemed harmless.

"No, not really," Emma finally answered. "They're all beautiful."

"Wow." Justin shoved his hands in his pockets and rocked back on his heels. "Way to make it easier on a guy."

The sales lady didn't say a word. She just produced a key from seemingly thin air and opened the case. "Wait just a bit, young man." The woman pulled out a tray and set it on top of the case. "This isn't something a young lady does every day. It takes some trying on and holding out and thinking."

Emma met the other lady's eyes and saw professional confidence. "You choose for me, first."

The woman pulled out a small pear-shaped diamond solitaire. "This seems plain at first, but the cut will look beautiful on your long, slim fingers."

Emma slipped it on and splayed her fingers in the air. The diamond glittered in the incandescent lights, just like in songs and fairy tales. "It's beautiful."

"It's a little big, though." The woman slipped the ring off, and Emma almost tried to stop her. "I'm Betty, by the way, Betty Peek."

"Emma, and that's Justin." Introducing Justin to someone in this second version of their relationship seemed so natural. "Thank you for your help, Betty. I wouldn't know where to begin."

Betty slipped a piece of paper around Emma's ring finger. "Size five, I think, if my twenty-five years of doing this mean anything."

Justin came back into the picture and pointed to a round diamond with a ring of smaller stones set around it. "How about this one?"

They lost track of time, trying on and taking off, talking about what looked good and what didn't. Finally, Emma stepped back and held up both hands. "I think I need a nap, as my four year old would say."

Betty nodded. "Now, you just need to sleep on it and see what comes up in your dreams. This is a heart thing."

Emma watched Justin's face to see if he would freak out at the cost or if there was any hesitation. There was none. There was just a smile plastered in stone. He glanced at Betty. "It was nice to meet you. Do you have a card or something?"

The woman tapped a finger on one of three card holders next to the cash register. "Right here. And may I say, it was lovely to meet you both. I hope you have a wonderful rest of the day."

Justin pocketed the card without looking at Emma and then started walking for the door. She went through the door, the bell jingling as they exited, and stepped out into the bright afternoon sunshine. "I really do think a nap would be a gift from God."

"Your wish is my command." Justin motioned for her to start down the sidewalk.

"No, not really." Emma bumped against his side. "No one should have that much power."

Justin bumped her right back and then grabbed her hand. "Right now, Emma, I don't know where I end and you begin. It blows my mind to think how much I love you after just a few months. It's as if those years between were a hibernating period, and my feelings for you were growing instead of dying away."

Emma stopped in the middle of the sidewalk, her abrupt change causing a couple behind them to have to go around on the edge of the walk and the road. "You just said..."

"I love you, Emma." Justin's gaze was intense, his green eyes fierce. "I mean it. It's not exactly the best location for the declaration, but sometimes a man has to say what he has to say."

Her hand went to her face, covering her mouth, pushing back tears. "If you knew how long I needed you to say that... I'd given up, on us, on everything. All I could do was take care of Haley. That's all I had left when you were out of the picture."

He brushed away a tear that she thought she'd prevented. "I'm sorry. I wish I could give us back those years, but I can't." He took her arm and led her to a bench. "Here. Let's sit for a minute, get ourselves together."

For the first time, Emma reached up and kissed him. "I love you, too, by the way. I never stopped."

Justin sobered. He brought them both down to the bench, and he stared off in space for a minute. "It would be a bad look if a big, scary Army dude cried in public, right?"

"Right," Emma said and leaned her head against his shoulder. Last night, she'd been shunned by most of his friends and their wives. She'd probably–okay–definitely lost her second job, and left her phone charger at home. None of that mattered when her heart was so full. "But I wouldn't tell."

"Good." They sat there for a few minutes, his arm around her shoulder, and her head on his, silent, maybe watching the passersby and maybe seeing nothing at all.

Emma yawned.

She got her nap, they had a wonderful dinner at a little Italian restaurant that was more pizza place than anything else but still made pasta from scratch, and they watched a romantic movie with Justin saying she owed him an action flick and she better be prepared to pay up when the time was right.

The kiss in the starlit night, under the porch light, reminded her of their first kiss, and she shoved that unpleasant memory out of her mind and focused on the dozens, if not hundreds, that had come between their first and a last kiss that hadn't turned out to be the last after all.

"Good night, Emma." Justin kissed her on top of the head, after he thoroughly kissed her lips and rendered her speechless. "May I say that this new version of us, behaving like good Christians, is killing me?"

She would have laughed if temptation didn't perch on her left shoulder and murmur in her ear. "I'm sorry."

"No, I mean, really. Like I may not make it to the truck without keeling over." His humor was the needed medication for what ailed them.

Emma did laugh and pulled away. "Good night, Justin."

"Good night."

The one blight on the day was the fact that her phone was dying, and buying a charger somehow slipped both their minds until she sat on her bed ready to text Tiffany and ask about Haley. There was nothing to be done but wait until she got home the next day. She would normally check in, but sometimes, work got busy, and she didn't get to her phone until after Haley would be asleep. She should save a little battery in case it looked like she was going to be late rather than cause real worry tomorrow.

Excuses. She was making excuses rather than lie to Tiffany about where she was and what she was doing.

Sunday morning, they went to a local church. Emma hadn't been to church other than Christmas Eve and Easter for years. With her heart as happy as it had been in some time, she felt ready. The church was old-fashioned, similar to the one she'd grown up in and similar to the one Tiffany attended. They had hymnals, and she recognized some of the advent hymns, ached for the classic Christmas songs. Too many years lost, and there was a hunger for God that made her hoarse.

When the pastor came out of the pulpit to talk to the congregation, her first instinct, a hold-over from her teenage years, was to let her mind wander. Her reflex was to stare at her shoes. But the man got her attention by raising his voice.

"Wake up." Pastor Mike grinned. "Yes, I know you're already here so, technically, you're awake. But this is my sermon, and I'm saying wake up. Wake up to the decisions you're making. Wake up to the habits you started maybe years ago. Wake up to the choices that are all yours. God gave you life for a reason. Are you living up to your purpose?"

Emma leaned forward. The sermons she remembered had been dry and boring and not applicable to her.

"So, I'm going to use the acronym of Wake up to help this stick with you longer than it takes for us to get to communion." There was general laughter. The pastor held up his hand. "First, the W— what. What is your purpose? Why are you here? What talents and gifts do you possess that you are meant to use for God's glory? If you don't know, then find out. There are all sorts of tests online and career counselors and life coaches and there's always me."

Emma pasted the ghost of a smile on her face, but she felt too intense to waver in her attention.

"A is for Assess. Are you fulfilling that purpose? By the way, you can have more than one purpose. But pick one for now—are you doing it? Are you getting it done?"

Emma didn't remember how to dream for herself. Now, Justin had opened the possibility of a whole new life with him.

They would be moving, and that would mean new places and new jobs. She could maybe go back to school. She had truly never thought about what she wanted to do.

"K is for Kiss your past goodbye."

Everything the pastor said sent her mind skittering down paths of how this applied to her. Could she let go of her fears? Her guilt for her father's death? Could she see a future?

"E, well, I got stuck on E because I want it to mean several things. First, E is for everyone. God made each and every person for a reason. But E can also be for enable, not in a bad way, but in terms of preparation. Get the training, the education," he waggled his eyebrows, "see what I did there? Yet another E. We need to lay the groundwork so we can do what we are supposed to do. There are no shortcuts."

Emma ran her hands along her thighs, nerves getting the better of her. There was no reason to believe this shiny future could be for her. The pastor was paid to say hopeful things. This could not be real.

"U, well, that's a tough one. My mind wandered back to you, but that's cheating because these words start with the letter I'm discussing. I thought of up, but that's cheating again. The only word that came to my mind that works is under. We are under God, and sometimes, we're under the weather, and sometimes, we're simply under-equipped. Sometimes, we have things in our past that weigh us down and prevent us from moving forward. Sometimes, we have disabilities that make life hard. So, I'm back to the word, 'up.'"

He seemed to be talking directly at her, a stranger. "If it's okay for your purpose to help others, then it has to be okay for someone else's purpose to be to help you. Accept that help. Let them pick you up.

"So, back to P. Purpose. Find it. Assess it. Kick your past to the curb so you can do what needs to be done. Everyone has a purpose, including you. Get up and live the life God wants you to live." He paused for a few seconds. "Seriously, get up. We're going to do the prayers now."

They stood and laughed as a disjointed group. The sermon was among the shortest and most impactful she'd ever heard in her life.

After church, they dropped by Justin's apartment and picked up a whining Jimbo, changed, and got on the road. They'd stashed her bags in the back seat before church.

"When he stops complaining, I want to tell you how much this weekend has meant to me." Justin gave the rearview mirror an evil eye as if Jimbo would pay the slightest attention. "And I want to ask what you were thinking about during the sermon."

Emma stretched out her legs in the wide truck cab. Then, she tucked them under her hips and turned toward Justin. "This weekend has meant the world to me, too, Justin. Even if we break up."

Justin slammed on his brakes at a traffic light. She sent up a grateful prayer that they were driving on a back road. His GPS had warned that there was an accident on the interstate and had sent them out into the North Carolina countryside. "Whoa. Sorry about that, but don't even think those words, much less say them out loud."

The red light switched to green before she could give an explanation. He looked down at her and then started moving forward. There was a tractor trailer on their left. Justin's position put them in the truck's blind spot, yards between them and the light.

If Emma hadn't been searching Justin's face for every minuscule change of expression, she wouldn't have seen the car rushing at them as if the other driver had the green light.

Her head jerked up, and a scream tore out of her. "Stop. Oh, God."

The intersection had a yellow flashing light in the opposite direction.

The tractor trailer truck driver waved the other car on, not seeing Justin's truck.

Tires screeched. The eerie whine filled her ears, followed by the sound of metal scraping steel. The stench of smoke permeated their closed windows.

The impact spun them across the highway. Her body flung forward. Emma braced herself against the dashboard as the airbags deployed. The windshield shattered into a million plastic shards.

Seconds, minutes, forever, passed before they came to a stop, off the road on the wide, flat shoulder. Somewhere else, and there would have been trees. A few miles down the road, they had just passed a river. The truck came to a stop in a field of stubble.

A few lifetimes came and went before she had the courage to turn toward Justin, who had taken the brunt of the impact. If he was hurt... he couldn't be, not now.

"Emma, Emma. Are you okay?"

Jimbo whimpered on the floorboard behind them.

"Yes, I think." Pain stabbed up and down her arms. "Me? Justin, the car hit on your side."

"They hit the front, didn't T-bone me exactly." His voice sounded strained. "Thank God for airbags."

For a few minutes, all Emma could hear was the blood pounding in her ears. Then, the sirens started.

Something pounded on the car window. A man's face appeared, and the door opened. "Miss, miss. Are you alright? I swear I didn't see you. I was letting that woman cross in front of me, being a gentleman. I'm so sorry."

She pushed the airbag off her, got out of the car. "My boyfriend. He's on the other side."

"I'll go see."

Emma wandered a few feet into the grass and then looked back. The other vehicle was a small car, and the front of it looked like a sardine can lid pulled back by the tab. "The other girl?"

A woman came toward her. "No one can get her door open. They're going to have to get the jaws of life."

"Emma." Justin sank down on the grass beside her and placed Jimbo's crate on the ground. She hadn't even registered when she'd sat down on the grass. "Emma. Honey."

"Are you okay?" She'd already asked. She knew she had, but there was a need for reassurance. "I mean."

His arms went around her and they just held on. "I'm fine, just some scratches. I think we'll both have some whiplash. We were in the big truck, though. She was in a miniature car."

Time slowed to a crawl, but the minutes were foreigners in a strange land. The police came and asked them questions. The fire trucks and EMTs took at least an hour to peel apart the other vehicle and take the girl away on a stretcher. The tow truck let them get their stuff out of the truck. Jimbo was fine and silent as a rock next to her on the grass. Justin's truck was totaled.

"Can I drive you folks somewhere for the night?" The police officer stood over her like a giant.

Justin had his phone out, but they could all hear someone's dial tone switch to voicemail. "If you could, that would be fantastic. None of my buddies are answering."

Emma blinked at the phone. The sun had set, and they were sitting in the highway lights. "Where are we?"

"About an hour from the state border," the state patrol officer said. "The nearest town is barely a town, but that's where they took your truck. Not that they can fix it. That thing is totaled."

Justin ran his hands through his hair. "I have insurance. I have credit cards. What I don't have right now is a way to get anywhere."

"I'll take you to the nearest motel." The man reached down and grabbed Emma's suitcase. "I'll let you take Killer over there."

Jimbo chose that moment to growl at the world as if it had just tried to kill him. "I've got him. Poor thing," Emma crooned. "I'm so sorry, baby."

They placed the bags in the trunk. Emma shivered when the police officer held the back door for her. "Can't say I've ever wanted to ride in a police car."

The man waggled his eyebrows. "Oh, it's a lot more comfortable than you'd think."

The drive took them down yet more back roads before they came to a little constellation of buildings and a motel. When the officer dropped them off, he gave them his card. He'd already filed his report. "I'll be in touch, send you the official report for your insurance. I'm just glad you both walked away."

"I'll check us in," Justin said, leaning over to kiss her cheek. "I'm going to leave you and Jimbo out here. The last thing I want to do is be dishonest, but if they don't take pets, we're up a creek."

There was nothing else on the horizon except a Waffle King. Emma's belly complained on cue. "We'll be right here."

Justin had no clothes, nothing. They'd have to share a room. The cost would be prohibitive for two rooms.

Justin didn't take long, and she didn't ask about the pet policy. Exhaustion hit her about as hard as hunger. They let Jimbo run around the edge of the parking lot and then made their way into the room, which had two queen beds. Neither of them said anything; she claimed one, and Justin claimed the other.

"I could eat a waffle." Justin peered at her, and the statement implied a question.

"They have more than waffles." Emma went in for yet another hug. There didn't seem to be enough touching in the world. The woman in the other car was in intensive care, her right lung punctured. "That could have been us."

"Yeah." Justin swayed a bit. "If anything had happened to you..."

"A little girl might not have a mother."

"There was nothing I could do."

"No, there wasn't." The police had placed the blame on the

other driver and the truck driver. "You didn't do anything wrong."

"Maybe if I had pulled up farther, if I had..." His grip tightened, and she had the unusual experience of being the strong one in the relationship for a little bit, long enough for him to take a few ragged breaths before straightening. "We need to get you some food. You haven't had anything since breakfast."

She leaned back, the strength of his arms supporting her weight. "Yeah, it's a wonder I'm not dizzy. Might be the tension."

"Whatever it is, let's not push our luck." His hand went into his pocket. "Forgot. I don't have any keys. We'll be walking."

"Wait." Emma grabbed his hand on impulse. "Can we pray?"

Justin's mouth opened and closed. "Yes, yes, of course."

"I'll–I'll do it." Emma took both his hands. She did pray, just not often. She said grace before meals whenever Haley was around. She led her daughter in the bedtime ritual. This last month, she'd even started to fall into a quiet time in the evenings after Haley went to sleep. But this was different somehow. There was another adult who could judge. "Dear Lord, thank You so very, very much for our safety. You are a God who still works miracles. Please also be with the other driver. We didn't even get her name. Please let her recover and go home. In Jesus's name, amen."

"Amen." Justin lifted both her hands and kissed her fingers. "Emma, I can't say how happy it makes me to see you getting back to your faith."

Waffle King was crowded, and they ended up sitting at the end of the counter. Emma found herself throwing caution to the wind and giving into the craving for comfort food. She slathered butter and drizzled butter pecan syrup over a pecan-studded waffle. She ordered extra bacon and dumped cream into her coffee.

"Wow. You're going to sleep good after that meal." Justin ordered eggs and hash browns in addition to his waffle. "On the other hand, I'm probably going to go into a food coma and still not be able to shut my eyes. I don't know when I'll stop replaying those few seconds in my head. I wish."

She rubbed his shoulder.

They were walking back to the motel when she looked at her watch. The face had two veins of broken plastic, but it was still ticking. "It's almost midnight. Tiffany is going to be beyond herself."

"You never called." Justin stopped in the middle of the sidewalk. "Of course, you didn't. Everything has been so crazy. You can't tell her we were in an accident. She'll blame me."

Emma stared at Justin. This was not the old Justin talking, the one who didn't want his parents to know he ever screwed up until it was too late to get help. On the other hand, Tiffany would be worried sick.

The roar of engines behind them had them both shying away from the road.

"Motorcycles." Justin turned to her, then held a hand up to the sky. "Why?"

The frontage road led to their motel and nothing else. Dozens of bikers were headed toward their motel. The noise would not be conducive to the sleep they both craved. She could cry.

They slipped into their room, and she dug her phone out of the side pocket of her purse. The nightmare continued as she saw the charge was down to 3%. She'd kept the cell off for most of the weekend, conserving the charge, but there was only so much she could do.

"I'll take Jimbo out for a walk, give you some privacy," Justin said and then followed his words with action.

Her eyes closed in pain when Tiffany picked up. "Tiffany?" Crackles and pops inserted themselves between the syllables. "It's..."

The connection was terrible.

"Emma, you're alive? Emma, we've been so worried." Yeah,

there was no way she was going to tell them she had been in a car accident.

"I'm okay. We're safe but can't…" The 'we" slipped into there without conscious intent on her part.

A train rattled not far from the motel. Tears burned at the edge of her eyes. There would be little sleep that night.

"Wait—we? Who's we?" Of course, the months of evasions and half-truths came back to bite her now. Tiffany, no one in her family, had any idea that Justin was back in her life.

"I don't think I can talk long on this phone." The charge evaporated in front of her eyes. "Our car broke down. I forgot my charger." Emma scrambled to determine the most important words when the clock was running down. "I'll be back soon, when I can't say." They had no vehicle and no one to call. "As soon as I can."

"Emma, I need to ask about Haley." The concept that her daughter wasn't at the forefront of her thoughts for even a minute stunned her, but the accident had set her mind on edge.

"Tell her I love her." Tiffany could take care of her. She'd been a second mother to her daughter since Haley's birth. The phone flashed red. "The charge is running out. So sorry. Bye."

The phone went dead.

Emma crumpled to the floor.

She was a horrible mother and terrible sister. This was abandonment. She'd almost died in a car wreck and the reality hit her almost as hard as the car running the yellow light.

If she lost Haley, there was no almost about it. She would die.

CHAPTER 22

*J*ustin came back in the hotel room, toy-sized dog tucked under his arm, leash lolling behind, and about had a heart attack. Emma was curled up on the floor in a heap.

He dropped the dog on the nearest bed and rushed over to touch Emma's neck. Nothing made sense. The woman was in her twenties, in perfect health, and no one could have come into the room without him seeing. Her pulse beat under his two fingers to the rhythm of a drummer in a classical piece, slow and erratic, but there. Her skin felt clammy, and he pushed damp hair from her face.

"Justin." She stirred and reared back from his touch. "No, you can't know. No one can know but Haley."

"Know what, sweetheart?" He braced his legs and lifted her as far as she would let him. "That you suffer from depression? I think I've known that ever since your dad died. I just didn't know how to handle it when I was a teenager."

"No." She shook her head, pushed at him as if she'd ward off evil. "I'm not depressed. I just got upset. The phone call. Tiffany thinks I abandoned my child."

"Do you think she called the police because she didn't know where you were?" He should have forced her to tell her family, at least Tiffany. At the same time, she was an adult and had to make her own decisions.

Emma moaned and backed away, catching the corner of the cheap bedframe with her shins. She fell to the mattress in a heap. "I don't know. Yes, I think so. The connection was bad. She couldn't hear me."

Voices from outside could be heard coming closer, and Justin hurried to shut the door. He sent up a quick prayer of gratitude that the dog hadn't seized the opportunity to seek freedom while it could. The Army had trained him to handle stress, but dealing with a prostrate woman and a lost Yorkshire terrier at the same time might be more than he could handle.

Sliding the deadbolt into place, he flicked on the light only to turn it off again when Emma covered her eyes. Instead, he twisted on a bedside lamp and sat beside her on the bed. "Sweetheart, first things first. No one is going to take Haley from you."

"She's all I've got."

He knew a little about depression and over-generalizations. More than one of his soldiers had been given the choice to either join the Army or go to jail. Serving was a great motivator to leave home and put yourself through mental and physical torture, but blackmail did not guarantee your readiness. Several of the raw recruits he worked with had needed serious help, some more than even the chaplain could provide. He had driven two in the last six months to the clinic.

"No, honey, she's not all you got." He rubbed her back in slow circles. "You have me and your sisters. Even if Shelby isn't around all the time, she loves you. Tiffany is definitely there for you."

"Yes, she is." Emma sat up and shoved at her falling hair. "Justin, what makes you say I suffer from depression? Can't I just be upset?"

He held out a hand, and she took it. She either recovered fast or was faking it. He'd put money on the latter. "You can be what-ever you need to be, baby girl. Have you ever talked to anybody about your father's death?"

She shook her head like she couldn't keep up with the speed at which he'd changed the topic. "What? I mean, I've talked to Tiffany."

He rubbed his thumb along the back of her hand. "That's good, but maybe not enough. Not with the guilt you've carried around."

The hand in his hand almost pulled away. "I never said." Her eyes shuttered, lids at half-mast. "I did tell you, when we were younger. I told you everything."

"And it scared me out of my skin." Justin tugged her closer, pulling her to his side. "Why do you think I ran like a coward?"

"I thought you agreed. I was responsible for my daddy's death. If it hadn't been for me distracting him, he would have been more careful."

He kissed her forehead, and the words drifted to a stop.

"No, you weren't. The stupid kid who pulled the trigger killed your daddy. He went to jail, and he'll have to live with what he did the rest of his eternal life."

"I know, but." She buried her face in his shoulder, and he inhaled her scent. The same cowardly voice that had goaded him to leave as a teenager told him it was now or never. If he signed on for this relationship, there would be moments like this the rest of their lives.

Depression could be treated, but it could also come back.

"Emma, would you consider talking to Pastor Mike?" He knew when he was out of his depth. If Emma had carried this guilt for so many years, she needed more than any help he could give. "Remember that I told you I went to him for counseling? When I got back from Afghanistan, I carried so much survival guilt it was like a rucksack on my back weighing me down to my knees."

She pulled away from him, creeping away from the threat

and going around to the other side of the bed. "No. I don't need therapy. I just need sleep. This has been one of the worst days of my life."

The words hit him like a blow. She needed a lot more than sleep. "Yeah, being in a wreck is no fun. It is late, but I also really need you to consider therapy. Haley told me about the nights she puts herself to bed because you can't get up."

She glanced from side to side as if there was a group of accusers surrounding her rather than just him. Maybe he should back off, let her have a good night's sleep and try again.

"You know she's just a kid, right?" Emma got up and started unpacking her bag, as if nothing in the world was wrong.

"Yeah, that's the point. She's a young child who shouldn't be left on her own." Complete beat-down exhaustion, and anger at the danger she could be putting their daughter in, had him saying words he would give anything to take back. "Emma, there's no more hiding from this. You've been fighting depression for years. You need to get help. In fact, if you don't..."

The unspoken threat hung in the air like a sniper's bullet. There was no pulling back the trigger.

"If I don't?" Her eyes reverted to the wild desperation that had been lingering in the corners. "If I don't, you'll take her from me, won't you? Or maybe you'll just disappear again. You'll leave." She crumpled to the floor. "Why don't you just go? Get it over with."

Justin dropped to his knees in front of her. "Emma. That's not where I was going with this. I was only going to say that I was going to take you to therapy."

Her hair fell like a curtain between them. She lifted one hand. "I said go. I don't need you. I never even put you on the birth certificate. I'm breaking up with you."

"Before I can break up with you?" Justin reached out to touch her, but she was present enough to scoot away from him. "I'm not breaking up with you, Emma. I'm going to go for a walk and give you some time to calm down. We were picking out engagement rings yesterday. I will fight for you. I will fight for us."

Despite her resistance, he picked her up and laid her on the bed, and drew the covers over her ball of a body. Not at any point did she make eye contact with him or acknowledge that she understood his reassurances.

"Emma, please hear me. I will stand by you. I will get you help. Please try to sleep."

Her sobs blocked out most of what he was saying. He had no idea how much she'd absorbed. The guilt at even looking like he was threatening her had him up and out the door.

The chill of the night air smacked him like a woman in an old-fashioned movie. He almost surrendered and went back into the hotel room.

The click of the lock behind him shocked him in place.

Emma crept back into the bed farthest from the door. Fear of someone breaking down the door layered on top of the terror of being alone. Her father had always checked the closet and under the bed, tucked her safely under the blankets so no body part was exposed. Then, her father was gone, and no one watched out for her.

Justin had come back into her life, but he had lied. He'd said he wouldn't leave her. He'd said he wouldn't take Haley away from her, but he would. If he believed she was a danger to the daughter he loved.

Maybe he should.

The voice was female and weak. Haley was precious. The times Emma lay in bed, prostrate, unable to rise, the child could get into anything. She already climbed counters and snuck candy. She could fall. Last week, she'd come up with the idea to heat up water for hot chocolate. Emma had been functioning at that point, but another time she might not be. Haley could have burned down the whole complex.

Haley could die.

Emma whimpered.

Going to therapy wouldn't fix her. Nothing would.

She needed to give Haley up.

Agony clutched her chest.

CHAPTER 23

*J*ustin walked into the pitch black past the final parking space. There wasn't much road, and the ditch led to a fence blocking off a patch of woods.

He didn't know if he had done the right thing speaking up, and he wasn't sure if Emma needed time alone or if that was a bad decision. He did know the almost threat had been one of the biggest mistakes of his life.

No, worse than that. It had been a sin.

He leaned his forehead against the mesh iron fence. The cold metal burned against his skin, but no physical pain could touch the agony within. What if he had destroyed any chance to be with Emma? If she decided to prevent him from seeing Haley, it would break his heart.

If she left him herself, it would break him.

The realization that he had maybe not made the distinction crystal clear had him silent in the night, his heartbeat barely audible.

"God." That sounded like blasphemy. "No, really, God, I need You. I need help." He held on to the fence with both hands and closed his eyes, even in the darkness. "Lord, I'm so sorry. I've been trying to work at this relationship. I've been striving, but I haven't been asking. I'm asking now. Please show me how to help Emma. Please help her be okay. Please help us be okay."

His right hand cramped in the cold, and the jangling of keys behind him made him self-conscious. He dropped his hands and walked to the side, out of sight of the main parking lot. The night air was cold. He needed to go back in the room, but he had a suspicion that the deadbolt had been shut and Emma not in the mood to let him in.

His fingers alternately clasped the useless key in one hand and his cell phone in the other. An urge so strong it was a compulsion came over him, and he searched his contacts.

"Hello?" Two rings and Pastor Mike answered. "Justin?"

The time of night, make that morning, registered with him. "Hey, man, I apologize. I forgot the time."

"Never mind that." His friend was only a few years older, but the patience in his voice was eons wiser. "Where are you? I had a feeling that something was wrong with you."

Justin glanced at the motel signs. "I'm only about an hour away from base, but it might as well be a world away." He kept moving, needing to generate some body heat. "We're stuck at a motel. We were in an accident, and my truck got totaled. We're fine, not a scratch except maybe some whiplash." He hurried to reassure rather than provoke the anxiety that Emma had tried to avoid with Tiffany.

"Thank God." Mike's relief was heartfelt. "I'm so sorry that happened. What time? You should have called sooner."

"Yeah," Justin joked and ran his fingers through his hair. "It would have prevented this early morning wake-up call. Please tell Lori that I'm sorry for waking her if I did."

There was the sound of conversation on the other side as if the happily married couple were talking right then and there, and Justin grimaced. The apology could have waited.

Mike came back on the line. "She said that the baby wakes her at such odd hours that this was nothing. Do you need me to come get you?"

The thought hadn't even entered his mind. Pastor Mike had always been a notch above him, in his mind, not quite the buddy he'd call to come rescue him from the side of the road. On the other hand, his equals hadn't bothered to answer their phones or return his calls. "Yes, I'd appreciate it. Maybe finish out your night of sleep and then come?"

"So if that wasn't why you called right now...?"

Shame for having disturbed the other man's rest had his shoulders slumping. "Emma is in a pretty bad way. Her sister didn't know she'd left town, reported her as missing. Emma's freaked out, worried that she'll lose her daughter."

There was the pregnant pause on the other end before Mike finally said something to his wife. Justin leaned against the corner of the motel building. Standing still brought the cold back into play, though, and he got moving again. He told himself to pretend that he was standing guard duty, as if military training could keep frostbite at bay.

"Lori has an opening at eleven in the morning. Do you think Emma will come?" Mike said, the empathy in his voice warming Justin's heart, if nothing else.

"I have no idea. I can only suggest." Justin passed the hotel room where he should be sound asleep and kept walking. "It's pretty convenient that your wife is a counselor."

Mike laughed softly, no doubt to avoid waking their three-month-old. "Yeah, that's the one and only reason I married her." Somebody grumbled. "I'm going to the other room now."

Justin waited, concentrating on picking up his feet.

"I'm back. So, give me an address and a time."

Justin stared at the receipt he drew from yet another pocket. "Thank you so much, Mike. I appreciate you taking my call and for the ride."

"Wait to thank me for the second one until I get there," Mike said with some humor. "I have a tendency to get lost down dirt roads."

Justin returned dry wit for dry wit. "Well, there are plenty of those. We're in the middle of nowhere." He rattled off the address. "How does eight in the morning sound? We'll get sleep and whatever free breakfast this place offers first."

"Sounds like a plan." Mike didn't sign off, and Justin squirmed in the quiet. "Justin, I have to ask. How are you doing?"

The temptation to give the blanket, worthless, "I'm fine," almost overpowered Justin's good sense. He'd called Mike for one main reason. He shouldn't waste the man's time, or his own. "Not so good, friend. I almost threatened to take Haley away if Emma doesn't get help. These episodes scare me, to be honest. I love her, but is that enough? I am almost to the point of asking her to marry me, but there's so much."

Mike laughed, a subdued roar because of the baby. "That's a long list for this early in the morning. How much time do you have, Justin?"

"Right now?" Justin cringed once more at the time. "Quite a lot since Emma locked me out of the motel room."

Mike's laugh cut off. "Motel room? Man, it's cold outside."

"Tell me about it. Keep talking and maybe my toes won't fall off."

Mike was no longer laughing. "I can be there in an hour. All it takes is my throwing on some pants and getting in the car."

Justin circled the parking lot. He'd be fine as long as the local police didn't stop and question his sanity. "No, that's okay. Nothing I haven't dealt with before."

"So, back to all the questions you threw at me. I have pretty much a one size fits all answer: pray. Then, get some shut eye yourself. First thing in the morning, tell Emma you love her. No social worker is going to take her child because she was in a car accident." Except Tiffany didn't know that Emma had been in one, whether it helped her sleep at night or not. "Her family knows she's okay so the police will see no reason to be involved if she's in touch with her family. What did I miss?"

The pastor's yawn proved contagious even sight out of

sound. "Sorry about that. And oh, yeah—whether you should marry Emma. First off, if she's locked you out of the room, start there, get inside. Then pray some more, but my belief is marriage is for better or worse. Wait, I didn't make that up. It's in the vows. So this is part of the worst, and you live with it. Better yet, you love her through it."

Justin rested his forehead on the cold brick and prayed that he didn't stick. "I can't see life without her. I just have to convince her."

"To let you in or say yes?"

"Both." Justin would have smiled, but his teeth were chattering. "I'm going to go knock on that door now, pastor. Pray for me."

"Always, friend, always."

"Thank you," Justin said. "Good night."

"See you in a few hours."

The call ended, but Justin didn't move.

He prayed.

The Army did teach him to obey orders.

CHAPTER 24

*M*usic blared somewhere above her head, and Emma bolted out of bed.

The antiquated digital clock changed numbers. One forty-five in the morning. There was no reason any rational human being would have set an alarm for such an abominable time. Emma stood motionless, trying to remember where she was and why she was alone.

Shivers wracked her body, and she cried out. No one had turned on the heat, and the room was ice cold.

"Justin." She'd locked him out.

The lyrics of the song permeated her sleep-deprived brain. "I need you. Lord, how I need you."

Emma frowned, at the radio and at the door. In both cases, unwanted emotions stared her square in the face. Shame at her self-centeredness that would send a man out in the cold. Dear Lord, he didn't even have the truck to offer shelter since the truck was no longer there. She faltered on the way to the door.

Opening that door seemed like an admission that she needed help. His threat still hung in the air like a clothesline, heavy with obstacles in her path. Her depression, and she wouldn't hide from the label any longer, not after the way she'd acted earlier, presented a danger to those she loved.

Fear for Justin's safety overpowered her shame. She unchained the deadbolt and jerked the door open.

"Hey." He was standing right there, his knuckles posed in mid-air.

"I'm so sorry." The tears were coming mighty easy tonight. "I'm so sorry. I wasn't thinking. It's so cold."

He pushed past her and stopped two steps inside. "It's not much better in here. Did you? No, neither of us did, we were distracted with the dog, and everything else." He hurried over to the window unit and switched on the heat.

Emma had the mental presence to shut the door. "Justin, I..." The music invaded her consciousness. *Lord, you are my breath. You are the heart beating inside of me.*

"You were listening to the radio?" Justin looked at her, his cheeks red from the cold.

Without thinking, Emma walked over to where he stood and wrapped her arms around his waist. "No, the radio came on by itself and told me what I needed to hear. Make of it what you will."

The hands that came to her waist were ice cold, but she took her punishment. "Emma. I'm sorry for what I said earlier. I would never, ever do anything to harm you or Haley. I just wanted..."

Emma rested her head on his chest. "You just wanted me to get help. I understand. I would like to tell you that Haley's never been in danger because of my depression, but I can't." The body beneath her cheek stiffened when she spoke the words so calmly. The change in her had to shock him. It shocked her. Sleep often helped her, but it was more than that. "Justin, I think I hit rock bottom tonight. I never realized, or allowed myself to realize, what could happen when things got so bad. You could have frozen to death out there."

His breath warmed her hair. "Hey, give me some credit. I'm

tougher than that. Maybe smarter than that. I went and made friends with the front desk clerk."

Some of the weight lifted off her chest.

"Emma." Justin took a step back and stood in the small open area in front of the door. "There's something important I have to tell you, and then there's something I need to ask you."

The weight settled back in for a good night's sleep. "What?"

Justin went to one knee. "I love you, Emma Marano. I have since we were kids, and I think I always will. Wait, scratch the I think. I will always love you."

Emma couldn't look any worse. She'd had maybe one hour sleep total. He couldn't be doing this now.

"Justin, I love you, too." Her hand went out, willing him to a stand.

"Thank you." He reached into his pants pocket and pulled out a ring box. "I went back to the store and bought this after I dropped you off yesterday. Emma Marano, will you marry me?"

Emma's hand flew to her mouth. "Justin, I..."

He shook his head, his one dimple deep in the streetlight filtering in through the cheap motel blinds. "I know this is one of the least romantic times and places I could have picked. We had what I hope will be our worst fight ever. That's sort of the point. Marriage is for better and worse. I'm here for the worst, and I'm not going anywhere, if you will let me."

Emma couldn't find words.

Justin took her hand and held the ring up, his eyes questioning her. She nodded, tears pouring.

"Emma?"

"Yes, oh, yes. If you love me after you've seen me like this." She didn't want to label herself. "Justin, I've wanted to marry you since I was fifteen. Why do you think I broke all the rules to go out with you?"

"Because I'm such a fantastic kisser?" He stood, slipped the ring that she'd chosen on her finger, and lifted her chin. He made certain that this was a kiss she'd remember.

CHAPTER 25

"So, I think our guest will sleep the rest of the day." Pastor Mike walked back into the living room. "She's in some pain. Are you going to the clinic?"

"Tomorrow. I should have known the effects of the wreck would sneak up on us. It will take some time to fully recover."

"Are you at least going to get some sleep once you get back to your apartment?"

Justin shook his head. He should be tired, but he'd caught his second wind, or maybe it was his third. "No, I have a stop to make. You remember Friday night? How Emma was treated?"

Pastor Mike scratched a day-old beard that came from not being able to shave because some jerk had got him on the road early in the morning. "Yes, but what are you going to do about it? There's been gossip, but that would be expected given the circumstances."

Justin looked at the man sideways. The good pastor wasn't the kind of man who tolerated damaging rumors if he could help it. "Which circumstances? The spurned girlfriend or the best friend who didn't get into OCS?"

Mike's grin was slow, and the deep lines next to his eyes

deepened. "That would be for you to figure out, but you might be on the right trail."

Justin nodded once and held out his hand. The pastor took it, and his grip was strong, much like the man's faith. "Thank you, Mike. Someday, I'll return the favor."

"Oh, we're counting on that." The pastor winked. "Babies need babysitting, you know."

Justin laughed. Lori came in with said baby on her hip, the dark-eyed charmer with drool on her chin. "I've brought you a thermos of straight coffee, no chaser." The woman knew him too well. He might have been imposing on their hospitality a little too often.

"Thank you. I owe you a lot." And he hoped to pay them back, provided Emma could cook, and they got their own place. On second thought, that might take too long. "When I get back this evening, the pizza is on me."

"Sounds like a plan." Lori grinned. "This one slept through the night for the first night, but somehow, I still didn't get a full night's sleep. I need a nap."

Justin groaned. "Six o'clock?"

"We'll be here." Mike shoved him to the door. "Now, go do what you have to do before you collapse. And take a nap."

"Yes, sir." Justin saluted to a door shutting in his face.

He laughed and burned his mouth with hot coffee before reaching his rental car. The thing was the size of a postage stamp, and he ended up kissing his knees before settling in, but the car would get them where they needed to go around town. Turned out a replacement truck was going to take a few days, maybe a week to arrive, and then he'd be getting Emma back home. In the meantime, she'd had a visit with Lori in her professional capacity this morning.

It was a start.

The aftermath of the session and the upheaval of the night before had left her exhausted and weak. Her cell phone was dead. No one memorized phone numbers anymore so there wouldn't be any calling her family. She'd not planned on being gone for more than a couple of days so her planner with all her passwords in it rested in a drawer back in Summer Creek. If worse came to worse, he would message them via his accounts and give them collective heart attacks. From his side of the conversation, Tiffany still hadn't mentioned his name over the phone.

They had no idea where Emma was or with whom.

He braked at a stop sign that happened to be the proverbial crossroads.

Take a right and head to Kristi's apartment and wallow in guilt for not having made it clear they were done sooner. He thought he'd made things right, but by the way the women had acted at the company social, maybe not.

If he turned left, he'd reach Cody right before he left for the gym. Before he'd discovered Haley's existence, the two of them had worked out together like clockwork every afternoon after work. Morning PT usually involved aerobic activity like running into the ground. They also needed anaerobic to build muscles, plus when he'd been single, there had been an over-abundance of time.

One thing his father had taught him was to put the first things first.

Fifteen minutes later, five minutes longer than it should have taken but some idiot had decided to go the speed limit, he pulled in front of Cody's apartment. He was under a time pressure as far as Cody was concerned. He whipped the little car into a parking space—a plus for the tiny rental. His back cracked five ways to Sunday as he unfolded his long body—a negative and the reason he would be getting a new truck.

Cody jogged down the stairwell just as Justin reached the sidewalk. The big man stopped and looked around like he was being punked. "Hey, Justin, my man. What are you doing here?"

Justin walked over, and they clasped forearms, a manly greeting that had Justin remembering how many workouts he'd missed these last few months. "I just wanted to talk. You got a few minutes?"

Catching the man on his way out had not been part of the plan. Accusing someone of undermining his career and relationship with his girl was best done not in a parking lot.

Cody glanced at the deep sea watch they all wore even though they were in the Army. They never knew when they were going to be swept overboard in the desert. "Yeah, the gym doesn't close for hours. So, not really sure why I looked at my watch. What's up?" Before Justin could answer, his friend slapped himself on the forehead. "Wait. You called last night. I was asleep so I didn't see it until this morning, and I was already on the way to PT. Sorry, man. I hope it wasn't important. Wait. Where's your truck?"

Justin was glad the man had hit himself, saved him the trouble.

"I was in a wreck last night. I called to see if any of my friends could pick me up off the side of the road," Justin said, not attempting to keep the sarcasm from seeping through.

"Well, shoot." The man scanned the parking lot, never meeting Justin's gaze. "I'm sorry. How did you get here?"

Justin twitched. That wasn't the first question someone asked after learning their best friend had been in a car wreck. In the face of his so-called friend's lack of concern, Justin resorted to answering the question. "I got a rental car while my insurance works out getting me a new truck."

"Oh. Man, you loved that old truck. Well, I'm sorry I didn't call you back. Is that why you're here?"

Something settled in the back of Justin's mind. He didn't want to accuse this man of anything. He didn't want to end up punching his lights out for besmirching Emma's reputation. He didn't want much of anything to do with a guy who couldn't care if his friend had been injured. "Emma and I are engaged. I just thought I'd let you know. You can spread the word."

Cody's eyes shifted from side to side as if the gears turned slow. Then, the implication must have hit him where it hurt because he leaned over and placed his hands on his thighs. "Wow. Have you told Kristi yet?"

Justin searched for the peace that had been a part of him ever since Emma had said yes. "No. Do you think it should come from me, or should it come from you?"

"Me?" Cody gave him a sideways grin. "Listen, she and I were only talking and mostly about how we were both missing you. There was nothing going on there. You broke it off with her, nice and clean. So, I don't think either of us need to talk to her. She'll find out soon enough."

Which answered Justin's question in reverse. He'd be calling Kristi as soon as he drove out of the parking lot. A visit seemed pushing the envelope too far, though.

"Well, I guess I'll be seeing you around." Justin turned to go back to his stupid car. "Have a good workout."

"Wait." Cody dragged him around. "That's it? Not to be rude or anything, but who's going to be your best man? Will I even be invited? What the hell happened between us?"

Justin had hoped they wouldn't come to this. Cody outweighed him by a good twenty pounds, but Justin had the height advantage. "What did you say to Emma Friday night? What have you been saying about her for months?"

At least Cody manned up. "I told her the truth, just like I've been telling everyone the truth. I'd have told you the truth if you weren't head over heels with someone who lied to you for years. She's bad news, man. You're on the fast track to success, and she's derailing the train. Don't you see that?"

Justin inhaled and spread his fingers rather than let a fist start on its way. "Be careful. You're talking about my future wife. My first loyalty will be to God, followed by her. Don't you speak to her or about her again. Got it?"

Cody got in his face for a few seconds. Justin waited for his temper to kick in, but it didn't. Instead, a Bible verse about trust trotted itself through his brain.

"Sure." Cody backed up, walked away, waved a hand at Justin. "Got it. Done. See you at work."

"See you there." Justin watched the man rev his jacked up four-door truck and drive away.

Justin felt nothing but relief.

God had a plan, and He was letting Justin in on some of the details.

Worked for him.

CHAPTER 26

$\mathcal{E}$mma got off the phone with Tiffany and buried her face in Justin's rib cage. A week of therapy had put her in a very good place, and one phone call with her sister devastated her. She wasn't helping her case by sticking to the story of the truck breaking down, even elaborating on it. He understood the way lies worked—once someone started down that path, it was almost impossible to retrace their steps.

"I'm so proud of you for telling her about us. Baby steps, baby girl." She lifted her head enough to glare at him. "Yeah, I know the nickname is getting old. You're a grown, responsible woman, but you're my woman, and you'll always be my baby girl. Same person, many sides."

He lifted her up, took her seat, and pulled her into his lap. He was encouraged when he met no resistance. They might be engaged, but their relationship had a ways to go as well.

"They worried about me." He couldn't see her face, but he could hear the tears in her voice. "She did call the police and let them know I was fine, but I may have to meet with Social Services. Haley was crying. What's wrong with me?"

He wrapped his arms around her, held her as tightly as he

could without cutting off circulation, he hoped. "Besides the obvious of being human, you know full well the answer to that. You've been struggling with clinical depression for the better part of a decade. You needed this week. At some point, you had to focus on you."

"I could have told them." There lay the crux of the matter.

She could have told her family just how badly she'd been struggling with her father's death and her guilt at maybe having contributed to his bad decision to confront an armed robber with nothing but a taser. She could have told him about Haley. He'd forgiven her, but maybe she needed more than that.

"You could have, but that would have taken more strength than you had at the moment." He took a deep breath and said yet another silent prayer that God would give him the right words. "It took me a while to understand, but I do now. You needed every bit of courage, every little bit of energy, to make it day to day. Your functional depression meant you functioned. And that's all you could do."

The lights in her eyes when she looked up at him and finally met his gaze almost blinded him. "Thank you. Thank you for understanding. I can't tell you how much that means to me."

He kissed her, softly and gently. "I had some help. God and Pastor Mike, a powerful combination."

"Amen." She settled back down, and they stayed like that for some time. He could have held her like that forever, but one or both of their stomachs, their closeness made it impossible to tell, growled as if starvation was imminent.

"Hungry?" He grinned down at her.

"I guess so," she said, untangling her body from his lap. "Since I'm in charge of the kitchen right now, it's either order pizza or Chinese. Take your pick."

He tilted his head toward the baby monitor. "I can't believe Chloe is still sleeping. We have some way of repaying our hosts. She'll keep them up all night."

Emma grinned and then held her head. "Pizza it is."

$\sim$

Haley clung to her, her small fingers clawing the fabric of her shirt as if she'd attach herself bodily to her mama and there would be no escaping ever again.

"I'm going to let Mama know you're here." Tiffany broke into the reunion.

The bitterness and anger in her sister's voice was something Emma would have to work at repairing, too. Lori had told her to expect it, accept it, and love on it. There was nothing else she could do.

"Do you have to?" Emma heard her own voice, recognized the defensive posture of her body, and squared her shoulders. A week and one day of therapy would never have been enough to prevent her old mechanisms from showing their ugly heads, but said therapy was enough for her to know what she needed to do. "Thank you."

Tiffany left the room as soon as their mother and Shelby got there. Emma could have explained everything to her during the fifteen minutes of wait time, but she couldn't find the words. Maybe since Tiffany had been the one to stand by her all along, her disappointment was more difficult to bear. Her reaction to finding out that Emma had been suffering all these years and hadn't confided in her would be yet one more burden to bear.

Haley followed Tiffany as fast as her little legs could carry her. Now that Emma was back and she felt secure, there was the dreaded grandmother to flee.

Mama held on to Emma as if there had never been the distance between them that had marked their relationship for years. "My baby. My girl."

Shelby stood off to the side, arms crossed, separate.

Emma pried her mother's arms from her sides and motioned

to the kitchen table. "I'm sorry. For everything. Will y'all sit down? I need to talk to you."

Her mother fumbled in her purse and came up with one of those little packets of tissues that only mothers seemed to carry. "Here."

Emma took the tissue, but she shocked herself at the lack of tears. "I'm not crying. Ain't that a first?"

Shelby even pushed her chair farther away. "I don't remember you crying that much in the past. It was always Tiffany. Why are you surprised you're not crying now?"

Her younger sister didn't cry either, but Emma focused on what she needed to say rather than go on the attack. "Because I've done nothing but cry for the last week. I've been seeing a therapist."

Mama reacted exactly as expected. "What? Why would you do that? You're not crazy."

Emma smiled. "No, I'm not. I'm depressed. I have been ever since Daddy died."

Her mother dabbed at her eyes with a wadded-up tissue. "Well, of course you've been sad. You were his special tomboy. Plus, you drove him crazy that night. I wouldn't be surprised if he was so distracted by your bad behavior that he made a mistake that got him killed."

Shelby's sharp indrawn breath caught Emma off guard. Shelby looked aghast at their mother. "Oh, my Lord. I can't believe you just said that, Mom. Emma, is that what you thought?"

Emma couldn't believe someone had taken up for her. All these years, she'd just believed the worst about herself so why argue? Now, the tears came. "I did. I don't remember Mama ever saying it, but it's what I believed. Then, when Justin broke up with me and I found out I was pregnant with Haley, it was all I could do to get out of bed every morning."

Shelby stood and drew her into a hug. "I'm so sorry. That's

awful. If I had only known. Who am I kidding? I was too young to understand."

The look her younger sister sent their mother could have held venom.

"What?" Their mother dabbed and blew her nose. "I was a grieving widow who had never lived on my own. I did the best I could to put food on the table and buy you clothes. I don't know why you are looking at me."

"Mama." Emma wished with every fiber of her being that she could have brought Lori with her. "I'm not blaming you. I'm asking you to come to therapy with me. We need help. What happened to Daddy was a horrible tragedy. I understand that people of your generation saw getting help as a weakness. But that's okay. I am weak. I need help. I need God, and I need therapy. Will you come?"

Her mother rocked backward in her chair. "Me? Go to a therapist? No. I'm not crazy. I don't need counseling." She stood and gathered her purse to her chest. "Shelby, we're leaving. Emma, I'm glad you're safe, but I'm not going to no therapist. I have work to do and a husband to take care of."

Emma reached over and squeezed her mother's hand. "I understand. Just remember, the offer still stands if you change your mind."

Shelby turned her back to the both of them and wandered to the couch. She retrieved her own across-the-shoulder designer purse and held it to her like a shield. "Okay, Mama. I'll take you home, but I can't stay. I have a date."

Emma worked at keeping her expression neutral. Her sister had her ways of coping, and Emma had hers. All she could do was ask her mother, be there for her sisters. "Tiffany, Mama and Shelby are leaving."

Tiffany came into the living room, lugging Haley's overnight bag, which seemed to bulge a lot more than it had when Emma had last seen it.

"Hey, baby." Her mama gave Tiffany a side hug. Her expression had reverted back to approval for the one daughter who never did anything wrong, especially not ask her to attend some insane therapy session.

"Hey, Mama. I'll see you on Sunday for the church potluck?" Tiffany never stopped. A tease of a smile hinted at the corner of her lips. Big sister never gave up.

All three sisters' mouths dropped open when Mama responded with, "Call me and let me know the details."

Emma glanced at Shelby. So, church was a more acceptable alternative than counseling. Would wonders never cease? She'd like to tell Tiffany that her nudge had granted her sister's wish of getting back to church, but this wasn't the time.

Shelby hugged Tiffany, and then they were gone, leaving Emma alone with Tiffany and Haley in the back somewhere.

Emma could feel Lori pushing her forward. "We need to talk."

Tiffany's anger was like a shawl she wrapped around her chest. "Um, sure?"

Emma closed the door and marched to the couch. "Okay. What did I hear about the police?"

Tiffany raised her voice, and Emma shrank back. "What did you think you heard about the police? You disappeared without letting anyone know where you were; you didn't show up for work. By the way, Jasmine's fired you, you know."

"I would have had to quit anyway." Emma tried to exude calm and regret. Part of her was still in Justin's arms and the idea that there was someone else to share the burdens.

Tiffany took in a breath and ignored Emma's answer. "Most important of all, you left your daughter with me, and as far as I knew, you'd been kidnapped by some guy you met online. That was the only clue I had."

Haley came running back into the room. "Aunt Tiffy, what's wrong?"

Emma knew she deserved Tiffany's anger, but she didn't want Haley to be part of it. She knelt beside her daughter and brushed back the little girl's bangs. "Aunt Tiffy is mad at me because I did something wrong. She has the right to be angry. Sometimes, it's okay to be mad."

Haley nodded. "As long as you don't do anything bad because you're mad."

Emma was rocked back on her heels. "Where did you learn that, honey?"

"Church." Haley glanced at Tiffany. "You're not going to do anything bad, are you?"

Tiffany shook her head. "No, Haley. I'm not. Can you go back into your bedroom and check under your bed? I forgot to look for your stuff there."

Emma's heart ached at the thought that her daughter possessed a room here that was as just much as hers as the one in Emma's apartment.

"Yes, ma'am." Haley raced off like a rabbit.

Emma started again. "So, you were right to contact the police. I understand completely. I mean, what do I do now?"

Tiffany started to feed Bunny Foo Foo. Emma would have been insulted, if she didn't recognize yet another distraction. Her sister needed the distance. "I already called, and they closed the case. You might be contacted by Child Services, though."

"Dear Lord." Emma found her way to a chair. "Okay. I deserve that, too. While I sit here and beat myself up, I have to ask. Something Haley said earlier has been nagging me. What's this about Mr. Nick and Elloree?"

Tiffany blushed. "What did she say?"

Her sister was hiding something. "Is Nick back in your life? The boyfriend who joined the Marines and never looked back?"

Tiffany was still feeding the infernal rabbit. "It's not the same. Turns out Nick wrote me letters that I never received."

Emma's hands flew to her cheeks. "Oh no, oh no."

"What?"

"It was me." Emma couldn't believe this. Just when she was crawling out of the hole, some past mistake shoved her back in the pit with no ladder. "I did it. I was angry at you for telling Mom about me sneaking out with Andy." This had happened when she and Justin had been on one of their breaks, breaks that happened because she couldn't handle a real relationship. "So, I hid your letters. I'm so sorry."

Her hatred of herself had been so bad that she couldn't stand when Tiffany and Nick seemed so happy, and she was so miserable. She'd tossed the letters in the trash so there was no going back once she came to her senses.

Tiffany walked out of the apartment.

A month or two ago, maybe two weeks ago, Emma would have dissolved. Tiffany had been her rock. Without Justin, she would have felt completely alone.

Instead, she sat there and prayed. She couldn't have told anyone the words, other than God help her and her sister and her family and everybody in the world. She may have repeated the words like a chant.

Still, by the time Tiffany returned, Emma could feel the tears of conviction running down her face. Without making the conscious decision to do so, she held out an upturned hand and begged forgiveness.

Her beautiful sister said the words she needed to hear. "I'll work on forgiving you. It may take some time. Besides, like I said, it doesn't really matter in the long run."

"Why?" Emma choked out the one word.

Tiffany went to the couch, more distance. "Nick and I aren't meant to be."

Emma's chest hurt. She hurt for herself, and she hurt more for her sister who deserved so much love. "Why?"

Tiffany shook. "Because he's a police officer."

Emma closed the distance and sat right next to her sister, with nothing between them but a throw pillow. "Are you telling me you're going to give up the love of your life, for the second time, because of fear? Aren't you the only one of us who's stuck it out at church? Where's that faith now?"

The irony of her urging her sister to cling to her faith, the transformation of their roles, almost had Emma breaking down.

Tiffany stared at her mutely.

Emma reached over and placed a hand on Tiffany's where her older sister had them clasped on her lap. Her engagement ring gleamed in the sunlight.

Tiffany stiffened, her breath coming in small pants, her eyes wide.

Haley came out of nowhere. "Mommy, can we go home? I'm sleepy."

Emma looked at her sister, wanting more than anything to make everything better. She didn't have that power.

Instead, she reached for her daughter and held her until the child complained, loudly.

Justin waited outside Tiffany's apartment. If not for going against everybody, including his mother's and pastor Mike's advice, he would have barged in and inserted himself into the equation. Emma had been through so much, struggled so long. She needed his support.

She also needed to feel strong. She was strong.

So, he sat in the truck.

His phone rang.

His immediate reaction was to groan. Then, he checked the screen just in case the caller was someone important and not a robocall. His father.

Justin snickered even as he accepted the call. God was bringing his loose ends to him rather than waiting on him to get on with it already. "Hey, Dad."

"Justin?" His father had made the call and should have expected him to answer. "That you, son? Your mother and I have been worried sick over you."

"What?" Justin wracked his brain trying to remember a

missed phone call or a birthday or something. "Why have you been worried?"

"Are you kidding? Did you forget that your insurance agent is my golfing buddy? That you totaled a truck over a week ago and haven't bothered to call?"

Justin leaned his head against the steering wheel. "Yes, to all of the above. I'm sorry. I figured it would be easiest for all involved if you didn't find out about the wreck. I had no idea that Mr. Wilsea would spill the beans."

"It wasn't that he was being unprofessional," his father was quick to defend his old friend. "He just assumed that I knew. Are you okay? Was Emma with you?"

Something clicked into place in his chest. His father had asked the right question. He'd always asked the right questions. Justin had resented his father's perfection. His father was not only his hero, but an actual hero. How did a guy live up to that?

"Yes, to both questions. We're both fine. It wasn't my fault, and the truck was totaled. I now have a new truck, and we're back in town. As soon as she finishes visiting with her family, we're heading over. We have some news to share."

"Yes!" His father's fist pump could be heard across the miles. "Son, I can't tell you how happy that makes me. Your mother. Sarah, come here."

Justin cracked up. "Dad, I was going to tell you in person. Anyway, that's not all."

"More?" His dad sobered. "Son, did you not learn your lesson?"

"What?" He watched Emma come out of the apartment building, leading Haley by the hand. His sunshine girls caught the afternoon rays in their hair and in their smiles. "Dad, I am going to OCS. I am actually going to end up following in your footsteps."

"I have to sit down." There was a shuffling sound.

His mother came on the phone. "Justin, I don't know what you did to your father. I've never seen him like this."

Justin sucked at waiting. He'd have given anything to see his father's face. "I think those are happy tears, Mom."

"You hush. Your father doesn't cry."

Emma buckled Haley behind him. The fact that they were going to be a real family struck him like a hammer.

"I do, Mom. I do."

EPILOGUE

*E*mma stood in the vestibule of the small church. The Christmas tree on the other side of the narthex was decorated with white paper angels, each with the name of a boy living at the local foster care ranch, in need of a loving family and material goods.

"Mama?" Haley stood beside her, for once in her life, still. "Are you ready?"

"Yes, sweetheart, so ready. Are you?"

Haley nodded, her eyes wide, her hair piled on top of her head in a sophisticated up-do that had taken her stylist, Emily, hours to accomplish.

A few feet away, Shelby smiled at them both, and the ushers opened the double doors that had been closed after the grandmothers had been seated to give the illusion of a big entrance.

Shelby started down the aisle, one of only three bridesmaids.

Sandra followed, her dark hair out of place among so many blondes, but the million-watt grin and sparkly eyes fit.

"Ready?" Tiffany asked one more time, not because she doubted Emma and Justin's love, but because things had happened so fast.

Christmas Eve had somehow snuck up on them.

"Yes. I feel like I've been engaged five years." Emma held up her bouquet of pink roses against the ivory fabric of her wedding gown. "And loved my whole life."

"That's because you have." Tiffany did her half-wink thing and faced the front of the church.

Emma took Haley's hand. "Do you have your flowers, sweetheart?"

"I do." Haley giggled, a nervous little sound.

Emma squeezed her daughter's hand, so very grateful for this precious child's love and place in her life. The organ filled the small sanctuary, and they started walking together.

Once they passed the threshold of the church decorated for Christmas, Emma searched for Justin. The few seconds required to locate him, to the right of the pastor, in front of the altar, exactly where he was supposed to be gave her heart time to settle.

There was not a single doubt that this was the man God had made for her.

His blond hair reflected the candles lit behind him. The red handkerchief poking out of his dark suit jacket matched the rows of poinsettias that would be part of the service later that day. He looked like the hero of her dreams.

Her extended family, aunts and uncles, friends from work, both the office and Jasmine's, filled the left side of the church. She had always had more people in her corner than she'd realized. The right side of the church held soldiers and their wives and more of Justin's family than she'd yet to meet. Their support helped her keep walking even though all eyes were on her.

And her beautiful angel child who answered the pastor.

"Who gives this woman to be married?"

"I do!" Haley shouted.

Emma joined everyone else in laughing and enjoying, and then she saw Justin's eyes.

The look on his face was so intent. He leaned down to Haley and gave her a kiss on the cheek. "Thank you, baby girl."

The kiss turned to a raspberry, and Haley squealed. "Silly Daddy."

Justin straightened, and Haley stepped over in front of her Aunt Tiffy.

Pastor Mike waited until the uproar died down and addressed the congregation. "Amen. Justin and Emma, if you will step forward?"

Justin held out his hand, and Emma took it. Together, they approached the altar and their good friend. Without realizing it, Emma found her free hand captured by the man who held her heart.

"Dearly beloved." Mike stopped and scanned the room. This hadn't been in the rehearsal. "I want to stop and say something about that, if you don't mind."

Justin shook his head that they didn't mind.

"I'm glad because I'd have probably spoken my mind anyway. I mean, what are friends for but to co-opt your buddy's wedding?" Mike grinned, and everyone laughed again. Never had she attended a wedding so full of joy. Of course, Emma could be biased.

"Have you thought about what that means? Beloved." Mike held up the Bible he cradled. "This is before the ceremony. It's not about the couple, even though they're included. It's about all of you here. The beloved of whom you could ask? God. You are God's beloved." His blue eyes could have pierced everyone there with conviction. Emma could only hope. Shelby was still in question. Emma's newfound faith wanted her whole family with her in heaven someday. "And don't you forget it. God loves you."

He returned his attention to them. "Now, that didn't last long, did it? God loves you, too, Emma and Justin. He has loved you since before He formed you in the womb. He has loved you from the beginning of creation. He loves you so much that He sent his only begotten son so that you might have everlasting life. If the God of all creation loves you that much, you should really feel loved, don't you think?"

Mike opened his Bible. "Justin and Emma opted to stick to the traditional vows, but don't think these ancient words don't carry meaning because they do. They have already carried a lot of weight as these two young people have faced difficult times in their relationship and incredible obstacles. Justin has fought in a war. Emma lost her beloved father to a senseless tragedy. And still, they were loved, by God and by each other. Don't you ever forget that." He said those last words to just the two of them this time.

"Justin, repeat after me. I, Justin Grady Lee, take thee, Emma Grace Marano, to be my wedded wife, to have and to hold from this day forward, for better, for worse, for richer, for poorer, in sickness and in health, to love and to cherish, till death do us part, according to God's holy ordinance, and thereto I pledge thee my faith."

Each phrase was repeated in Justin's strong, steady voice. When he said, "for better and for worse," he winked at her, bringing the strangely perfect proposal to her mind. When he said, "in sickness and in health," he lifted both her hands and kissed them, and when he said, "to cherish," they leaned toward each other.

Emma focused on projecting her vows, making sure that everyone knew she was stronger, and she meant them, and she loved this man.

There were more words, Pastor Mike reading from the scripture, but her dazed brain only registering sights and sounds.

"I now pronounce you man and wife, Mr. and Mrs. Justin Lee."

The applause was deafening for such a small church.

"You may now kiss your bride."

This was her first kiss as a wife. Emma tried to blink through the tears that would come.

"Huh," Justin whispered next to her ear. "I do believe it's better to ask forgiveness than permission."

He dipped her halfway to the floor and deepened the kiss for the whole world to see.

ACKNOWLEDGMENTS

Thank you to Kara Leigh Miller for her hard work in editing. Thank you to my colleague, Dr. Susan Jones, for her answers to questions about clinical depression, and I miss you being in the office down the hall!

Thank you to my church family at Grace Lutheran for being my cheerleaders and buyers of my books and attendees at my book signing. Thank you to the ACFW LowCountry Chapter and Main Street Writes for your writing insights and friendship.

Thank you, always and forever, to my husband and children for their support of my writing and everything.

Finally, thank You to the God who grants every gift and loves despite every flaw. Bless you, Jesus.

ABOUT THE AUTHOR

A charter member of the LowCountry American Christian Fiction Writers, Christina Sinisi writes stories about families and faith and the love that binds them. By day, she is a psychology professor and lives in the LowCountry of South Carolina with her husband, two children, and crazy cat Chess Mae. You can learn more about Christina and her works on her website: www.christinasinisi.com.

ALSO BY CHRISTINA SINISI

Christmas Confusion

Sweet Summer

Christmas on Ocracoke